MAGNETIC SLEEP

BOOK 4: THE PARANORMAL CASEBOOKS OF SIR ARTHUR CONAN DOYLE

VAUGHN ENTWISTLE

MASQUE PUBLISHING LLC

The Revenant of Thraxton Hall; The Paranormal Casebooks of Sir Arthur Conan Doyle

Ebook edition: ISBN 978-1-8381568-2-4
Print edition: ISBN 978-1-8381568-3-1
Large Print Edition:

Published by Masque Publishing LLC

Note: This book uses British English spellings and grammar throughout (As did Arthur Conan Doyle and Oscar Wilde).

GET A FREE BOOK!

CHAPTER 1: A FATAL CASE OF SOMNAMBULISM

She appeared to be a ghost, a phantom, a Lady in White, the type of spectre reputed to haunt every ruined hall, crumbling castle, and ancient manor house in Britain.

Only she haunted not a gothic castle nor a derelict mansion, but the rooftops of London. And now her spectral form glided along the six storey heights of Mayfair mansions. Some roofs were flat, some steeply pitched and all giddily precipitous. Still, nothing seemed to daunt her as her bare feet trod slate tiles surrendering up the heat of the day. Cat-agile, she skipped across the dizzying heights with the high-wire grace of a circus aerialist.

It was a sultry summer night and the woman, a slender girl still shy of twenty years, was dressed for sleep in a diaphanous nightgown. As she fluttered along the rooftops, the full moon rising from the Thames shot her nightgown through with milky light so that it glowed translucent, revealing a lissome body quite naked beneath. In one hand she clutched a lit candle on a brass dish. In the other hand a flash of silver revealed that she gripped a knife. Up close, her eyes were heavy-lidded and blank—the glassy gaze of a sleepwalker. And so, oblivious to her perilous situation, she moved unerringly toward a mysterious goal. As her fleet feet skipped balletically, she seemed to move to the liquid rhythms of a strange celestial music that pervaded the air, soaring over the Mayfair roof≠≠tops, and echoing along the empty streets. A music both eerie and unearthly, as if plucked upon the crystalline harps of angels.

Six storeys below, on the gaslit avenue, a hansom cab clopped along the cobbled thoroughfare of St James' street. At this late hour the road was empty of pedestrians, apart from a lonely uniformed constable tromping the pavement, whose dazzled eyes now squinted into the beam of the approaching hansom's coach lights as it clattered past.

Inside the hansom, Arthur Conan Doyle and his friend, Oscar Wilde, jostled shoulders on the leather bench seat.

"It's awfully late," Conan Doyle fretted. "Perhaps we should do this another time. Jean will be thinking I've been kidnapped."

"Nonsense, Arthur," Wilde gently scolded, "I know you are a devoted slave to your beautiful young wife, but you two are in the formative years of your marriage. Now is the period that you, as husband, must establish that you are the rule maker. If you wish to stop for a night cap, Jean, as a dutiful wife, must accept that."

Conan Doyle frowned at the admonishment but said nothing. In truth, he was totally in thrall to his beautiful young wife, and he counted the minutes they were apart.

"And besides," Wilde continued, "we are on a very special mission. After tonight you will never again be the same."

"It's that special, is it?"

Wilde threw his head back and jetted cigarette smoke at the cab ceiling. "In a world of mediocrity, it is the acme, the apogee, an elysian encounter where the ineffable collides with the sublime."

At that moment the hansom drew to the side of the road and pulled up at a modest premise. The cabbie perched on the back of the hansom yanked a handle, the folding doors flung open, and the two friends spilled out.

"Lo! we have arrived," Wilde announced theatrically. "Behold, the holiest of holies."

"This is it?" Conan Doyle asked, frowning skeptically. He squinted up at a weather-worn sign swinging above the door that the years had stripped of most of its gilt and paint. "O'Hooligans," he read aloud. "Looks rather like a gin shop."

"The name is O'Houlihan's," Wilde corrected. "And comparing it to a gin shop is a brazen insult. Inside you will discover a curated collection of some of the best whiskeys produced in every foggy corner of these sceptred isles."

"Ah, yes, O'Houlihan's," Conan Doyle corrected himself. "I have heard of it but thought it was merely a rumour."

"I assure you it is. Like most mythical things it exists somewhere between rumour and legend. You stand before the Lyonnesse of liquor, the Camelot of alcohol, the Valhalla for whiskey aficionados. Come along, Arthur, we must not tarry. We are squandering valuable drinking time."

Wilde thumbed the latch. The door opened, and they stepped inside, crashing through an oceanic surf of malty aromas. For a moment they paused on the threshold, eyes squeezed shut, noses raised as they inhaled an olfactory nirvana.

"My word," Conan Doyle breathed, "That really is the most wonderful smell!"

Wilde smiled indulgently. "Rhapsodic, is it not?"

After bathing their sinuses for several moments, the two men stepped fully inside and pulled the door shut behind them.

On the opposite side of the street from the whiskey bar, six storeys up, the somnambulist reached a section of rooftop that required her to leap up onto the wall of a narrow parapet. Although the mansions belonged to London's wealthiest, the rooftops here were in disrepair, furred with moss and soot-slippery, with bricks barely held together by cracked and broken cement. As she stepped onto the next lintel slab, chunks of brittle mortar shattered and crumbled and for a heart-stopping moment the lintel pitched downward, see-sawing dangerously beneath her weight. But as she sprang clear, the loose lintel rocked back into place.

By now the constable that Conan Doyle and Wilde had passed in their hansom cab had fetched up outside O'Houlihan's where he was met by another constable, for the whiskey bar marked the end of both officer's beats.

"'Howdy, Charlie," the first constable greeted.

"Bleedin' hot one tonight, eh Jonesy?"

"My tongue's as dry as a burned kipper."

"I'll say. I'm well parched."

"Quiet night though."

"Too true. It's too hot even for the bloody thieves to be about."

"I'll nip inside and cadge us some water, shall I?"

"Grand idea."

But as the first constable gripped the door latch his partner, distracted by a flurry of motion in the corner of his eye, jerked his head around to peer upward at the rooftops of the houses opposite.

What he saw made him gasp aloud.

W ith the aromas of malt, peat, and barley purling in his sinuses, Conan Doyle finally cracked his eyes and looked about at the bar.

The space was tiny. He vacillated between describing it a nook or a cranny, for it barely exceeded the dimensions of the average airing cupboard.

Squeezed into the tiny space were six or seven patrons. Most sat at the few lopsided tables. In a far corner perched two ancient men whose faces were a net of wrinkles and who resembled nautical caricatures carved from scrimshaw. Nearby, a toff in a tilted top hat, who undoubtedly should have been at home with his wife and squalling brats, sat with a heavily rouged and flouncily-dressed young lady perched upon his knee as both sipped from glass tumblers. And before the bar, a bevy of red-faced businessmen with rotund bellies sprawled spread-legged in an unruly brawl of odd chairs. All of the patrons gripped glasses and tumblers and, apart from an occasional grunt of appreciation, all sipped their whiskeys in reverential silence.

There was little room for more patrons as huge casks of whiskey had been rolled into every empty corner. And then, behind the bar and stacked atop it was a wall of whiskey bottles which sparkled beneath the electric lights and refracted beams of tawny light upon the faces of the two authors. Wilde introduced the bar with a wave of his hand and said, "Feel free to genuflect." And like supplicants before a high altar, they were drawn irresistibly closer.

After narrowly surviving the loose lintel, the sleepwalker now found her progress thwarted by a gap between houses of five or six feet as the neighbouring buildings were separated by a narrow ginnel designed to allow access to the rear gardens of the properties. Here she hesitated for a moment, her blank stare measuring the drop. A fall here would mean a sixty feet plummet to the bone-shattering cobblestones below. After blankly staring at the gap, she backed up a dozen steps, and then ran and leapt the chasm, her nightgown fluttering wildly as she soared over the dizzying drop. She landed spritely upon the opposite rooftop, absorbing the impact with her knees and stood up tall again. On the brass dish, the candle guttered, dimmed to a faint spark, but then crackled back to life.

Now she stood upon on a flat rooftop. Before her was a pair of French windows, cracked to allow the heat of the day to escape. From inside, a susurrus of soft snores emanated, suggesting a rooftop sleeping apartment. She raised the hand that held the knife, pushed wide the French window, and silently slipped inside.

As the two friends shouldered up to the bar a tiny, wrinkled man, who looked suspiciously to have evolved from good leprechaun stock, stood polishing a glass with a tea towel.

"Prepare yourself for bliss," Wilde muttered to his companion as both men rested their elbows upon the burled chestnut bar.

"What'll ye have gents?" The Leprechaun asked in a strong Dublin accent.

"I think you know what I have a thirst for, Eoin," Wilde said familiarly to the barman and with that he peeled loose a large bank note from his billfold and slapped it down on the bar. "And the same for my friend. And I want you to keep them coming until you require either another bank note or an ambulance to take me home."

I nside the French windows, it took a moment for the somnambulist's eyes to adjust. And then she scanned the room. She was in a bedroom. A large bed, opulent with lacy pillows and comforters, held a single occupant: an older woman in a negligee. The bed clothes had been tossed aside because of the warm night. The somnambulist crept closer, set the candle down upon a bedside table, and stood looking down upon the woman.

The sleeper was a middle aged woman, matronly and plump. An immense necklace sparkled on her bare throat and bosom. Under the sharp-edged moonlight slanting in through the open window, rubies, emeralds and diamonds coruscated and flashed. The sleepwalker leaned close, brought forward the knife, and slipped it beneath the necklace. She was carefully lifting it when the woman snuffled, snorted, and her eyes creaked open.

"Hummnn, Florence, is that you?" The lady asked groggily. But as she came fully awake, the matron's eyes widened with fright at the ghostly figure bent over her. And then she noticed the knife at her throat, slowly lifting the necklace, and a squeal of terror squeezed from her throat. The sleepwalker did not react and as the knife raised higher, the matron obligingly lifted her head so that the necklace slipped from around her neck. Wide-eyed and rigid with fear, the matron breathed in shallow gasps as the sleepwalker retreated to the French windows, threw the necklace about her own neck, and then turned and slipped out, dissolving back into the night as silent as a ghost. It took several minutes before the matron's drumming heart finally slowed, her trembling subsided, and as her throat finally unclenched her first scream shattered the silence.

· · ·

A s he snatched up the note, the bar tender grinned like the devil welcoming sinners to hell, and then clambered up on an empty crate to draw down a cobwebbed bottle from a shelf high up in the roof beams. Next he set down two chunky crystal tumblers on the bar before them, squealed the cork loose, and then carefully gurgled two fingers of dark amber liquid.

"Looks wonderful," Conan Doyle said. "What are we drinking?"

"It is called *Bruichladdichm*," Wilde smiled. "And it is from your homeland, or more specifically from a distillery in the Isle of Islay in Scotland.

"*Bruichladdichm*," the author of Sherlock Holmes repeated. "A name in Scots Gaelic."

Conan Doyle was just reaching for his drink when Wilde stopped him short with a *Tut-tut*. The Scotsman stopped and threw his friend an enquiring look.

"Not yet, Arthur. You must engage all your senses before imbibing. Your first experience with this whiskey must be like your first schoolboy kiss. It must be an event to be savoured and fondly looked back upon in the years to come. First you must look, I mean really *look* at the whiskey. Study it. Note the peaty colours, the ocherous depths, the way the light dances off the surface."

"Yes," Conan Doyle agreed. "It is a magnificent colour." He was reaching for the drink a second time when Wilde stopped him with another Tut-tut! "No, Arthur. Next comes the most critical part of drinking whiskey. Now you must *nose* the whiskey."

Conan Doyle frowned. "Did you say, *nose the whiskey*? Do you mean smell it?"

"*Nose* is the correct term," Wilde insisted. "Observe." Wilde picked up his glass and brought it slowly toward his large Irish face. "But before you *nose* you must first *swill*. This allows the whiskey to breathe and liberates all the volatiles." Wilde then carefully swirled the whiskey in his glass and Conan Doyle followed his example.

"Very good. You have looked. You have swilled. Next you must *nose*. Now hold the rim of the glass to your bottom lip—careful!—be sure to keep the glass level. This helps funnel the various notes to your nose."

"Notes?" Conan Doyle echoed.

"The first notes you detect will be the peaty notes, but there are also fruity notes, sweet notes and grainy notes, and lastly, there are the oaky notes."

The distant scream interrupted the two constables' conversation, and when the second one looked up, his eyes were caught by a flash of movement as the somnambulist glided along the low parapet of the rooftop opposite.

"Bloody hell!" Officer Charlie started. "Lookit that!"

The second officer followed his point and gawped. "It's a young slip of a girl. What the bleedin' hell is she doing up there?"

"I reckon she's a jumper!"

"Stuff me, I reckon yer right, Jonesy. She's gonna jump!"

"We need help. Let's call out the lads!"

The first constable took out his regulation police whistle, put it to his lips, sucked in a deep lungful and then and gave an ear-piercing blast on the whistle, while the other constable drew his truncheon and began to rapidly drum on the pavement.

"Oaky notes?" Conan Doyle asked. "The oaky notes derive from the wood used for the barrels. If you can detect melon, or citrus notes, the chances are your whiskey was matured in an American oak barrel. If you detect apricot or peach notes, those are indicative of a European barrel."

"That's an awful lot to remember, Oscar. Should I be taking notes?"

"Now tip the glass away from you and dip your nose into it. Go on, Arthur, don't be shy. Dip your nose beneath the rim. This is where you will detect sweeter notes like vanilla or maple. And if there is a lot of vanilla, that's a good indication the whiskey was aged in a bourbon cask."

"I'm afraid I shall never remember all of this. Couldn't I just take the tiniest sip?"

"Tush! Be patient. Now hold the far rim of the glass to the tip of your nose and inhale. You should be able to narrow down the grain used to make the whiskey. You might smell barley or wheat, or just a bready sort of aroma."

"Just a tiny sip? A mere taste?"

Wilde finished nosing and then brought the glass slowly to his lips and took the teeniest sip. "Mmmn," he said, smacking his lips appreciatively. "Nirvana."

He noticed that Conan Doyle was not drinking and threw him a look.

"Well, go on, Arthur. What are you waiting for?"

"You mean I can drink now?"

"Yes, of course. Why are you lollygagging?"

"I didn't know if I would first be required to stand on my head and wiggle my toes."

"Don't mock, Arthur, I'm providing you with an education."

"I must point out, Oscar, that I have been enjoying whiskey my entire adult life."

"No you have not, Arthur. You've merely been guzzling it. Now you will begin to truly appreciate it. Go on, imbibe!"

"Finally!" Conan Doyle, said, releasing an exasperated sigh. He fixed his friend with a gruff look, but gently lifted his whiskey from the bar, took one last savouring sniff and had barely touched the whiskey glass to his lips when he was interrupted by a cacophony of noise from outside.

The two friends looked at one another in consternation at the blasting of police whistles and the hammer of truncheons coming from the other side of the door.

"What on earth?" Wilde exclaimed.

"That's the police! Come, Oscar."

Both men set down their glasses and then crashed out the door to find one constable blasting on his whistle, while the other pounded on the pavement with his truncheon. Answering whistle blasts approached from the distance as two more constables ran pell-mell toward them.

"What the deuce is going on?" Conan Doyle shouted at the two officers.

In response, one of the officers merely pointed to the rooftop of the opposite row of houses.

When Conan Doyle followed the officer's point, his mouth fell agape.

The young somnambulist was tight-roping along the top of a narrow facade wall, seemingly indifferent to the six-storey drop beside her.

"We reckon she's a jumper!" The officer said.

Conan Doyle threw an urgent look at Wilde, "We must get up there, Oscar. Come along!"

Conan Doyle set off running toward the houses opposite, with Wilde lolloping behind.

After brutally thrashing the brass knocker, the door was eventually opened by a sleepy butler. Conan Doyle breathlessly related the story, and then all galumphed up multiple flights of stairs to the sixth floor where the butler threw open a hallway window and they stepped out onto the rooftop.

Both men were panting and breathing hard. Conan Doyle frantically scanned the rooftop. And then they saw her, up ahead, a ghostly form gliding away from them, the edges of her white nightgown licked by tongues of darkness.

"There!" Conan Doyle pointed and set off after the woman with Wilde and the two constables following close behind. They had to dodge around chimneystacks and vault over short walls, but they finally overtook the young woman who was walking, one-foot-ahead-of-the-other, along the low parapet.

"Quick, grab her!" One of the constables shouted.

"No, wait!" Conan Doyle cried, restraining them with a thrown out hand. "Look at her eyes. She's clearly sleepwalking. From my medical journals I have read that it is dangerous to violently awaken a sleep-walker. The shock to the heart can be too great."

"So what shall we do?" Wilde demanded.

Conan Doyle thought. "She's dangerously close to the edge. We must be careful. I say we follow her and when she steps down from the parapet we gently guide her away from danger. Perhaps rubbing her arms or gentle slaps to her cheeks will bring her around."

But at that moment, the somnambulist reached the loose lintel that had rocked beneath her weight the time before. This time, as she placed her weight upon it, the lintel teetered once again, and then the rotten mortar beneath shattered into dust and the lintel gave way. The heavy slab of masonry tipped up and tumbled into space, shattering on the pavement below with a mighty crash. Off-balance, her footing suddenly gone, the sleepwalker spun around, arms windmilling, and then began to topple backward.

Conan Doyle had time only to lunge forward and make a wild grab at her. He missed her flailing arms but grabbed a handful of the flimsy night gown, but as he took her weight, he too was ineluctably dragged toward the sheer drop. Instinctively, he threw out his free arm behind him and shouted, "Oscar!" Wilde leaped forward and grabbed Conan Doyle's outstretched arm, planting his feet, and straining to hold him back, but the slick leather soles of his fine shoes were sliding on the moss-slippery roof slates, so that he too was being dragged toward the drop. Luckily, one of the constables grabbed Wilde's arm and then his fellow constable grabbed his. Now the four men formed a daisy chain, with the sleepwalker dangling limp above a six-storey drop, suspended only by the fistful of nightgown clutched in Conan Doyle's steely grip.

By now, two more constables had arrived on the street below and were shining their bullseyes lanterns up at them and blasting their whistles.

"Back up?" Conan Doyle asked through gritted teeth. "Can we back up at all?" But as the chain of men attempted to draw back from the edge, the front of the sleepwalker's nightgown began to tear with a horrifying ripping sound.

"No, no!" Conan Doyle breathed, but then a huge swatch of material suddenly tore loose and the sleepwalker tumbled backward into open space. The Scots author let out an anguished wail and could not look away as the young woman fell in seeming slow-motion toward the pavement below, her body uncoiling into space, her half-lidded eyes lit with the gleam of starlight, her long brown hair and night-gown fluttering as she fell with no scream or noise until the sickening SLAP of a human body hitting the pavement.

Together, the three men hauled Conan Doyle back from the precipice, where he sank to his knees, dropped his head, and gasped out, "Dear God, no!"

CHAPTER 2: LOOKIT THEM SPARKLERS!

The somnambulist was dead. Conan Doyle knew that with dread certainty. No one could possibly have survived a fall from such a height.

Still he hoped against hope as all four of them trudged down the staircase to the street. When they reached the body crumpled on the pavement, (her arms and legs unnaturally splayed and bending at the wrong angles) the young woman's eyes were still open, her lips parted slightly. Her baffled expression suggested that she was still lost in a dream from which now, tragically, she would never awaken. Conan Doyle looked down to find that he was still gripping the swatch of fabric torn from the front of her nightgown. He balled it in his fist and crammed it into a jacket pocket.

The four policemen, along with Wilde and Conan Doyle, gathered around the sleepwalker's broken body. The Scots doctor reached down and gently closed the woman's eyes. In the soft throb of gaslight, she might have been a sleeping angel, save for the widening pool of blood spreading from the back of her cracked skull.

"I waited too long," Conan Doyle lamented in a torn voice. "If only I had acted sooner . . ." His throat closed with emotion. "A beautiful young life lost . . ."

Wilde laid a comforting hand on his friend's shoulder. "You did what you could, Arthur. You must not blame yourself."

"That you did, sir," agreed the constable named Charlie, and his fellow officers murmured their agreement.

One of the newly arrived constable's head jerked up and he stood listening a moment. "Here, it's stopped."

"What's stopped?" Wilde asked.

"That music."

"Music?" Conan Doyle echoed. "What music?" He shared a puzzled look with the other constables, but all were nonplussed.

"I don't remember hearing any music," said Constable Charlie who looked around at the others. "Anyone else hear music?"

Conan Doyle shook his head. "I'm afraid we were all a little too preoccupied. What kind of music did you hear?"

The constable pushed his police helmet back on his head and scratched his scalp. "I dunno. Queer sounding music. Like somefink I never heard before."

But before the subject of music could be pursued a brash cockney voice interrupted.

"Cor, she wassa looker, this one," The owner of the voice was a short, boyish figure in a jacket and a newspaper boy's cap and now he stepped over to the corpse and brazenly lifted the dead woman's nightgown, ogling her slender legs and buttocks. "Nice arse, too!"

Conan Doyle flared with anger at the open disrespect. He stepped forward and forcefully shoved the short figure away. "You cheeky young . . . Who the devil are you? Show a little respect or I'll . . ." Conan Doyle balled his fist, but it seemed ridiculous threatening such a diminutive figure.

Although he appeared to be a young lad of fifteen, the short figure now pushed his cap back on his head and grinned up at Conan Doyle. "Here, I knows who you are. You're that cove that writes them Sherlock Holmes stories." And then he noticed Wilde. "And you're that fancy feller wot writes them plays that posh people go to see, Alfred Wilde."

"*Oscar* Wilde, if you don't mind," the Irishman replied, regarding him with a sour look.

At the news, the young man produced a notebook and pencil and began scribbling notes. "Strewth," he chuckled, "Arthur Conan Doyle *and* Oscar Wilde! This story is writing itself. And can I add that you two gentlemen bravely tried to rescue the lady? That makes you both heroes, I reckon. Our readers will eat that up."

Conan Doyle took an instant dislike to the young man throwing questions at him. He cast a look at the constables. "See here, who is this chappie? He's not with the police. What's he doing here?"

Jonesy, one of the older officers volunteered, "It's just Billy, sir . . . Billy Brash. He's a reporter for the Illustrated Police News. Always Johnny on the spot, eh Billy? As usual?"

The young man flashed a cheeky grin. "You know me, Jonesy, I gotta nose for news. When I heard all them police whistles, I cut along, sharpish like."

The newcomer was wearing his paperboy's hat pulled low, so that his face was hidden in shadow. But when he approached Conan Doyle, he raffishly pushed his hat back, and grinned up at him. The gaslights peeled the shadows away and Conan Doyle saw that what he had taken for a schoolboy was in fact a young man in his early twenties. His short stature had fooled Conan Doyle and he suspected that Brash used that illusion to his own benefit.

"Sherlock Author in the mystery of the dead sleepwalker," the young man said, "That's a headline wot'll sell papers," he smiled cheerfully, "Or how's about: famous writers watch helpless woman plunge to her death?"

Conan Doyle ground his molars in irritation. If this young scallywag wanted to publish such a story, he was powerless to prevent it. However, Wilde was concerned about other considerations. "If you're going to write about me you must at least mention my name, Oscar Wilde . . . playwright, wit, and raconteur. Author of the play *An Inconvenient Woman* currently enjoying a boffo run at the Theatre Royal, Drury Lane. And if you miss-spell a syllable I will drag you and your rag of a paper through the law courts!"

Further discussion was precluded by the arrival of a Black Mariah, sent for to transport the body. But when it arrived, as two constables went to lift the corpse, the sleepwalker's arm fell to one side and revealed what hung around her neck.

"Crikey!" Lookit them sparklers!" one of the officers exclaimed. His expression caused Conan Doyle and the other constables to gather closer, many of them letting out gasps of amazement.

The necklace was large and heavy. The many strands of garnets, diamonds and precious gems flashed and sparkled in the gas light.

"That's worth a million pounds, that is!"

"Not quite a million," piped up the young reporter. "It's called the "Pride of Tashkent and it's been valued at a hundred thousand pounds."

Wilde and Conan Doyle exchanged a stunned look. "How on earth would you know that?" Conan Doyle challenged.

The young reporter grinned. "I wrote about it, that's how. About six months ago. The Marquess bought it for Lady Geldsachs. But then he snuffed it shortly after giving it her. His family took her to the law courts to try and get it back, but she wasn't having none of that."

"So is this Lady Geldsachs?"

The young reporter laughed and nodded at the corpse.

"Naw, Lady Geldsachs is a fat old biddy. This 'un musta stole it."

Despite the fact that he knew nothing about the sleepwalker, Conan Doyle felt obliged to defend her innocence. "If she did steal it, I doubt she meant to. She was clearly sleepwalking. I'm sure the poor girl had no idea what she was doing."

Billy Brash guffawed. "Oh yeah, sleepwalking was she? And then she just happened to nick a necklace worth a fortune. That's a good excuse ain't it?"

Even though he had no reason to believe in the sleepwalker's innocence, still Conan Doyle's distaste for the impertinent young reporter only grew stronger."

Wilde was less invested in the sleepwalker's innocence. "She probably works for Lady Geldsachs. I imagine she's a maid or something."

Under the crossfire of several policemen's bulls eye lanterns the gemstones flashed and sparkled, throwing refracted beams upon the dead girl's face.

While the argument continued, the body of the sleepwalking woman was wound in a shroud and lifted inside the Black Mariah.

The most senior officer, a sergeant named Ned appeared and spoke to Conan Doyle. "Course, you gents will need to report to our station in the morning to make a statement."

"Yes, of course," Conan Doyle said."

The sergeant was about to walk away but then turned back to the two authors. "You gents might wanna cadge a lift with us. There won't be no hansom cabs at this late hour."

"Yes, thank you," Conan Doyle said. "We'd be grateful for that." Conan Doyle threw a glance at the guttersnipe reporter and happened to catch a surreptitious exchange. Brash turned his back and held something in his hand which the Constable named Jonesy discreetly lifted from his fingers and slipped into his own pocket. It happened in a flash but then Conan Doyle realised what he'd just seen exchanged: a screw of snuff or tobacco. Evidently, Billy Brash rewarded his contacts on the force so he could be sure of getting the scoop on stories. No wonder he was "Johnny on the Spot" so often.

Everyone clambered on board the Mariah and took a place on the hard bench seats. The body lay on the floor between their feet, bleeding through its shroud onto the scuffed wooden floor, Before they closed the rear door of the Mariah, sealing them up in the darkness, Conan Doyle heard a chiming noise and when he looked out the open door, saw the Boy Reporter whiz past on a bicycle, cheerily jangling its bell as he swerved around them.

"That young rascal needs his ears boxed," Conan Doyle remarked grumpily.

The Mariah set off with its occupants' eyes fixed upon the corpse rocking with the motion of the wagon. Wilde and Conan Doyle said little as they rubbed shoulders with the other constables crowded into the boxy space. The Mariah's tiny barred windows provided little view of the outside, and so Conan Doyle had no view as the Mariah trundled through the next cross street. As a result, he missed seeing a black, four-wheeler carriage (commonly known as a "growler") idled at the kerb. Two figures stood close by; a grey haired and stooped old woman and a young man in a top hat and a cape. Sitting on the driver's seat of the carriage was an incredibly tall figure who wore a grey fur Cossack hat and a long wool coat despite the balmy evening weather.

The tall young man threw a severe look at the old woman and bitterly commented. "She's not coming, is she? The police have been called. No doubt she's fallen to her death. I'm quite certain that was her body they were taking away in the Black Mariah. I told you it was too big a risk."

The grey-haired woman shot a look at the young man and warned, "Hold your tongue and get back in the carriage."

The young man climbed back into the carriage and angrily slammed the door.

The grey haired woman threw a look at the Cossack and barked, "Load the instrument . . . and be quick about it."

The Cossack climbed down from the driver's seat, picked up some kind of instrument housed in a wooden cabinet, and carried to the back of the carriage. He set the instrument in place, and then drew a tarpaulin over it and lashed the cords down tight to secure it. The woman climbed back into he carriage. Then the Cossack clambered back up to the driver's seat and shook the reigns so the two horses drawing it whinnied and pulled away into the darkness.

In the back of the black Mariah, Conan Doyle's eyes were constantly drawn to the slender form wrapped in its death shroud. In his mind the young woman's fall played over and over. As she tumbled away into the darkness there had been no terror, no understanding that her young life was about to be suddenly and horribly cut short. And then his vision starred and he looked away into the shadows, for his eyes were filled with tears. Had he grabbed her sooner, would the shock of awakening have killed her? Now all he felt was remorse, for he had failed to save her and he knew that, for the rest of his life, his mind would retain that terrible image of the young woman tumbling away into empty space.

3

CHAPTER 3: DROWNING IN NIGHTMARES

Jean Doyle was asleep when Conan Doyle crept into the bedroom of their Norwood home. For long minutes he stood over his young wife, watching her sleep. Her beautiful face in peaceful repose resembled the face a Renaissance angel. After what he'd just been through, the sound of her drawing in each breath and then peacefully releasing it was a balm for his turmoiled soul, a promise and reassurance that his happiness would continue. After the tragic events of the night he felt as if his skin had been flayed from his body, exposing every raw and throbbing nerve. He had witnessed death up close. As a doctor, as a man, as a human being, he had reached out to try to save a human life . . . and he had failed. Now a dull fatigue suffused his weary body and his exhausted soul. He ached for sleep.

For release.

Jean had left the bedside oil lamp turned down low and so he quietly undressed, pulled on his night shirt and then lifted the bedclothes and slid into bed beside her. After several minutes he let out a deep sigh and allowed his head to sink deep into the pillows, willing his body to relax. But still the tragic events of the night played over and over in his mind. Again and again, he saw the young woman's face, her half-open eyes spilling over with starlight, and that inscrutable, seraphic smile as she fell away from him toward the merciless pavement that rushed up to meet her. Again and again, her heard the sound of fabric tearing, felt the nightgown rip loose in his hand and watched the helpless girl fall to her sudden death. But eventually, after an hour of listening to his wife's relaxed breathing he finally fell into a peaceful doze . . .

. . . only to awaken with a cry of terror.

"What? Darling husband? What's the matter?"

Conan Doyle was grappling to hold onto his wife's slender form, murmuring incoherent cries of terror. Finally, he came fully awake, realised where he was, and lay clutching his wife as shudders wracked his large body.

"What? Arthur! What is wrong?"

Conan Doyle slowly eased himself loose of the nightmare, although he could not let go of Jean.

"Arthur? What's happened?

"N-n-nightmare," he finally managed to stammer out.

For an hour they sat up in bed together, the bedside lamp turned up full, as Conan Doyle haltingly related the tragic events of that night. Jean wept to hear of the young sleepwalker's demise. But then Conan Doyle told her something in a voice suddenly torn to rags.

"I dreamt of the young woman. Again, she walked along the parapet until she stepped upon a loose lintel slab. It gave way under her weight and she began to fall backward. I seized hold of the front of her nightgown but then it began to tear. And when I looked up into her face . . ." Conan Doyle's voice cracked and broke. ". . . it was your face. Not hers. Your face!"

Jean Doyle paled, her mouth opened, lips twitching, but his story had stolen her voice.

Conan Doyle gathered her up in his arms and hugged her to his chest. "Oh, my darling wife. I could not lose you. Not so soon after . . ."

He did not finish the sentiment, but Jean knew what he was referring to. It has been two years since Louise Doyle, the Scots author's first wife, had finally succumbed to tuberculosis. They had waited a full year—a respectful time after Louise's death to marry. These days, although Jean and Arthur were very happy together, she knew that Louise's death still affected Conan Doyle deeply.

'I am so sorry," Conan Doyle apologised. "I should not have told you about this incident. In fact, on the way home, I resolved never to tell you."

Jean's face betrayed her deep shock and unease at the revelation, but then she pulled her face back together and laughed carelessly. "Oh, but it was just a silly dream, darling husband. Here I am with you now. And we are both safe and snug in our bed."

She hugged her husband and snuggled into him, but as her head rested on his shoulder, he could not see the deep look of fear that swept across her pretty face.

CHAPTER 4: INSPECTOR CRUMPET

Even before Conan Doyle strode into the briefing room of the police station, he knew that Wilde was already there, for he smelled the piquant aroma of his Irish friend's Turkish cigarettes. Upon entering, he found Wilde in characteristic pose as he lounged in a chair, one leg crossed over the other, the elbow of his smoking arm cupped in his hand. He looked ridiculously crisp for such an early hour in the morning in his pinstripe jacket, cream cravat, and even his trademark green carnation in his boutonniere. Somehow Wilde always managed to usurp any space he occupied and make it his own, so now he reposed like a prince on his throne, rather than an eye witness dragged into a grubby police station.

Conan Doyle, stepped into the room, his sleep-deprived eyes pouchy and bloodshot. He squinted around and then shuffled over to where Wilde was sitting and collapsed into the chair next to him.

"Ah, Arthur, " Wilde drawled. "So glad you could finally join us."

"Sorry," Conan Doyle apologised. "I slept poorly last night."

I was only then that Conan Doyle realised why the smell had been so pungent—everyone in the room seemed to be smoking one of Wilde's Turkish cigarettes. Evidently, the Irishman had been passing around his silver cigarette case.

Wilde smiled lazily. "At last I have put your Hibernian timeliness to shame. I arrived early, while you, Arthur, are shockingly late. I know I always say that punctuality is the thief of time, but I assure you it was an accident. I promise never to be on time again."

Standing stiff-backed to the windows was a bald-headed man with a voluminous moustache and beard, whom he correctly guessed to be the Chief of Police. Also present were a pair of moustachioed constables, and then, sprawled in a chair rocked back to the wall, was a portly Sergeant with enormous bushy sideburns of a fiery ginger colour. Just then the Sergeant took an enormous bite from the giant wedge of pork pie he was gripping and a trail of bright yellow mustard dripped onto the lapel of his uniform. He wiped the spill up with a thick forefinger which he then placed in his mouth and sucked clean and then dozily daubed at the remaining stain with a handkerchief, merely succeeding in smearing it farther.

"I am Chief Dalworthy," the bald man announced. "Our precinct will be handling the investigation of your ill-fated sleepwalker—just a matter of tidying up loose ends, really. After you've given your statements, I'd appreciate it if you gentlemen would accompany Inspector Crumpet as he conducts his investigation. First, he is to return the necklace to Lady Geldsachs, and then he will visit the household where the unfortunate young lady was employed as a maid. This was a most unusual tragedy, and you two gents were eye-witnesses. I think if would be helpful if you went along too."

Conan Doyle threw a glance around the room, but saw no one dressed like an inspector. "And is this Inspector Crumpet to arrive soon?"

With obvious unease, Dalworthy nodded toward the portly sergeant whose jaws were feverishly working away at his pork pie. "That, ahem, is Inspector Crumpet."

"Inspector?" Conan Doyle asked. "Forgive me for pointing out that he's wearing a Sergeant's uniform."

"He has recently been promoted to Inspector . . ." The Police Chief answered dryly and then added, ". . . after first being demoted back down to Sergeant . . . again."

Inspector Crumpet grinned around a mouthful of pork pie, and waggled his fingertips cheerily at the authors.

After giving their statements, Conan Doyle and Wilde trooped outside to a waiting Black Mariah—their transport. They clambered inside and took a seat on one of the bum-bruising bench seats. But after a twenty minute wait, the two authors were beginning to wonder where the Inspector had got to.

"Isn't the Inspector supposed to be coming with us?" Wilde asked.

"I would presume so," Conan Doyle noted grumpily. "He is supposed to be leading the investigation. I must say, his appearance does not inspire confidence. The man's a disheveled mess. I'm not surprised he was recently demoted."

"Inspector Crumpet," Wilde mused. "He is certainly aptly named: fat, round and doughy, just like a crumpet."

"From the sound of it he's regularly demoted and then promoted again," Conan Doyle noted. "So perhaps he's a good inspector, even if he does look like an unmade bed."

"Yessss, well, I have my doubts."

At that moment Crumpet appeared, grunting extravagantly as he clambered up into the police Mariah and plunked down heavily on the bench next to Conan Doyle, huffing and puffing from the exertion. The Scots author smelled pastry and suddenly noticed that Crumpet was clutching a grease-stained paper bag. As the Mariah set off with a jerk, Crumpet rustled open the bag and offered it up to the two authors. "Would you gents care for a sausage roll?"

Wilde visibly recoiled and covered his mouth with the back of his hand. "I'm afraid I never eat a bite before noon."

"I have already breakfasted," Conan Doyle replied, although the aroma of pork and pastry was heavenly and he found himself salivating.

"Yes, so have I," Crumpet answered. "In fact, this is my third breakfast of the morning. I find that it's important that I eat sufficiently so that I'm not overly hungry by dinner."

The doctor in Conan Doyle could not resist commenting, "And

now you're going to eat three enormous sausage rolls? That hardly seems a healthy diet."

"Not all three. Only the one," Crumpet retorted looking hurt. "I'm not a complete pig." And then he rustled in the bag, drew out a fat sausage roll and crammed it into his mouth, devouring it in three huge bites. He carelessly brushed pastry flakes from a moustache the size of a scrub brush and then eructed loudly, unleashing a pork-scented belch that wafted about the Mariah's confined and poorly ventilated space.

Conan Doyle threw Wilde a look and rolled his eyes.

"So where are we visiting first?" Wilde asked.

"Back to the scene of the crime," Crumpet volunteered, in between sucking his teeth. "The necklace belonged to Lady Geldsachs, widow of the banker, Lord Geldsachs. I am to return it to her."

After a moment's thought, Wilde released a titter.

"What?" Conan Doyle asked.

"The name," Wilde explained. "Geldsachs is a German surname. It literally means 'gold sacks.' We're on our way to visit Lady Moneybags!"

CHAPTER 5: LADY MONEYBAGS

The Police Mariah trundled through the traffic-choked streets of London and finally drew up at a huge mansion in Mayfair. The handsome residence was just two streets distant from O'Houlihan's, the whisky bar Conan Doyle and Wilde had visited the previous evening.

They soon stood on the elegant doorstep of 42 Adam's Avenue, with its Greek-style Corinthian pillars and massive double doors with red paint so thick and glossy it reflected the image of the two tall and broad shouldered writers standing beside the shorter and decidedly rounder reflection of Inspector Crumpet.

Crumpet seized the brass ring swinging in jaws of the brass lion and punished the door knocker with three sharp raps. After a short wait, the door was opened by a balding butler who, upon glimpsing the visitors, assumed the expression of a man whose nostrils have just caught a whiff of something nasty.

He asked them to follow him and then led them along a gloomy and rather morbidly decorated hallway. Apparently, the Late Lord Geldsachs was an enthusiastic murderer of exotic animals, for they trooped past an elephant's foot umbrella stand, nearly tripped over the snarling mouth of a leopard skin rug, and past walls perched by taxidermied examples of exotic birds that had apparently been stuffed mid-squawk. Finally, he conducted them into a stuffily decorated parlour where two ladies reclined on a pair of sofas facing one another across a small occasional table upon which a tea service had been placed. As they entered, the nearest woman stood up from the sofa. She was short, and had red hair which was slashed across the crown by a sinuous wave of pure white. Conan Doyle estimated the women to be in her early forties, but the shock-white stripe was not a sign of age. Thanks to his medical training, he recognised the white streak as poliosis, an hereditary condition. The woman was dressed in a simple taffeta dress across which she wore a sash which ran from shoulder to hip. At first Conan Doyle assumed the woman was a campaigner for women's rights, and thought the banner proclaimed her as a suffragist, but when he read the words written there, they said "Marylebone Refuge for Fallen Women."

Thanks to the sash and the collecting tin and tray of pins resting on the couch next to where she was sitting, Conan Doyle quickly deduced the woman was collecting money for a cause, but Crumpet was apparently oblivious to such clues, because he now stepped up to her, ducked a bow and spoke, "Lady Geldsachs? I have come about your missing necklace."

"I'm afraid I am not Lady Geldsachs," the woman replied, causing the Inspector's smile to collapse. "I am Madame Xylander, the operator of a charity for distressed women. I am here on a social visit." She looked to her right at the woman sitting on the opposite sofa, who now rose to her feet. "This is the lady of the house."

"I am Lady Geldsachs!" The female voice boomed. When the three men looked to their left they saw the large owner of the large voice. Lady Moneybags was a solid, rather stout lady, pushing sixty, if not older. She steamed toward them across the parlour with the gathering mass of a dreadnought bearing down upon a rowboat. As she drew close the cloying scent of her perfume preceded her like a bow wave.

When the cloud of scent bowled into Wilde, he physically recoiled as if back-handed across the face. Snatching a handkerchief from his breast pocket he clamped it over his nose and mouth as he muttered in Conan Doyle's ear, "The lady is drenched in so much perfume she's leaving a stain on the ceiling!"

The comment burst a laugh from Conan Doyle that he masked as the start of a coughing fit.

Lady Geldsachs stopped and turned to directly address the other woman. "I'm afraid I shall have to cut our visit short, Madame Xylander, I have business to attend to of a rather private nature." She clearly read the curiosity on the other woman's face and hastened to explain. "It involves a precious belonging of mine that was stolen. I am sure your charity is very worthy. Perhaps we can discuss my support of it at some future date."

Madame Xylander seemed crestfallen. "Oh, but I was hoping . . . I would only take a moment of your time . . ."

Lady Geldsach's face concertina'd with irritation. It was clear she had been hoping to be rid of the charity beggar before the news of its return was released.

"I shall leave you to attend to your precious necklace, Lady Geldsachs. I'm sure you rejoice at its return. Perhaps I might visit you again—at a more opportune time to discuss your assistance in my charity for fallen young ladies. In the meantime, I hope you will consider supporting our cause."

"Yes," Lady Moneybags replied. "Perhaps I will think of it." She tinkled a bell and the bald butler reappeared. "Charles, would you please see the lady out?"

The charity lady, clearly realising she was being given the bum's rush, lacked the time to utter the meagrest complaint before she was ushered out of the room.

"Bravo!" said Wilde, addressing Lady Geldsachs directly. "I have always maintained that the profession of charity worker is the perfect disguise for a scoundrel. I am always not at home when one knocks at my door. Indeed, I would gladly fling myself out the nearest window as soon as receive them. Imagine a profession where your job is to intrude upon people's privacy and then beg money from them. I'd rather give my cash to the street beggar who ties his leg behind him and begs money for being a cripple. At least he has added an element of theatricality to his begging and he does not intrude upon my reading of the morning newspaper. As I have often said, charity is not a solution to poverty: it is an aggravation of the difficulty. Have you ever looked out your window and remarked. Oh, splendid, here comes a charity worker. I do hope they stop at my door."

Conan Doyle stepped in before Wilde had chance to expound further. "Yes, thank you, Oscar for sharing your views upon the subject of charity workers, but we have some about the theft of Lady Geldsach's necklace."

"Very well," Lady Geldsachs agreed. She waved her arm toward the sofa her unwanted guest had just vacated. "Please, gentlemen, take a seat."

As the three men found a place on the sofa, Inspector Crumpet's face lit up when he saw the tea service.

"Lady Geldsachs, if it wouldn't seem presumptuous of me, might I help myself to a cup of tea? I've only had the two cups this morning and I am quite parched."

The lady made a fussy face but assented. "Yes, by all means, help yourself."

Crumpet seized a spare tea cup and saucer, carefully ladled in two teaspoons of sugar into his cup, added a splash of milk, and then hefted the large floral teapot and poured himself a steaming cupful. His stirring technique seemed to follow a pattern of two clockwise stirs followed by two counter-clockwise stirs. Having stirred, he then took a sip and a look of pure bliss flashed across his face. "Ah, this is Harrods' special blend of Indian and Ceylon tea if I am not mistaken?"

The lady looked puzzled as to why they were discussing tea. "I am not certain, but I do know it comes from Harrods."

"Yes," the Inspector agreed, the special brew number four. A bit expensive for me on a policeman's salary, but worth every penny. I compliment you, Lady Geldsachs, on your fine taste in the brown cheer."

Lady Geldsachs made a puzzled face. "Thank you but I am sure I have no idea what kind of tea it is. It is something my housekeeper procures for us. Now Inspector, there is the matter of my missing necklace. I am quite eager to have it back."

Inspector Crumpet set his cup down and began, "Lady Moneyb—He just managed to stop himself before he called her Lady Moneybags and now he shot Wilde a caustic look—I mean Lady Geldsachs. I have news that I am certain you will find welcome. I am here to return your necklace to you."

"Thank goodness!" The lady smiled at her visitors and confided. "I have not slept a wink since it was snatched from me at knifepoint!"

The rotund inspector released breathy sounds as he dug through the many pockets of his uniform jacket, which gaped like the drawers in a bank after it's been robbed. Finally, he tugged free a paper sack and proudly held it out to her as he bowed slightly and said, "Lady Geldsachs, I am right proud to return this to you."

The Lady frowned as she uncertainly took the crumpled paper sack from him. She opened the bag, peered in, and looked up at with a scowl on her face. "This appears to be a rather crushed sausage roll."

Crumpet double-taked, snatched the bag back and also peered inside. "Ah, yes. So it is. Sorry, wrong bag."

Conan Doyle and Wilde shared a pained expression. Crumpet appeared to be a bit of a buffoon, seemingly capable of bungling the simplest task.

He crammed the paper bag back in his pocket and rummaged the opposite pocket, finally drawing out a black velvet bag.

"Sorry, ma'am. This one's got your necklace in it."

The lady doubtfully took the bag from him, but then she opened it and lifted out the stunning necklace, which even in the gloomily-lit room managed to flash and coruscate. Lady Geldsachs put a hand to her bosom, emitting a deep sigh of relief.

"Yes, it seems quite undamaged." She appeared about to put on the necklace but Conan Doyle interjected, "Ah, there might be some blood on it."

The lady's smile dissolved into a scowl of disgust and she quickly held the necklace at arm's length. Once again she reached a small china bell from a side table and tinkled it. A moment later a shy maid cowered into the room. Lady Geldsachs gestured her over, "Florence, have this sent to the jewellers to be cleaned at once. And then have it forwarded to my bank. The insurers have decided it must be kept in our vault when I'm not wearing it."

Crumpet crossed his arms behind his back. "Now Lady Moneybags, I must ask you about the circumstances of how you lost the necklace. The uh, the lady burglar what took it."

The matronly Geldsachs put a hand to her bosom and drew a shaky breath. She rose from the sofa, moved to the window and stood looking out, the back of her hand pressed to her forehead. Conan Doyle glanced at Wilde who rolled his eyes and muttered under his breath. "With that standard of acting, I would not give the role of lowest understudy in one of my productions."

"As you might appreciate," she began, "the nights of late have been warm and close. On such occasions I abandon my usual boudoir for one of our sleeping rooms on the roof. Because of the heat, I had thrown the bedclothes aside and was wearing my most revealing negligee. And so I was practically naked . . . if you can imagine it."

"I'd really rather not," Wilde muttered *sotto voce* to Conan Doyle, who stifled a laugh with great difficulty.

Lady Geldsachs paused to throw him a sour look and then resumed her narrative.

"I cannot express the full terror of that moment," she said. "I was deep asleep. The burglar who crept into my room was clearly a hardened thief, a skilled assassin. I awakened to find a knife levelled at my throat."

She threw a gesture at the end table next to where she'd been sitting. "Why that is the very knife there. My assailant dropped it as she stole away from my room. I awakened from a restful sleep to find her coiled over me, the wicked blade held to my throat, ready to slash my windpipe. It was clear the vixen would not hesitate to murder me if I offered the least resistance."

All now looked at the shiny silver knife sitting atop the small table next to her .

"And did your . . . your . . ." Crumpet grappled for the correct term. ". . . your assailant say anything?"

"She said nothing. There was no need to. She was a cold blooded murderer. I saw death in her eyes."

Conan Doyle leaned forward in his seat. "You did not notice her gaze? The heavy-lidded, blank stare of a sleepwalker?"

"Not at all!" The lady countered. "Her eyes were cold and calculating. The eyes of a murderer."

"And how could you see her eyes in the darkened room?" Wilde asked. "With the window behind her, surely her face would have been concealed by shadow?"

"It was, save for the reflection from the blade she held at my throat, which threw a line of light across her eyes."

"So you awakened with the knife at your throat. Crumpet ventured. "What happened next?"

"With devilish resolve, she slipped the blade beneath my necklace. I felt cold death press against my beating heart."

"Heart? That's a bit lower down surely?"

"By heart I mean my bosom."

Conan Doyle shrugged. It was hard to argue that point. The lady's bosom was prodigious.

"And why were you wearing such a priceless necklace to bed?" Wilde questioned.

"I do not customarily sleep in it, but I had returned late from a soiree. I was tired and simply went to bed wearing the necklace."

Custard put it in, "So, there you were, laying in bed, when you awakened and a shadowy figure had a knife to your throat? What then?"

"And then she used the pitiless blade to lift the necklace and violently snatch it over my head. I started to cry out, but she put a finger to her lips to shush me and then, as she left the room though the French windows, she flashed a wicked smile and slowly drew a finger across her throat to threaten what she would do if I cried out."

Conan Doyle jumped to his feet. "If I might I'd like to examine the knife."

He retrieved it from the table. "And this is the knife?"

"It is. I am lucky it is not soiled with my own blood."

The Scots author frowned at the knife. "This is a butter knife. Very blunt." He sawed at his palm with the blade to demonstrate its dullness and turned to offer it to Inspector Crumpet. "She could hardly have cut your throat with a knife such as this."

Wilde commented, "Perhaps she meant to butter Lady Geldsachs to death, a slippery and rather delicious way to die."

Inspector Crumpet pointed the knife at Lady Geldsachs. "Did you recognise this girl? Had she ever been in your employ?"

Lady Geldsachs took umbrage at the very notion. "Certainly not. All our people in service only come from very best households with the highest recommendations."

Crumpet threw a glance at the two authors. "Can you gents think of any other questions?"

Conan Doyle shook his head."

At that moment a Coach clock on the mantlepiece chimed the hour. Taking that as a signal, Custard snapped his notebook closed and struggled to jam it into a pocket of his overly-tight uniform.

"It's ten o'clock gents and we have another household to visit. I suggest we move along and allow the Lady her peace once again. Plus it's only two hours until my lunch."

The lady chimed her bell and the butler appeared to lead the the three men back through the macabre menagerie to the front door.

As they were walking away up the front path, the three men were still comparing notes. When they reached the road, they stopped to confer.

"I think Lady Geldsachs is a large lady with an even larger imagination," Conan Doyle confessed. "I think her testimony was laced with exaggeration and dramatisation."

As the three men clambered back into the Police Mariah, they failed to notice the black carriage snugged up against the opposite kerb. The driver slouched over the reigns looked neither right nor left, and appeared to be doing his best to appear inconspicuous, which was impossible due to his towering height and the fact that was oddly dressed for the London summer in a long wool coat and a Russian Cossack's fur hat. If the carriage bore any occupants they were concealed behind windows tightly curtained apart from where the curtain was parted slightly so that anyone inside could discretely observed the comings and goings from Lady Geldsach's residence.

Just as the police Black Mariah lumbered away, the curtains of the black carriage opened slightly as a hand reached up and lowered the glass. Then the hand tossed something out of the window: the still-smoking butt of a short cigar which hit the cobbles and rolled a few feet.

CHAPTER 6: THE DEAD MAID'S ROOMMATE

The Police Mariah next took them to an elegant but less upscale residence in Fitzrovia.

On the journey over, Inspector Crumpet was uncharacteristically silent, mainly because he was busy munching away on the last (now rather crushed) sausage roll, as well as the saveloys, biscuits, and boiled sweets he kept pulling out of the pockets of his uniform like some kind of magic trick.

"I wonder if any of our inspector's family hails from Mexico?" Wilde muttered *sotto voce* to Conan Doyle.

It seemed an odd thing to say and Conan Doyle's face showed his puzzlement as he whispered back, "Why do you say that?"

"Because the man is a human piñata. Whack him with a stick and I swear all types of sweets would burst out."

When they arrived at the house in Fitzrovia they were informed that the master and mistress were holidaying in Venice, and that they would be seen by the housekeeper. With that, the butler conducted them up four flights of stairs (with Crumpet huffing, puffing, wheezing and moaning up every one) to the servant's quarters. As they stumped up the final set of stairs, all were panting slightly but

Inspector Crumpet was wheezing like a steam calliope about to explode.

Conan Doyle leaned close to Wilde's ear and whispered, "I fear that poor Crumpet is but one floor shy from a heart attack."

"On the plus side the climb has kept him from eating another bite."

Thankfully the rotund policeman survived, staggering lead-legged to the top of the stairs where he collapsed into to a convenient chair someone had been thoughtful enough to position there. He wiped his red, sweating face with a handkerchief as he fought to slow his panting breathing.

The housekeeper approached them. She was an older lady whose eyes were red with weeping and who broke into sobs upon sight of Crumpet's police uniform.

"I can't believe she's gone. I'll never believe it," the woman wailed, her eyes sparkling with fresh tears as she crushed the hanky she clutched to her mouth.

The housekeeper, whose name was Agnes, led the three men down the hallway and into a small bedroom. The room was typical of austere servant's quarters: two single beds huddled against opposite walls. A cheap deal dresser with a tiny mirror hung on the wall above it. A crucifix nailed above the door. A chest for clothes at the foot of each bed and scant other furniture.

Also being interviewed was Gertrude, a rather plain girl of just fifteen—a scullery maid who was the dead girl's room mate.

Conan Doyle took the lead in interviewing the two women as Inspector Crumpet slumped on one of the two beds, still red-faced and panting from the stairs. "And the girl, her name was Fanny I take it."

"Fanny Jones," the Matron said with a hitch in her voice. "A good girl from a family in Wales."

"And had she even been in trouble before?" Conan Doyle probed.

The matron stifled a sob and shook her head. "No, never. She was as good as gold."

"And had she ever been suspected of stealing anything from the house?" Inspector Crumpet managed to put in.

The matron shook her head vigorously. "No. Never. She was from a good Christian family and honest and hard working as the day is long. Like many girls from the provinces, she had moved to London to find a job and sent what little she could afford back to her family. I'da been proud if she'd been me own daughter." The woman broke down into tears and shook her head. "Forgive me, but I gotta go write to her poor parents." And with that the woman rushed from the room, although they could hear heart-wrenching sobs as she hurried away down the hallway.

Conan Doyle turned his attention to the teary-eyed roommate, Gertrude. "She was your roommate. Were you two close, my dear?"

The young woman merely nodded, her eyes bright with tears.

"How long had you been roommates?"

"Six months, sir, ever since I come here. Fanny took me under her wing. Helped me. She was ever so lovely."

Conan Doyle nodded thoughtfully as if carefully considered the girls' words, and then casually asked, "Did Fanny ever sleepwalk?"

"Su-sleepwalk, sir?"

"Did you ever find her out of her bed at night?"

"No. Well, yeah, but only the last month or so."

Conan Doyle and Wilde shared a look freighted with meaning.

"When was the first time you saw Fanny out of bed?" Wilde asked. He paused and made a face. "Which sounds like the punch line to a rather rude joke."

The innuendo was lost on Gertrude, who continued, "Like I said, about a month ago. I woke up one night and she was standing at the window. She give me ever such a fright, I can tell you."

"And what happened?"

I asked if she was all right. I figured she'd had a bad dream."

"And what did she say?"

"Nuffink. She didn't say a word. She was fumbling with the window, as if she couldn't figure out how to open it. I jumped out of bed and took her by the arm. Shook her. That's when I noticed her eyes."

"Her eyes?"

"Yeah, she just stared like she couldn't see what was in front of her."

"Her gaze was glassy?"

"Yeah, that's what it was. Glassy. Empty."

"And did that ever happen again?"

"Yeah, a few times. Once I woke up and she was bumping about the room, trying to open the bedroom door, but I'd bolted it. Then there was last Wednesday."

"Yes?"

"I woke up. Felt a cold draft, and when I looked, I saw that the window was wide open. And then I saw Fanny outside, on the roof. So I climbed out the window after her. She was standing there, like a statue. It took me a while but I managed to guide her back inside and put her to bed again."

"And this sleepwalking only began recently?"

"Yes, sir."

"And had anything happened in the last month? Anything that may have upset Fanny?"

The girl mulled the question over, but then frowned. "No. Nothing, sir. Just the usual."

As they were preparing to leave, Conan Doyle cast one last look around the tiny room. There were no personal possessions in sight and nothing, save for the small crucifix nailed high up on the wall, to give any kind of clue as to the personal lives the young servants lived, but then his eyes moved across the dresser and he noticed something stuck in a corner of the mirror frame. He stepped over and pulled it free.

It was a paper flier for a music hall show. The coloured illustration showed a handsome, top-hatted young man with jet-black hair and elaborate, waxed moustaches which stood up at an exaggerated angle.

The ornate calligraphy arcing above his head identified him as *Morpheus the Magnificent.*

"What's that, Arthur?"

Conan Doyle frowned at Wilde and shook his head. "Looks like an advertisement for some kind of music hall conjurer."

Apart from that, the flyer was unremarkable. It was the kind of thing one could find among the litter blowing along any London street. Conan Doyle flourished it beneath the roommate's nose and asked. "Is this yours, Gertrude?"

The maid shook her head. "No, it was Fanny's. The show was playing at the Alcambra Music Hall."

"And did you and Fanny attend?"

The young maid shook her head, shamefacedly. "No, sir. It cost a farthing, and I ain't got no savings. But Fanny went with her friend."

"Her friend?" Conan Doyle's ears perked up. "Do you know the name of her friend."

The young maid shook her head. "No, sir, but I know it was someone she knew from back in Wales. Another girl wot come to London to work in service."

"Ah, I see." Conan Doyle said. He flashed an avuncular smile as he casually tucked the flier into his pocket and said, "Never mind. And thank you for speaking with us today. You've greatly helped our investigations. I am deeply sorry you have lost your friend."

He threw a look at Crumpet who, having finally caught his breath, had produced a Bakewell Tart from one of his pockets and had just taken a huge bite . "Yeff," Crumpet added, speaking around his mouthful of marzipan and pastry. "Fink you vewwy mush."

As they followed Crumpet's waddling form back to the waiting Mariah, Conan Doyle and Wilde discussed the case.

"This girl Fanny hardly seems like the ruthless, master burglar, Lady Moneybags described," Wilde noted as they clambered inside the waiting Mariah.

"Unless the young lady was living a secret double life," Conan Doyle added sceptically. "Which I would say would scarcely be possible for a young, hard-working chambermaid."

" Oh, I dunno bout that, sir," Sergeant Crumpet put in. "I seen a number of slippery customers in my time. Simpering angels who butter wouldn't melt in their mouth. Course their thieving was usually confined to their own households. I never seen one what could would traipse the roof top tiles in order to slip into an occupied lady's boudoir. It's like something outta the IPN."

"The IPN?" Wilde repeated. "What on earth is that?"

"The *Illustrated Police News*. You met one of their reporters the other night."

"Ah yes," Conan Doyle agreed. "That young scallywag. What was his name again?"

"You mean Billy . . . Billy Brash, Boy Reporter as he likes to be known."

The name gave Conan Doyle a sudden inspiration. "I believe they have offices in the Strand. If you could be so kind as to drop me, Inspector, I'd like to interview this Brash chap."

CHAPTER 7: BILLY BRASH, BOY
REPORTER

The Black Mariah dropped Conan Doyle on the Strand, directly outside the offices of The *Illustrated Police News*. The IPN, as it was known to most, was one of the best selling newspapers on the newsstands of London. As opposed to sober journals of record such as *The Times*, the *IPN* was a sensationalist broadsheet filled with accounts of murders, hangings, tragic accidents, ghastly goings-on, and all things eldritch, melodramatic and sensational. The magazine's pages were lovingly illustrated with lurid depictions of things such as the Ripper's murder victims with their bruised and slashed faces lying bleeding in their open coffins, or of fiendishly grinning monkeys snatching babes from their cribs only to dash their brains out in full sight of their hysterical mothers, of axe murderers, poisoners, arsonists, and bridge-leaping suicides. Blood, guts, gore, death, horror and human suffering in all its bizarre and macabre forms was a favourite topic, and the London public had an insatiable appetite for it. It was the best-selling periodical of the time, for there is nothing more interesting to the public than the death and suffering of their fellow human beings.

The location of the publication's offices on the Strand was indeed fortuitous, as many of the crimes it reported upon were committed in the immediate vicinity, and so it was convenient for the paper's reporters and illustrators who were often dispatched to the scene of a crime as soon as word came in, so that many of the locations of outrages could be accurately sketched by the paper's artists, and many of the crimes could be reported upon before the blood spattered on the pavement had had a chance to dry.

Conan Doyle stepped into the front office and asked to see Billy Brash. He was conducted into the news room, a riotous scene of reporters crouched over typewriters, hammering away at the keys, and "copy monkeys," young boys running up and down the news room snatching proofs from the hands of reporters as they finished their copy, raised it aloft, and shouted "Copy!"

The Scotsman scanned the rows of desks for Billy Brash. Conan Doyle had only seen him just the once, and that was in darkness, so he was uncertain he would be able to recognise him. But then he noticed an empty desk with a familiar bicycle propped against it and what appeared to be a rumpled sleeping palette beneath. The magazine's illustrators all sat at drawing tables pushed to the sides of the room. Now he saw what appeared to be a child perched on a stool looking over the shoulder of one illustrator as his hand moved across the paper, sketching. From his boyish stature, Conan Doyle recognised the diminutive form of Billy Brash.

As he strode over, Conan Doyle eyed the drawing being worked on and was disconcerted to see the events of the previous evening being depicted, including (much to his chagrin) a very recognisable likeness of himself and Wilde struggling to hold onto the young somnambulist as she dangled over the sheer drop below. It was an uncannily accurate reproduction of the scene, only for Conan Doyle it disturbingly echoed his nightmares, in which he always watched the action from a similar perspective, looking down from somewhere outside his body and slightly higher.

Before they became aware of him looking over their shoulders, Conan Doyle was able to eavesdrop on their conversation.

"Okay, Griggsy, that's not half bad, but can't you make her nightgown a bit more see-through? Or maybe it's being blow up by the breeze, so we get a cheeky glimpse of her curvy arse."

The illustrator was clearly struggling with Billy's suggestions and grimaced with frustration. "I can't get no more suggestive than that, Billy. You'll get me sacked and the paper pulled into court."

Conan Doyle realised he'd been standing there far too long and cleared his throat noisily.

The illustrator and the boy reporter looked around and Brash's face lit up with a big grin.

"Stap me, it's Mr Sherlock Holmes hisself!"

The snatch of conversation he'd just overhead had only helped cement Conan Doyle's jaded opinion of Brash's character. Nevertheless, he tried to keep a civil tone. "Mr Brash, I see you remember me from the other night."

"Are you bonkers? It's an honour, Mistah Doyle. And look, Griggsy here is immortalising your heroic deed."

Conan Doyle let his gaze scrape across the drawing once more. "Perhaps I'd be more enthusiastic if we had been successful in saving the young woman."

"Wasn't your fault, sir. Ya did yer best. You and your pal Albert Wilde."

"His name is Oscar . . . Oscar Wilde. Please don't get that wrong. He's very sensitive about it."

"Yeah, alright. Oscar Wilde. I'll remember that."

The Scotsman threw a quick look around the busy room. He wanted to get this over quickly, so he tried to change the direction of the conversation. "Can we talk a minute . . ." he eyed the illustrator, who'd been listening to every word. ". . . in private?"

They moved back to Billy's cluttered desk, well out of anyone's earshot.

"From the sleeping palette I take it you sleep under your desk?" Conan Doyle asked.

The boy reporter smiled slackly, "Too right I do. I don't never leave here. I live's here. Eats here. And sleeps here. That's how come I'm always Johnny on the Spot."

"Well, that and bribing the police to give you tips when news breaks. I saw you passing that screw of snuff to the constable last night."

Brash's face twitched in a wicked smile. "You could call it a bribe. You could call it that. I call it paying the constabulary a 'con-sul-tay-shun' fee."

Despite himself, Conan Doyle smiled at the younger man's moxie.

"You said something the other night. When you saw the young lady's dead body. You said, 'another one.' What did you mean by that?"

"You ain't a regular peruser of the Illustrated Police News, is you, Mister Doyle?"

The comment made the author of Sherlock Holmes squirm a little. "As you might imagine, with my own writing taking up so much of my time. I don't have the time to read every journal on the news stand."

At the comment Billy snatched open his desk drawer, revealing an impenetrable miasma of clutter, but he dug into the pile and fished out a dog-eared copy of a book that had lost its cover and slapped it down on the desk in front of Conan Doyle.

When he examined it, the Scots author was surprised to see that was a copy of his collection of Sherlock Holmes Stories, obviously well-thumbed.

"I've read your stories. Every one. Dozens of times. I even copied them all out. See, I never had no proper education. But I learnt grammar, spelling and whatnot from your Sherlock Holmes stories. So, in a way, you was my teacher."

Something caught in the back of Conan Doyle's throat and his eyes misted slightly. Perhaps he had been too quick to judge the young fellow. From his cockney accent and demeanour, it was obvious he'd had a tough upbringing in the mean streets of London. In a city where the weak were ground down and buried in the trash, through hard work and native cunning, Billy Brash had pulled himself up by his bootstraps. By comparison, Conan Doyle had had a privileged life, but the family had experienced just enough adversity that he had compassion for those who had had it even worse.

Brash's boyish grin lit up his face. "Like they says, reading broadens the mind. But I meant "another one" because she's the twelfth sleepwalker in as many weeks."

Conan Doyle's jaw dropped at the news. "Did . . . did you just say the *twelfth* sleepwalker?"

The Boy Reporter stood up from his chair and signalled with a nod. "Follow me and have a dekko." He led Conan Doyle to the other side of the room where shelves held a stack of illustrations waiting to be filed. Each illustration was mounted on pasteboard and now he lifted the stack and riffled through them.

He stopped and slid one from the pile to show the Scots author. "This is from last week."

Conan Doyle studied the illustration. It showed a group of fire-fighters milling around the base of a house. their faces taut with consternation. They were throwing a rope up to a young woman who (once again) was wearing nothing but a suspiciously flimsy night-gown. The young lady was in the process of tumbling off the roof of a house. What throwing up a rope to young woman was supposed to accomplish Conan Doyle could not guess at. (He suspected that, like most of the IPN's illustrations, a shocking amount of artistic license was employed.) But as the young reporter paged through the illustra-tions, there were more, many more: "Death of a Somnambulist" showed a woman tumbling backward from the rooftop to her death. For Conan Doyle the image sent a icy jolt of deja vu through him. More followed: a somnambulist walking across a narrow plank sepa-rating tall buildings. A somnambulist falling from a pier, and so on.

"I had no idea this was such a common occurrence," Conan Doyle said.

'Not usually," Brash agreed. "But lately there's been a whole rash of 'em."

"And did they all die?"

The young man pulled a frowny face. "One or two. But most just disappeared."

"What do you mean, disappeared?"

The reporter shrugged. " Stepped out a bedroom window onto the rooftop and was never seen again."

Conan Doyle responded to the news with a stunned expression. "Never seen again . . . ?" A gasp tore loose from his lungs. "Surely . . . never? But how is that possible? Surely their families searched . . . I don't . . ."

'Never seen again," the Boy Reporter repeated. "And knowing some of the doings in this city like I knows, I can't imagine what grief they come to."

Conan Doyle's gaze went blank as his mind swarmed with dreadful images of scantily-clad young sleepwalkers helplessly wandering the filthy streets and brimstone alleyways of the Capitol— the deadly and dangerous streets of London.

"Like lambs walking into a tiger cage," he muttered to himself.

His eyes refocused as he finally came back to himself and fixed his young companion with an urgent gaze. "Names, dates, addresses!"

"Wot?"

"Information. You must give me everything you know about these disappearances."

The young reporter replied with an unenthusiastic scowl. "Sounds like a lot of work. I'm a newspaperman. I got deadlines. Stories to write. I can't just—" He shook his head. "I mean, I'd have to try and find me notes, and all that stuff. Might take a while to get it all together."

"I'll pay you," Conan Doyle said.

But the young man shook his head sulkily. "I dunno. You're asking a lot, guvnor. I'm a busy man . . ."

Conan Doyle held out a fist with a five pound note crumpled in it. He guessed that five pounds was likely a few months salary for the young reporter. "If you're too busy, maybe someone else in this office could help me."

Without hesitation, Billy snatched the note. He flung open a desk drawer, grabbed a notebook and tossed it on the desk. "There ya go. It's all in there."

Conan Doyle snatched the notebook up and also grabbed the stack of illustrations.

"Hang on just a minute!" Brash objected. "You can't take those. They belong to the magazine."

"I'll bring them back," Conan Doyle called over his shoulder as he walked away. Before exiting the press room, he threw a look back at the Boy Reporter. "And if you hear anything else, contact me. I'll make it worth your while." Conan Doyle rubbed his fingers together in the universal short hand for money, and the Boy Reporter flashed him a knowing grin before he stepped from the office.

CHAPTER 8: A PLAGUE OF
SLEEPWALKING

When Conan Doyle strode into the echoing vault of Victoria Station, he immediately stopped at a newspaper kiosk to purchase a copy of *The Times*. But then his eye was caught by the cover of the *Daily Mail*, which had the screaming banner headline: *Sleepwalking Hysteria Hits London.*

He tossed down a handful of coins to pay for both papers and tucked them under his arm along with the stack of illustrations he had commandeered from the IPN office before dashing to catch his train.

After settling into his seat in the First Class carriage, he unfolded the *Daily Mail* and his eyes skimmed a breathless article alleging that London was in the grip of a "sleepwalking plague." The screaming headline was followed by a grab-bag of rumour, innuendo, half-truths, bald-faced lies and groundless speculation as was typical of the Mail's high journalistic standards. In rabid and histrionic prose it told of how young women (and as with the IPN, all those illustrated were lissome and scantily clad) were climbing out their bedroom windows and tumbling off rooftops or vanishing into the night. The article contained few concrete details and devoted precious column inches to hand-wringing fear-mongering while offering nothing in the way of reasoned analysis. It was obvious that most of it was invented by journalists idly lounging with their feet propped up on their desks, or cribbed from the equally groundless speculation of other newspapers. He dragged his jaundiced gaze across the article and then tossed the paper aside. While it contained nothing of substance, it did, however, confirm the notion that, true or not, there seemed to be an uptick in public awareness of a very rare phenomena. Seeking a more substantive read, he snatched up his *Times* and started to catch up with the real news, politics and events of the day.

Conan Doyle was lost in his reading when he heard the squeal of brakes as the train began its long, rumbling deceleration into Norwood station. But just then his eye fell upon a headline in the Announcements section of The Times on page 4. It was a dry notice of the latest in the series of scientific lectures regularly run by the Royal Institution. The upcoming lecture, which was scheduled for the very next day, was entitled, *Sleep Walking, Sexual Suppression, and Female Neurosis*. From the brief description the lecture promised to focus upon the root causes of sleepwalking in men, and especially in women, and how it should be dealt with. It sounded like the perfect source for answers and so he made a mental note of the time and location of the lecture. It was in the afternoon, and Conan Doyle's chest tightened as he wondered if he might still be able to secure a ticket— perhaps even two tickets, if in the unlikely chance he could persuade Wilde to accompany him. His eyes rescanned the lines of newsprint seeking the name of the lecturer, which he finally located: *Professor Sigmund Freud.*

Conan Doyle had attended many lectures at the Royal Institution, but was disappointed that the lecturer's name sounded distinctly foreign and he worried that the man might possess some impossibly thick and indecipherable foreign accent. But still, it might be worth attending. He changed his mind about inviting Wilde and then changed it back again. Perhaps this Sigmund Freud chap might possess some genuine insights into the human mind.

But then he was startled back to the present by a whistle blast followed by a jolt of the train. The steady chuff-chuff of the locomotive grew louder, and when he looked out the window he saw to his dismay the station sign for Norwood sliding past the window. He had been so engrossed in the announcement he had missed his stop which was even now moving away behind him.

When he finally stepped through the front door to his home, nearly an hour late, Jean bounced up to Conan Doyle, threw her arms about his neck and bussed him on the lips.

The Scots author laughed at her infectious enthusiasm and hugged her back, giving her a squeeze that made her oof and then giggle.

"You are in high spirits today," he said.

"I'm just happy my darling husband is home," she beamed.

"I'm sorry I'm late. I was engrossed in the newspaper and missed my stop."

"I hope you are hungry for dinner."

"When am I ever not hungry?"

Mary the maid floated up and curtseyed to Conan Doyle. "Beggin' yer pardon, sir but we've been holding dinner back for you. Are you and Mrs Conan Doyle ready to dine?"

"Ah, yes, Mary, thank you. Tell cook to dish up. Mrs Doyle and I will be waiting in the dining room."

The maid bobbed another curtsey and left on her errand.

Conan Doyle stopped and examined his wife's mischievous expression. "But you seem especially pleased with yourself my darling. Do you have a secret to tell me?"

His words made her laugh carelessly. "No secret. Am I not always happy to see my husband?"

He smiled. "Well, yes."

"Oh, and Constance Wilde and I are going out together tomorrow."

"Very good! I am glad you two ladies have become such firm friends. What are you both up to?"

"Oh, nothing, just shopping. But I promise I won't spend too much."

"Well, I hope you two have a good time." He inhaled and smelled dinner cooking.

"What is for dinner? I could eat a bear."

"Come along, I've had the cook make your favourite: Shepherd's pie."

"Sounds splendid."

For the first time Jean noticed the leather portmanteau Conan Doyle carried over one shoulder and the stack of pasteboard covers he had borrowed from the Illustrated Police News tucked under the other arm.

"But what is all this you have brought home?"

Conan Doyle did not want to upset his wife by sharing more lurid images of sleepwalkers, so he quickly made up a fib. "Oh nothing, dear, just some research for my next historical novel. I'll just pop it into my office. You go ahead to the dining room."

Conan Doyle hurried to his writing room and laid out the materials on his writing desk. It was then that he was struck by a memory of something he wanted to study further—the flyer from the Alcambra Music Hall. He had left it on his dresser, so he left the writing room and thundered upstairs to his bedroom. But when he stepped inside the bedroom that strange phenomenon that afflicts most human beings struck Conan Doyle. Upon entering a new room the reason he had come upstairs totally evaporated from his mind. He looked around the space, straining to remember what he had come upstairs for but it was gone. He heard his wife calling him from downstairs and so reluctantly gave up his search and hurried back to her.

Jean was waiting at the bottom of the stairs. "Darling, cook has been holding dinner for an hour. Were you changing for dinner?"

"Uh, I had thought about it," Conan Doyle agreed. "But then I changed my mind." He hugged her again and kissed her on the forehead. "Come along darling, let's go through."

But his expression was perplexed and Jean was especially intuitive that she noticed it.

"What is it?" her eyes searched his face and found trouble there. "What's wrong? I sense your unease."

"The other night . . ." he began before his voice frayed at the edges and he had to begin again. "The other night well . . . I must apologise."

"Apologise? What for?"

"For my behaviour which was . . ." A pained grimace swept across his features. " . . . which was less than manly. I . . . I am deeply ashamed—"

Before he could continue the thought Jean gently put her fingers to his lips to shush him. "Arthur, you are virile and strong but your heart is caring and thoughtful. You witnessed something terrible that night. It filled your dreams and made you fear for me. Never apologise for what you are, for that is why I fell in love with you."

When they reached the dining room, Mrs Hague, their Scottish cook, was hovering outside the door, waiting for them.

"Doctor Doyle your dinner is going cold on the table. The children are seated at the table and waiting. Shall I return it to the oven or are you and Mrs Doyle finally ready to sit down to your supper?"

The two took their scolding with chagrined good humour.

"You must forgive me, Mrs. Hague, I do apologise. We are now ready to sample your fabulous cooking. Shepherd's Pie, my very favourite!

Conan Doyle linked his wife's arm and said. "Shall we go in, my darling?"

CHAPTER 9: JEAN FINDS THE MORPHEUS FLYER

The next morning Conan Doyle left in a rush after breakfast. He told his wife Jean that he had to get to the Royal Institution just after it opened in an attempt to secure tickets for himself and Oscar for an afternoon lecture.

Jean spent the morning in her usual routine, playing with the children, overseeing the domestic staff, proofreading Conan Doyle's latest pages (the historical novel he was penning) so that when she looked up and saw the time, she realised she had to get ready for the visitor she was expecting.

She ran upstairs, rushed into the bedroom and gave her curly, honey-blonde hair a quick adjustment with a hair brush. Jean's dressing table was on one side the room, Conan Doyle's on the opposite. As she set down the hairbrush and her focus shifted, she looked in her mirror, and in the reflection spotted something lying on the marble top of her husband's dressing table on the far side of the room.

Conan Doyle was fastidious in his personal habits and usually ensured that the top of his dresser was kept clear of any objects. He couldn't abide clutter, and so his combs, hair brushes, hair oils, moustache wax, and other grooming aids were snugly settled into the dresser's drawers. But he had been in a hurry that morning and so it looked as though he had left something lying on the surface. It appeared to be an old rag and at first Jean wondered if one of the servants had absent-mindedly left behind a dust rag. Up close it proved to be a swatch of raggedly-torn fabric. Jean picked it up and studied it. It was a thin and sheer material, almost like something from a night gown. Then Jean suddenly remembered her husband's midnight confession of the horrible death he had been witness to. This was the swatch of the sleepwalker's night gown that had torn loose before she plummeted to her demise. Jean realised that the fabric held the taint of death, and with a horrified shriek she threw it back down. It wafted loose a colourful rectangle of paper which floated to the floor. She snatched the paper up and studied it. It appeared to be an advertising flier. On the front side it had a depiction of a handsome young man in a top hat. Figurative lightning bolts quivered in the air around his extended hand as a young woman swooned before him.

But before she could study it further, Mary, one of their domestics, called up the stairs to announce that a carriage had just drawn up outside. Jean set down the flier and tripped down the stairs to find that her visitor was Constance Wilde whom she had invited over for tea and then a shopping trip.

Constance stepped inside the Doyle residence and the two ladies bussed one another on the cheek and hugged.

"Constance, thank you for coming," Jean greeted her friend, smiling.

"I am always happy to visit. Oscar is at rehearsals at the Haymarket and my boys are visiting with their grand mama, so I am a free woman all afternoon."

"Wonderful! My children have just gone to the boating pond with their nanny, so I too am free."

Thanks to Wilde's and Conan Doyle's friendship, Constance Wilde and her boys were frequent visitors to the Doyle household and everyone got along very well together. Free of their children, both women retired to the parlour together to drink tea. While they were waiting for the servant to fetch it, they both perched on opposite ends of the Doyle's rather lumpy horsehide sofa. A few minutes later, Mary the maid, bustled back into the room, carrying a tray chinking with a pot of tea and cups and saucers. She drew up an occasional table, arranged the tea service upon it and said, "I'll just fetch the sweet tray from the kitchen, ma'am."

While they waited for the maid's return, the two women made chit chat and, even though Jean had told herself that she would not repeat the story, she ended up relating the tragic tale of the ill-fated sleep-walker in the exact level of detail as her husband had told it to her.

Constance Wilde listened in wide-eyed horror to the story.

"Really?" Jean said afterwards, "I am surprised you have not already heard the tale. Did Oscar not mention it to you?"

Constance Wilde barked out an ironic laugh. "In truth, I have not seen Oscar in two weeks. He is always busy with rehearsals for the newest play, or he is up at Oxford visiting his university friends, or he is staying at his club in town. The boys and I seldom see him these days."

Constance knew that Wilde and her husband were going to see a lecture that afternoon at the National Institute, but she bit her tongue and said nothing. Mary finally returned with a three-level cake stand burgeoning with petit-fours, small biscuits and, of course, that most English of artery-clogging indulgences—home made scones with clotted cream and jam. Free of an audience to criticise them, both women felt free to ignore restraint, and eagerly fell upon the the scones, which were still warm from the oven and which smelled like warm pillows made from the clouds of heaven. And as is the custom, each woman lavished her crumbly scone with a dash of butter, a large dollop of Devon clotted cream, topped with a blob of jam. Jean's favourite was a nicely tart rhubarb, while Constance favoured strawberry. Each woman made an un-ladylike grunt of ecstasy as they bit into three layers of bliss. Their conversation lapsed as they ate.

Constance sipped her honey-sweetened tea, and then reached for another scone (her third) and paused to slather it with clotted cream followed by an extravagant blop of black current jam.

"Not another scone, Constance!" Jean scolded. "You have had two already. You will get fat and then your husband will stop loving you."

Constance Wilde bit into her scone and paused to lick the scone crumbs from her lips and then suck the cream from her fingertips.

"In truth, my husband has already fallen out of love with me."

Jean's face registered surprise at such a confession freely given. She reasoned that her friend must be joking. "Dearest Constance, do not say such wicked things, even in jest!"

Constance Wilde replied by throwing her friend a jaded look. "It is no jest, Jean. Since I birthed Vyvyan, Oscar has not so much as laid a finger on me."

It was a shocking thing to confess to another woman, especially someone who was little more than a casual acquaintance—it was not as if they had been friends since school days. Jean felt her face reddening and squirmed at being made a confidant of such intimate news. She forced a smile and offered breezily, "Oh, but men become preoccupied with their work from time to time and neglect their familial duties. I am sure that Oscar is very busy with his plays—"

"His plays and his young male . . . " Constance paused as she chose the correct word, then added the word acidly ". . . companions."

Laden with innuendo, the word *companions* seemed to ricochet around in Jean's head like an angry wasp looking to escape from the jar it was trapped in. Now Jean really did not know what to say or where to look.

"And what of you?" Constance asked. "Has Arthur been neglecting your needs . . . in the boudoir?"

It was a shockingly direct question, made doubly difficult to answer truthfully that of the last week or so, her husband was seemingly perpetually aroused, so that every morning end evening she found herself on her back, feet raised toward the ceiling and her thoughts fixed upon the Empire. Even if he walked into the bedroom and caught her bending over the bed to smooth the coverlet, she was likely to be tumbled on the spot. In truth Jean was thrilled at the constant attention, but she could hardly compound Constance's misery by admitting to it.

"Arthur is often very tired when he finally comes to bed," she offered cautiously. "Especially if he has been at his writing desk since the early hours of the morning, penning his latest creation. Other nights, however, he can be quite . . . vigorous in his attentions."

Constance Wilde looked away into space, a look of hurt and sadness creasing the corners of her pretty eyes. When she spoke again her brittle voice revealed how wounded she was. "Once, when the end of my labour with Vyvyan was near, I loosened the belt of my robe so that it dropped from my shoulders. I was hoping that the sight of my naked body, my breasts swollen with milk and my belly gravid with the child I was carrying, would fill Oscar with ardour at what he had done to me. At the child he had put inside me. But instead . . ." her voice broke on a hitch. ". . . instead I caught in his eyes a look of utter revulsion. As if he found my pregnant body deeply disgusting. We have not been intimate since that day."

Jean was struck dumb and could think of nothing to say. As she tried to lift the tea cup to her lips, her hand shook and the teacup made a porcelain rattle. Time ticked by as she thrashed her brain to think of a safe response. Thankfully, the deadly silence was broken by the maid bustling in to collect the empty cake tray and ask the ladies if they required any more tea.

"Yes, another pot, please," Jean quickly put in, grateful to say something to fill the silence.

The maid ducked a curtsey but as she was about to leave she remembered something and reached a hand into the broad pocket of her pinafore

"Oh, ma'am," she said turning back. I found this on the Master's dressing table. Should I keep it to light the morning fire, or would you like to hang into it?"

She offered up a crumpled scrap of paper to her mistress. Upon recognising it, Jean snatched the flier from her fingers. "Yes, we'll keep it, thank you," Jean answered. The maid curtsied a second time and hurried off to fetch another pot of tea.

"What is that you have to show me?" Constance Wilde asked.

"Oh, this? I don't know. I just found it on Arthur's dresser. I cannot imagine how he came across it."

She handed the flyer to Constance who studied it closely and remarked, "It appears to be an advertisement for some kind of Music Hall magic show."

"Really?" Jean said. "How odd. It's not the kind of thingArthur attends. Usually he is more interested in scientific lectures . . ." and then she added in a devilish voice, ". . . and other rather boring things!"

The two women shared a naughty giggle.

Constance's eyes dropped back to the flyer, and after a moment's study, her handsome face lit up. "Morpheus the Magnificent . . ." She read aloud, and added excitedly, "Oh, but I have heard of this chap. He's not a magician. He is a hypnotist. I have also heard that he is devastatingly handsome. If he is as handsome as this picture, I should love to see him in the flesh."

"Where is he appearing?"

Constance read the venue aloud. "At the Alcambra Music Hall."

"I so enjoyed going to the music hall when I was single . . . " Jean lamented. ". . . before I was a married lady. Arthur frowns upon such entertainment as vulgar, and I know he thinks of the Alcambra as a rather low establishment."

"Oh, it is!" Constance agreed. "It is in an unseemly area and has a very poor reputation. Some of its acts border on the obscene." She smiled and added, "All the more reason why we must go."

Jean laughed and rolled her eyes. "Oh I could not even bring myself to ask Arthur's permission. What if he expressly forbade it?"

"Then you must do what all married women do."

Jean threw her a puzzled look. "And what, pray, is that?"

Constance laughed gaily. "Simply don't tell him. My dear, you and Arthur are in the beginning of your marriage. Everything is new. Now is the time when you must train your husband. Before things become fixed."

Jean tittered. "Train him? You mean like a dog?"

"Not quite like a dog. Dogs have a brain and can be difficult to train. Men are much easier."

Jean squealed with laughter. "Oh, I couldn't *not* tell him. That would be like a lie."

"Not a lie. Nothing as grand as that. More like a white lie. An omission. You simply forgot to tell him. At the very worst, a fib. And fibbing is necessary to any marriage."

"And what if Arthur caught me fibbing? What then? What could I possibly say?"

"Then you fall back on the weapon every married woman possesses—tears. You rush to your husband. Hug him. Beg his forgiveness with tears in your eyes. Thank him for correcting you because, as a weak and simple woman, you rely upon his male better sense to correct you when you do foolish things. Soon you convince him that he has done you an enormous service that will make your marriage stronger and happier."

"I don't think Arthur would be fooled by such an act. He has a very penetrating mind."

"Believe me, Jean, when Arthur looks into your pretty blue eyes and sees your cheeks streaked with tears, he will not think with his mind, but with his heart. He will not only forgive you, in the end he will blame himself. He will probably bring home roses and take you out to dine . . . maybe even jewellry."

Jean Doyle had to cover her mouth she laughed so hard. "Constance, the things you say. You will scandalise me! Next you'll be insisting that women have the right to vote."

At that moment the servant, Mary, entered the room carrying a tray with a freshly charged teapot. She set the tea pot down on the small table positioned between both women. "Shall I bring the desserts around again ma'am?"

"Oh no," Jean said. "I think we're quite done with . . ." She trailed off and then a wicked smile creased her face. "Do you know, I rather fancy another scone and jam. "Yes, Mary, do bring the sweet tray again."

The maid bobbed a curtsey and whisked out of the room.

Jean Doyle looked at her visitor and laughed at herself. "Why did I do that? I'm not even hungry!"

"Because I am being a bad influence on you. After all my life of being the good girl and then the good wife, I am finally learning to do what I want. I want you to learn that lesson early, Jean. Please do not take as long as I did."

Constance picked up the flyer again and studied it. "Do you know, I've heard of this chap," she said, running a finger over the printed likeness. "In the letters to the Times I read an account of a lady who went to see the show. He asks for volunteers from the audience who he then hypnotises and makes them squawk like a chicken, bark like a dog, or perform all kinds of outlandish feats which keeps the audiences in fits of laughter, and afterwards the volunteers have no memory of any of it."

Jean's brow furrowed slightly. "How very odd. Why do people do such things?"

"Because he has hypnotised them, and they are totally in his thrall."

"Oh, I don't think I should like that."

"Really? But he is so very handsome. Can you imagine being totally in the thrall of a handsome young man? You are powerless to resist his every command. You are totally at his mercy."

Jean looked uneasy. "But . . . but he would be free to take all kinds of liberties . . ."

Constance Wilde's smile turned wicked. "Exactly, he is free to touch you. To caress you. To interfere with your most intimate lady parts." She brought her lips close to Jean's ear and whispered, "He could fondle your breast . . . or lift your skirts and touch you upon your . . ."

The last words were whispered into Jean's ear and were so shocking they made her shriek with laughter. "Stop, Constance! I blush to even think about such a thing."

"Oh, but it's not your fault," Constance assured, "because you are a helpless woman . . . under his spell . . . powerless to resist his licentious desires."

"You make it sound horrid."

"Really? Now that Oscar has lost interest, I would love to be ravished by a handsome young man."

Constance Wilde traced a finger across the hypnotist's handsome features on the flyer and suddenly blurted out an idea. "We must go!"

"What? Oh no! I couldn't!"

"There's a matinee. Today. We must go. It's only a sixpence for entrance. I have money. I'll pay. And I have our carriage outside."

"No, I dare not. Arthur would not approve!"

"You must do this, Jean. You must for the sake of your marriage, otherwise you will grow dull and predictable and Arthur will fall out of love with you."

Jean vacillated for several long moments but finally found her voice. "Oh . . . very well then."

Mary re-entered the room bearing the cake tray freshly laden with scones and confectionaries. Jean snatched a petit-four from the tray, and then jumped up from the sofa and spun around the room as she bit into it.

Mary looked rather shocked at her mistress's behaviour, but swallowed her surprise and remembered to ask. "Shall I bring another pot of tea, ma'am?"

"Uh no. No thank you, Mary. Mrs Wilde and I are going out for the afternoon . . . " And then she added with a devilish smile, the first fib of her married life ". . . shopping."

CHAPTER 10: FREUD'S LECTURE AND SLEEPING IRISHMEN

"I must warn you, Arthur, I might require a cup of coffee . . . or twelve. Last night our performance of *An Inconvenient Woman* was a triumph, as usual. But I'm afraid our celebrations went on till early morning."

"Exactly how early?" Conan Doyle asked.

"I've just come from there."

"So you haven't slept?"

"Not a jot. But fret not, the Wildean mind—which thrives upon intellectual stimulation—has little need for sleep. While at Oxford I rarely slept—I was famous for it."

"Really? I remember you telling me how you drew eyes on your eyelids with ink and learned to sleep with your head propped up on your hand."

"Oh, did I tell you that story?" Wilde laughed at the memory. "Yes, wizard wheeze. Got away with it through two years of Latin and won a prize from my professor for being the most attentive student in class. Yes, it was some of the most productive sleeping I've ever done."

"Anyway, I'm sorry, but we have no time for coffee," Conan Doyle said as the two men hurried through the hallways of the Royal Institution. "Because, as usual, we are late."

"By your tone I can't help feeling that you somehow hold me responsible."

"We're late, and not by a few minutes!" Conan Doyle announced to the air as they raced through the corridors. Conan Doyle ground his molars in irritation. Wilde was habitually late for every appointment and Conan Doyle was desperate to catch this lecture.

"But surely that merely enhances the gravitas of my appearance when I finally do arrive," Wilde insisted. "Instilling in all a sense of both relief and gratitude."

They reached the appointed lecture hall just as an elderly lady was closing the doors to prevent further admission.

"Two more!" Conan Doyle called aloud and waved his tickets frantically. The lady fixed him with a look that could curdle milk, but held the door wide as the two authors pushed past into a large lecture hall with a steeply sloping floor. Attendance was impressive as nearly all the seats were occupied by an audience buzzing with anticipation. But as is always the case with such lessons and lectures, the front two rows of seats were mostly empty and so Conan Doyle hurried toward them.

"Ah, perhaps we should find seats toward the back, Arthur, in the unlikely case that I nod off."

Conan Doyle spoke through gritted teeth. "Perhaps I should borrow a hat pin from one of the ladies to ensure you don't nod off?"

Wilde laughed nonchalantly. "No, no, that shan't be necessary. I ensure you I will be riveted to the lecturer's every word."

Conan Doyle took the seat directly opposite the lectern, front and centre, and Wilde, with obvious reluctance, dropped into the seat beside his.

As they were horribly late, they waited only seconds before the lecturer was announced.

"Please welcome to the Royal Institution Professor Sigmund Freud of Vienna University."

As the audience broke into polite applause, Wilde leaned close to Conan Doyle and asked in a low voice. "Who is this chap?"

"An Austrian fellow, Professor of neurology. He's to talk about somnambulism."

Wilde nodded and said, "Ah! How apropos. I definitely won't fall asleep now."

The man who walked up to the lectern was younger than Conan Doyle was expecting. In fact, he seemed to be about the same age and himself and Wilde. He was a handsome man with a dense black beard and side-parted hair cut short. His suit, ties and general grooming, exhibited typical Teutonic, almost manic precision. He carried an air of self-importance and his expression was serious almost to the point of self-caricature. He settled himself behind the lectern, gave a curt nod to acknowledge his audience and then made them all wait as he acted out an elaborate ritual. First he drew a humidor from his breast pocket. He removed the lid and drew out a short cigar. Next he produced a match box and fastidiously removed a single match. Struck it. Touched the match to the cigar and puffed it into life. Then he returned the burned match to the matchbox and both the matchbox and humidor to their respective pockets. Finally, he puffed away at the cigar, clearly enjoying it as he looked casually at his waiting audience. Keeping an entire lecture theatre hostage throughout the drawn-out ritual was a shocking act and Conan Doyle was taken aback, for it seemed disrespectful of the audience.

"That was magnificent!" Wilde breathed. "Did you see that? Talk about gravitas! I must remember to smoke on stage before my next premier. It certainly establishes dominance. Clearly, the alpha wolf has lifted his hind leg and marked his territory."

Conan Doyle shushed his friend, and when silence had once again been established, Sigmund Freud addressed his audience.

"Wilkommen to you all, ladies und gentleman. My name is Sigmund Freud. Today I shall be presenting a lecture I first gave in Vienna. It concerns somnambulism, or sleepwalking as it is vulgarly known."

Conan Doyle felt a stir of excitement wash through him. After the traumatic events of the past few days at last he would have an expert's view on the subject of sleepwalking. He threw a quick glance at Wilde, but the large Irishman beside him sat slumped in his chair, chin sagged down to his chest and was softly snoring. For a moment, Conan Doyle considered a well placed elbow to the ribs, but finally gave his friend up as a lost cause and turned his full attention back to Freud.

The Austrian psychiatrist began by introducing the concept of the unconscious, the existence of which he claimed explained many puzzling phenomena such as hypnotism and sleepwalking. At the mention of "hypnotism" Conan Doyle suddenly flashed back to the flyer he had found in the dead sleepwalker's room. He couldn't remember precisely, was the dapper young chap on the flier a magician . . . or a hypnotist. He made a mental note to look for the flyer again when he returned home.

Freud then went on to assert that sleepwalking was connected to fulfilling sexual wishes. This, he said, explained why sleepwalking was more prevalent with the very young, and especially adolescents who were maturing sexually and typically had no sexual outlet because they were not married. He provided a personal anecdote of the time he shared a room in an inn with his coach driver. The driver had warned him of his sleepwalking habit and Freud was able to witness it first-hand. In the middle of the night, the man climbed out of his bed and moved about the room, performing a number of behaviours—all as if he were awake. Freud was amazed that a person could move about, get dressed, open cupboard doors, and so on—all without interrupting their dream.

The Austrian smoked throughout the lecture. When the cigar he was smoking burned low, he dropped it to the floor, ground it out, and then immediately lit up another one. Conan Doyle liked a pipe now and then, but it was clear that Freud was addicted to his cigars. For the rest of the lecture the Austrian spoke with the small cigar clenched in the corner of his mouth and used it to gesture when making a point.

The lecture finally ended precisely at the hour mark. Five minutes was allotted for questions from the audience. Conan Doyle immediately threw up his hand and was the third person chosen. He rose to his feet and posed his question. "I need to know if it is dangerous to awaken a sleepwalker? I have read that the shock might be enough to stop their heart."

Freud puffed his cigar, the smoke wreathing about his head as he fixed Conan Doyle with his gaze, his dark eyes glittering. "There is a tradition that that is so; however, it has never been verified by scientific experiment. Indeed, how could it be? It would be unethical."

Conan Doyle frowned at the deeply unsatisfying answer. Other hands shot up but for once he was rude and continued, "Forgive me but I must ask a second question."

The Austrian assented with a curt nod.

"Can anyone be hypnotised, or only certain people who make suitable subjects?"

Again, Freud puffed his cigar before answering. "On that question, I can be more definite. "In my experience anyone can be hypnotised . . . with the exception of the insane." He gestured with his cigar at Wilde, "And people who area already asleep, like your friend there."

The response drew a burst of laughter from the crowd, which failed to rouse Wilde from his feet splayed, rocked-back-in-the-chair-mouth-open slumber.

As the audience filed out, Conan Doyle stepped forward to speak with the man. Freud was already surrounded by people who had jumped up from their seats to do the same, and he was presently engaged in conversation with several young women. In fact, the handsome young Austrian seemed exceedingly popular with the ladies, and Conan Doyle couldn't help but feel that his freely speaking about sexuality had stirred some juices. When his turn finally came, Conan Doyle stepped forward and introduced himself. If Freud knew who Conan Doyle was he made no signs of being impressed as he cooly shook the author's hand. Despite this, Conan Doyle explained that he was investigating a tragedy involving the death of a sleepwalker and wondered if he could invite Freud to dinner to discuss it further. The Austrian considered the Scots author's invitation for a moment, cigar smoke wreathing about this head, but finally nodded his assent and the two made a dinner appointment for that evening and exchanged information.

Conan Doyle was deep in thought as he followed the crowd out of the lecture hall. He was already composing the questions he would put to Professor Freud at their dinner that evening and was walking down the long corridor to the building's entrance when he was struck by the feeling that he had forgotten something. For a moment he pondered what it could be. The weather outside was fine so he had not been carrying an umbrella, nor had he brought with him his portmanteau and notebooks. Still, the feeling dogged him until he reached the front doors when he suddenly realised what it was he'd left behind. He turned and rushed back to the lecture hall and was just in time to find the older lady in the act of locking up. He breathlessly explained he'd forgotten something of importance and she unlocked the door for him, tut-tutting with impatience. Inside he found a large Irishman still slumped in his chair, head lolling, mouth wide open as he snored. He strode over, gripped his friend's shoulder, and shook him awake.

"Hmmmn? What?" Wilde mumbled, looking around dopily. "What did I miss?"

"Only everything," Conan Doyle retorted.

CHAPTER 11: MORPHEUS THE MAGNIFICENT

At the Alcambra theatre, Jean and Constance stopped at the box office to buy tickets and then shuffled through the doors along with the mass of middle-class Londoners filing into the music hall. As they transited the elaborate foyer, Jean squeezed Constance's hand, her face radiant with joy and excitement. "Thank you for this, Constance," she gushed. "I am so excited to actually be visiting the music hall after so long." She giggled. "And I do feel rather naughty for not asking Arthur's permission!"

Constance smiled at Jean's schoolgirlish excitement. "Perhaps this shall be the first of many adventures we share together."

When they stepped from the foyer into the vast open vault of the music hall proper, Jean gasped and looked around, wide-eyed. "Oh but this is wonderful!"

The Alcambra was a narrow but tall theatre, with three tiers soaring up from the sloping floor of the inner circle all the way up to the nose-bleed seats in the rarefied air of the third level. Like most music halls, the initial impression was of opulence, with plush rows of red velvet seats, balustrades of glittering gilt with gleaming marble columns thronged with gilt-winged cherubs and, floating impossibly high above their heads, the ceiling with its scalloped plaster and gold painted motifs.

As with all visitors, that was the first impression that struck Jean. However, a second, closer look, left a much different impression.The music hall's red velvet seats had been worn threadbare by the bums of many patrons. The chubby bellies of the cherubs were scabrous with peeling gilt. The building even smelled tired. So, like an ageing dowager, the theatre was settling gracefully into a state of genteel dilapidation.

Constance led the way as she towed Jean along by the hand, making a bee-line for the middle of the stalls at the very front. "Hurry, Jean," she urged, practically dragging the younger woman along. "I want to be close to the stage, so I can see the colour of Mr Morpheus' eyes up close."

The seats were quickly filling up, so when Constance reached row D she quickly said, "let's sit here," guiding Jean into a seat while she herself plunked down in the aisle seat.

Jean was thrilled with their seats. "Oh, look how close we are to the stage!"

The ladies were seated in the middle, row D, seats 14 and 15. Here they were close to the stage, but did not have to crane their necks to look up. The two women giggled and squeezed one another's hands with girlish excitement. Now that they had their seats, Jean had time to observe their fellow audience members as the theatre filled up.

Chief were the smells and sights of ordinary Londoners crammed into the rows of seats. Women in hats and bonnets and shawls. Men in all forms of dress from epauletted crimson army uniforms, to businessmen in white starched shirts, frock coats and ties, to labourers in worn black jackets, much patched and repaired. Seated on their row was a cross-section of lower and middle-class Londoners: an old soldier with shock-white hair in a red uniform jacket and shiny brass buttons, his chest mapped in campaign medals from Crimea. Next to him a large, gap-toothed lady bulged out of a tight-laced bustier straining to reign in her juddering bosoms. And looking around, a happy drunk with a boozy grin and a rubbery nose mottled with gin blossoms. An Indian gentlemen with brilliantined hair parted down the middle and a bushy moustache so enormous it concealed both his upper and lower lip and made him look like a grumpy walrus.

The aroma of fried food coiled greasy in the air, mingled with the smell of beer, armpit sweat, cloying perfume and floral hair oil. The show had yet to begin and the audience was already rowdy, some standing up in their seats and shouting and waving to friends they knew, others quaffing pints and belching volcanically to the amusement of their companions, gaggles of women cackling with laughter.

Conan Doyle's judgement of the Alcambra had been astute: it was rather a "low" place, and to the delicate sensibilities of Jean Doyle, came as a bit of culture shock. Previously her visits to the theatre had been to places such as the Haymarket Theatre to see one of Oscar Wilde's latest plays. Here they frequently lounged in box seats high above the stage, sipping champagne as Jean exulted in the heady experience of rubbing elbows with London's elite. On their very first sojourn to the theatre they had enjoyed a box that neighboured the royal box, which had been occupied by none other than Prince George and his rather buxom lady companion for the evening.

By contrast, the music hall's clientele comprised the lower levels of London society. Still, the place thrummed with cheerful bonhomie and had a vividness and sense of life that was somehow missing in places like the Haymarket.

Nevertheless, Jean felt guilty about being at the Alcambra, and suddenly realised she'd been playing with her wedding ring the whole time. She suddenly turned to Constance and said, "I'm taking my wedding ring off!"

Constance looked puzzled. "Why? Whatever for?"

"I feel like Arthur is watching me. Like I'm somehow betraying him."

"You're being silly!"

But Jean quickly slipped off her wedding ring and held it out to Constance.

"Please, hold this for me. Give it back once we leave for home."

"Jean, that's ridiculous!" Constance was about to argue, but just then the band in the orchestra pit struck up a jaunty tune, drowning out any chance to argue further. Constance slipped the wedding ring in her purse where it would be safe.

The attention of the music hall then focused on a tall figure striding onto the stage. The man bowed deeply and introduced himself as Alphonse McKee, the theatre manager. Alphonse was a balding man who had scraped together every follicle of hair left on his head and glued it into place with pomade. He gave a breathless welcome to the crowd and then announced the first act: Mr and Mrs Muddle. An appreciative roar went up from the crowd as the curtains swished open. The stage was set like a country market. A rather ugly woman (presumably Mrs Muddle) sidled in from the wings. Beneath one arm she clutched a basket filled with large cucumbers. As she wandered about the stage pretending to examine the wares for sale on the barrows, she sang a song in a queer, falsetto voice. The song was about the size of her husband's cucumber and she lewdly stroked one as she pretended to shop. Guffaws erupted from the audience, and as the woman began the next chorus, Jean finally caught on that the words to the song were filled with filthy double-entendres. She shot an astonished look at her companion, only to find that Constance's laughing eyes met hers, and that she was hiding a broad smile behind one gloved hand. Jean did the same as the third verse began, which was even bawdier than the first two. The ugly woman was suddenly joined onstage by a slightly-built moustachioed man in a constable's uniform. The two then engaged in a coarse repartee about the cucumbers and what the woman might do with them once she got home. Jean, felt her cheeks burning with shame, but she couldn't look away nor could she stop her giggles. And then she was hit by the stunning realisation that the ugly woman was in fact a man dressed as a woman, and that the sleight policeman was a woman dressed as a man. The faux policeman then began to sing about his wife named Fanny. As the song continued, Jane became swept up in the irresistible inertia of the crowd, and found herself laughing at jokes she couldn't even hear or understand due to the singer's impenetrable cockney accent.

Cheers, whistles and cat-calls went up as the song finished and the two performers bowed and curtsied as the curtains crashed together only to reopen a moment later as the pair bowed and blew kisses as they accepted the rapturous applause and cheers of the crowd.

The elderly woman sitting on Jean's left Jean painfully elbowed her in the side and flashed a grin comprised of more gaps than teeth. "That Mr and Mrs Muddle, oi fink they're a bloody good larf." For Jean it took minutes to sink in as she struggled to translate the woman's impenetrable cockney,

They were followed by a "straight" act: a young woman with an overly sweet voice who led the audience in a sing-song of the Music Hall favourite, "The boy I love is up in the gallery." Her voice was not strong, but still the entire audience, including Jean and Constance, were soon singing along with her.

What followed was some rough and tumble by Cameron and Johnson, a pair of knock-about comedians. Their best jokes were groan-worthy, while their worst drew hisses. They opened with one mediocre joke and then the performance quickly went downhill from there. The crowd soon began to hiss, then to boo, and then to hurl missiles (mostly oranges and overripe tomatoes). The duo were finally forced to flee the stage to the braying of shouted curses and catcalls.

Next, there was a slight delay as a stage hand stepped out onto the lip of the stage and slipped a painted sign into a waiting easel. The sign read, "Morpheus the Magnificent."

The band struck up as the instruments played a restless stir of notes, as ominous as the premonitory rumble of a thunder storm.

Constance clutched Jean's hand in excitement. "This is it. The next act is the man we've come to see: Morpheus the Magnificent."

The band abruptly stopped playing, opening a chasm of silence that begged to be filled. As then an eerie, celestial music oozed into the air. Audience members looked around them as the music seemed to come from all directions, the crystalline notes hovering in the air like blown-glass fairies, tremulous and fleeting as a soap bubble. The music seemed to grasp at the base of Jean's mind, lifting it up high into the open space above the seats, so that she was forced to grip the arms of her chair to avoid being levitated out of her seat. The curtain finally swished open to reveal the source of the music.

A lone figure sat at small instrument.

She was an old lady, grey-haired, stoop-shouldered, her face deeply lined, but her hands moved fluidly over the instrument, which Jean could not identify.

Jean leaned close to Constance and whispered, "What on earth is that thing she's playing?"

As if anticipating her question, Constance Wilde leaned close and whispered in Jean's ear, "A glass armonica, I heard one years ago. It has a series of glass bowls set end to end. It is like wetting your finger and then running it around the rim of a wine glass. The glass bowls are tuned to different notes."

The eerie sound made Jean gasp. "The music it produces. It's like being in a dream. I feel like it's going to lift me out of my seat and float me up to the ceiling!"

The music was having the same effect upon the audience, for the normally raucous crowd sat in absolute silence and looked about themselves wondrously as the familiar environs of the music hall turned suddenly strange.

To Jane it seemed as though the entire music hall had been transformed into a snow globe that had been given a vigorous shake and now the silvery notes of the glass armonica floated in the air around her, slowly settling onto her eyelashes and face.

Then the music shifted, morphing into three persistent chords that repeated over and over, heralding something about to happen. And then he appeared in the most dramatic way imaginable: a trap door in the floor opened and he rose up from the stage on a hidden elevator. As the lime light splashed over him, he seemed like a god ascending from the Underworld.

He was tall. Thin. Dressed in black except for a dazzling white shirt. A black cape was thrown about his shoulders, a black top hat worn tilted atop his head.

There was an audible gasp as it seemed as if every woman in the theatre sucked in her breath. The rumours did not lie. He was incredibly handsome. No, that was insufficient. He was beautiful . . . but in a strange way. He seemed otherworldly, as if someone had found an overgrown statue of a beautiful youth in a secret garden, pulled loose the green tendrils clinging to its perfect form, and brought it to life with a kiss.

"Look at those eyes!" Constance whispered. "I've never seen eyes so blue."

And he was young.

Very young.

Shockingly young.

Jean herself was only 24, and Morpheus seemed considerably younger than her. It confounded her expectations and made him appear all the less real.

Morpheus the Magnificent.

The name decidedly fit him.

He did not speak at first, but stood silently at the lip of the stage, his eyes moved steadily along the rows of seats, carefully scanning the crowd as the ethereal music continued to play. For a moment his gaze alighted upon Constance and lingered. The ghost of a smile floated upon his lips and then vanished as his gaze moved on. As he stood silently regarding the crowd the eerie music seemed to shiver and become more celestial as it poured into the open ears and minds of the audience and swirled there in metallic indigo clouds. Finally, he raised his hand and the music shivered into silence with the suddenness of a soap bubble bursting.

All watched, rapt, as he stepped to the very edge of the stage and spoke in a basso-profundo that seemed out of proportion to this thin frame. "Ladies and gentlemen. You are about to leave behind the mundane, the hum-drum and enter into a strange new realm of existence. I want you all to focus on the sound of my voice. We are about to leave this theatre and enter the theatre of the mind. In this strange new realm, all things are possible: human limitations, pain, fear, infirmity, lose their meaning. In this strange new realm human beings are possessed of amazing powers and are capable of astonishing feats.

I am Morpheus the Magnificent, a master of mesmerism. Through hypnosis, human pain can be totally eliminated. I predict that, in the future, child birth and major surgery will be performed under hypnosis, without the need for morphine or ether. Instead, the pain will be blocked by hypnosis so that the patient will not bleed. Will feel no pain. Will rise from the operating table and walk away, fully healed. He smiled and added. "As I shall now demonstrate."

To demonstrate, the hypnotist reached into the folds of his cloak and produced a slim metal rod.

"Behold, a bicycle spoke from a penny farthing. Only one end has been sharpened beyond infinity. Ordinarily, thrusting this spike through human flesh would cause pain, blood and trauma. But I am a trained mesmerist, and so, using the power of my mind, I can control the flow of blood. Alleviate pain. And heal myself instantly."

And with that the Mesmerist brought the spoke up to his face, and as the audience looked on, he calmly place the tip of the sharpened spoke to one cheek. The wicked spike impressed deeply into the hollow of his cheek. And then he calmly pushed the spoke until it pierced the skin, and he continued to push until the other end plunged through the opposite cheek and emerged. The audience let out a horrified gasp, punctuated by severals shrieks and squeals. For her part, Jean Doyle could not stand to look. She dropped her head and stared at the floor as she death-gripped Constance's hand.

On stage, the hypnotist remained calm and composed. He held his arms wide as he turned his face first left and then right, calmly displaying his pierced face to the audience, many of whom shielded their eyes and recoiled in their seats. When he had tortured them long enough, Morpheus calmly reached up, grasped one end of the metal spoke and then cringe-fully slowly he drew the spoke from his face, and wiped it with a white handkerchief before returning it to the folds of his cloak. He then stepped to the edge of the stage and offered his face for closer inspection. There was clearly two holes in his face where the flesh was slowly closing again. But not so much as a drop of blood.

"As you can see. No pain. No blood. No discomfort. With the mind in control, the body acquiesces."

A thin smattering of applause started at the back of the room. He allowed it to build until it overflowed the stage and then removed his top hat and dipped a bow.

The glass armonica started up again, filling the air with its heart-squeezing notes.

"The music you are hearing has long been employed in the studios of Franz Mesmer, the father of Mesmerism. It is played upon a glass armonica, an instrument comprised of glass bowls that are attuned to the angelic frequencies—the so-called music of the spheres. It is against the law to play such a glass armonica too close to a graveyard, lest the celestial notes tease loose the spirits of the dead from their graves and set them free to once again walk the earth."

The mesmerist's words, accompanied by the ethereal sounds of the glass armonica, set Jean's scalp swarming with pins and needles, and by the collective gasps, had the same effect upon the rest of the audience.

"But even greater wonders are yet to be revealed." Morpheus flashed his charismatic smile. "But I shall need volunteers. Please raise your hand if you would like to take part in the next demonstration."

But after his cheek-piercing demonstration, there were no takers in the audience. Morpheus studied the people sitting on the front row. And then he tripped down the three short steps from the stage and proceeded to walk up the aisle directly toward Jean and Constance. As he moved closer, Morpheus seemed to bend the light around him, so that the audience and the rest of the theatre appeared dull, smeared and sucked dry of colour, while he was the bleeding sharp edge of the eye's focus. The babble of whispering voices fell away as he approached, for his presence was magnetic, drawing all eyes and holding their gaze. As he stepped closer, Jean could see he was the most beautiful man she had ever seen. He was slender—the lean body of youth. His hair was gloss black. He was well over six feet in height with an athletic build. His face captured the sublimity of a Greek hero: high cheekbones, piercing blue eyes, a strong chin. His lips were sensuous, but manly and were pursed in a kind but confident smile.

He stepped up to a young woman who was sitting staring up

lovingly at him. Although she had dressed in her best for the music hall, her clothes were plain and cheap which meant she was likely a seamstress or casual labourer.

"You, my dear. Would you volunteer for me?"

He reached out a hand and the star-struck girl timidly grasped it. He pulled her to her feet.

"We have our first volunteer," he announced to the audience, then leaned in and asked the girl, "Tell me, what is your name?"

The girl bashfully managed to squeak out, "Ruby."

"Ruby," Morpheus repeated. "An apt name, for you sparkle like a gem." He looked to the audience. "Ladies and gentlemen, we have our first volunteer. Now we need one more." He cast his gaze once again at those sitting around him.

"Now, who will be our next volunteer?"

Timidly, slowly, Constance Wilde raised her head to meet his gaze. But then the mesmerist broke his gaze with her and moved on to Jean. He reached out a hand and asked, "Would you volunteer?" And then, despite her reservation, Jean found herself reaching up, taking his hand and being pulled to her feet. As he led them up the aisle to the stage, it seemed to Jean as though both she and the Ruby girl had been pulled into a shimmering bubble that surrounded Morpheus, so that the hubbub of the audience fell away, muffled and distant as though behind a pane of glass. The light outside also seemed dimmer, while the three of them seemed brighter and more colourful. She would later describe it as feeling like being in a waking dream.

In her seat, Constance Wilde dropped her head and looked down at her lap, crushed that she had not been chosen.

On stage, Morpheus now spoke to the two young women.

"The music of the glass armonica has the ability to loosen the bonds holding the soul to the body and so eases the mesmeric bond where the soul can be drawn from a living body where it may hover overhead. This is the essence of mesmerism, which I will now demonstrate. I will manipulate the animal magnetism, drawing it forth."

He turned to Ruby and began to make gestures, pulling motions with his hands, wild sweeps back and forth before her face, and then he made a pulling down motion beneath her chin while saying aloud, "Sleep!"

The young woman's head lolled and fell to one side, transfixed. He then turned his attention to Jean Doyle, waving his arms about her face and then making a fist and drawing it down before her face. Constance, watching from her seat, would later swear that she could see currents of energy flowing around Jean's body. Jean's eyes fluttered shut and then her head also lolled. He moved close to Jean and asked, "What is your name young lady?"

"Jean," Conan Doyle's wife mumbled.

"And now we have two prime subjects, Ruby and Jean. These beautiful young women may seem like delicate flowers, but I will show you that they have the hearts of lions. For within this theatre, they will defy all logic and performs feats of great danger. Feats that defy death. But through my mesmeric powers i can hold death at bay." He turned first to the girl named Ruby,

"What do you do, Ruby?"

"I'm a chambermaid."

"Now tell me, Ruby, what is your greatest fear?"

The woman was silent a moment and then mumbled, "Snakes."

He then turned to Jean and asked, "And what is your greatest fear?"

Jean faltered a moment and then said, "Heights. I'm afraid of heights."

He waved a hand over Jean's face, He had positioned her so that she was standing on the trap door. He made a gesture with his hand and the platform began to sink into the stage. As Jean slowly disappeared from view, Constance fidgeted in her seat with concern.

Morpheus nodded sagely, "Yes, snakes. A very common fear." A stage hand appeared and quickly set up a folding metal stand with rectangular object covered with a hood.

He reached over and snatched the hood from the rectangular object which proved to be a cage. Inside the cage was a live black mamba which now hissed and lashed out striking against the inside of the cage near Morpheus' hand.

The audience gasped. Several women shrieked.

"The black mamba is one of the deadliest snakes known to man. There is no antidote for its venom, and if bitten, victims usually die in agony within the hour. Like many snakes, the black mamba senses the fear of its victim and that is what makes it strike. I am now going to remove all fear of snakes from you." Morpheus began to make motions around the young woman, waving his arms. Pushing and pulling and sweeping his hands back and forth. When he finished he said, "Now Ruby I want you to reach into the cage and pet the mamba's head."

Constance felt her back muscles tightening. Surely this must be a trick. Surely he couldn't let this girl risk her life for a music hall show. Or could he?

"Yes," Ruby answered.

Morpheus lifted the cage from its stand and held it close to the girl. The mamba slowly raised itself from the floor of its cage, the snake's tongue flickering in and out, tasting the air.

Ruby seemed awake, although her eyes were glazed. She began to reach a hand toward the cage and the audience collectively cringed, many gasping with fear. As her hand entered the cage the snake hissed a warning and reared its head back, ready to strike.

Constance Wilde wanted to look away. She, too, had an abhorrence of snakes. But now she found she couldn't avert her gaze. The girl's hand moved into the cage and suddenly the snake lunged forward and coiled itself around her arm. Men shouted aloud and several women shrieked.

The hypnotist grabbed the snake, seized it by the the head, snatched it loose, and seemed to wrestle with it as the body flailed and whipped. But after several minutes he relaxed, smiled and held up the flaccid body of the snake to reveal—the reptile was a clever fake — something like a sock filled with stuffing.

Morpheus addressed the crowd. "This was not a magic trick. The snake was never real, but the mesmeric force can bend minds, change reality, alter what you think you see."

Morpheus turned back to the girl. He leaned close and whispered something in her ear. Then stepped back, waved his hands before her face once again, then snapped his fingers beneath her nose, and commanded, "Awaken!"

The young woman blinked her eyes open. She looked around dazedly.

"Applause for the lovely lady," the Mesmerist demanded and the audience erupted with clapping, whistles and cat calls.

The mesmerist resumed his position at the front of the stage, and his eyes once again scanned the crowed. "But what has become of Jean, our other volunteer? Ruby has a fear of snakes but she will no longer have that fear. And what was it our second volunteer Jean was afraid of? Ah yes, that was it: she has a fear of heights."

The orchestra played a blare of dramatic music as Morpheus looked up and directed the audience's gaze with a gesture of his hand.

Spotlights swivelled, their beams searching the higher reaches of the theatre and then converged upon an empty box seat on the third level. And then a figure stepped into the beams. Constance squinted up at the small figure: a woman in the aerialist's costume of green tights and a tight-fitting, spangly green corset. The woman had honey blonde hair like Jean's and then a stunning realisation struck Constance that caused her to suck in a deep breath—it was Jean.

Morpheus stood looking up at her. "Our volunteer Jean has a fear of heights, but I will convince her, by the power of mesmerism, that she is a skilled tightrope walker. Now we will put the power of mesmerism to the test."

The orchestra fell silent and the eerie music of the glass armonica began to play, the ethereal notes, too light to be constrained by gravity, floated up into the air, ascending to the highest level of the Music Hall, where Jean Doyle, holding only a parasol to assist her balance. Now she stepped to the edge of the box and set her one foot down on the rope in an experimental toe-touch.

And then Jean took her first step. She wobbled on the wire, the parasol held high as she fought for her balance. And then she took a second step, and then a precious third.

Constance Wilde watched from far below. She had both hands clamped over her mouth, her eyes wide and terrified.

Jean moved forward another step along the wire. She was now far enough away from the balcony that if she lost her balance she would fall into the rows of seats far below.

Constance's gorge rose and her mouth soured with the taste of acid. If Jean fell from such a height she would be killed, or at the very least horrible crippled. What had seemed a moment ago a delightful diversion, had turned into a horrible nightmare. Jean's legs momentarily wobbled, the rope whiplashing back and forth as she fought to keep her balance.

Many in the audience cried out in alarm, certain that Jean was about to plummet to her death.

Looking up from so far below, Constance clutched her throat, unable to draw breath.

Gradually, the rope slowed and then ceased its wild side-to-side swaying. Jean resumed her slow progress along the wire. She reached the mid-way point, directly over Constance's seat and then seemed to gather speed, moving along the rope with greater steadiness, and then she practically ran the last four steps and sprang into the safety of the far box.

The crowd erupted with cheers and thunderous applause.

Constance Wilde slumped back in her seat, sweating, her face pale, on the verge of swooning to the floor.

CHAPTER 12: THE TEA SHOP
INTERROGATION

"And you remember none of it?"

"No . . . nothing."

"Really?" the voice contained more than a hint of doubt. "Nothing at all?"

"No. Nothing after Morpheus brought me up on stage. I remember him waving his arms in front of me and then . . . the next I remember was stepping down from the stage and taking my seat next to you."

"I cannot believe it. You must remember some of it."

"Really. Nothing. Not a bit. Why do you ask so many times? Did I do something untoward? Did I compromise myself in some way? I'm afraid to ask. I did, didn't I? I can see from your face . . . but . . . go on . . . tell me."

Jean Doyle and Constance Wilde were sitting at a table for two in the front window of the *Tittle-Tattle Tea Room* conveniently located directly across the road from the Alcambra Music Hall. The tea room was busy with nearly every table occupied, mostly by patrons who had also just attended the music hall and who had walked across the road to refresh themselves with a pot of tea.

Morpheus had been the final act of the day, and when Constance returned to her seat, she seemed totally unaware of the amazing performance she had just put on. But before they could discuss it, the performance had ended and Jean and Constance, along with the rest of the audience had filed out of the Alcambra Music Hall.

Constance had dragged Jean across the street to the tea room, as she was dying to interrogate the young woman about the shocking and amazing performance she had just been witness to.

Constance looked across the table, over the tea pot and cups, at her friend. It was hard to believe Jean remembered nothing after her intense ordeal at the hands of Mister Morpheus. Incredibly, she had no recollection of walking a tightrope across the lofty span of the Alcambra, sixty feet above the seats and the sea of upturned faces.

"Please, Constance," Jean said in earnest. "You must tell me what I did that was so shocking."

Constance leaned across the table and put her hand atop Jean's, and then she drew in a breath and said, "Do you remember Morpheus asking you what you are afraid of?"

Jean's eyes narrowed at the question. "Yeeeeesss."

"And you said you were afraid of heights?"

Jean looked even more suspicious. "Yessssss?"

And then Constance began to describe in great detail the amazing and terrifying feat that Jean had performed in front a packed music hall. When Constance had finished, Jean sat silent for some time, emotions sweeping across her face: doubt, fear, amazement and finally, back to disbelief.

"Oh, you are making fun of me," Jean said. "I see you can barely resist bursting into laughter as you tell the story."

Constance smiled placidly, and then asked, "Jean, what stockings did you wear today?"

"What stockings? Oh, I see, you are saying that I walked the tight rope dressed like a circus aerialist in green spangled stockings and a tight green bodice. Really, Constance, you have a better imagination than my Arthur."

"What colour, Jean?"

"I wore a black pair of stockings as I always do. And not a new pair, I am ashamed to confess. They must be six month's old and have been mended in several places."

Jean smiled at her friend, but Constance did not return the smile and fixed her with an intense look. "Are you sure you wore your black stockings?"

"Well yes. Why are being so silly about it?"

Constance said, "Perhaps you should check?"

Jean thought Constance was being ridiculous, but she shot a quick look around the busy tea room. No one was looking their way. Then she quickly reached down and snatched up her skirt to her knees. "When she saw the spangly green stockings gracing her legs, Jean let out a shriek that made every head in the tea room turn her way.

CHAPTER 13: A DINNER DATE WITH FREUD

At dinner at the Savoy, Conan Doyle found Sigmund Freud disappointingly taciturn. He did not ask Conan Doyle a single question.

About his writing.

About his family.

About anything.

In fact, Freud seemed curiously incurious for a man whose professed goal in life was to understand the human psyche.

The only topic of conversation Freud could be goaded into was psychiatry, which he claimed to have invented (Conan Doyle was uncertain but doubted that claim). About this subject, once given the slightest encouragement, he would drone on about this study or that study—in excruciating detail. Apparently, he cared little for the niceties of chit-chat so that their conversation was stilted and seldom. Even getting him to speak required Conan Doyle to prompt him with constant questions, which he found exhausting. When their food at last arrived they both consumed it in a monastic silence unpunctuated by little more than the nerve-shredding scrape of fork and knife on porcelain. Conan Doyle also noted that the Austrian was a noisy eater, who made slurping noises—and not just when he was eating soup. But then he noted that the side of Freud's mouth that typically held the cigar had acquired a permanent dent so that his lips did not quite seal together properly. And more irritatingly, the man was like a factory chimney for he would fire up cigar after cigar between each course without regard for his dining partner or the couples sitting at adjoining tables, despite the fact that they were quite pointedly fanning the smoke away using their napkins. By the end of the meal Conan Doyle's eyes were red and smarting from cigar smoke.

All through this ordeal Conan Doyle had been patiently biding his time for an appropriate juncture at which to ask the questions he'd been longing to ask, and so as the waiter whisked away the greasy dinner plates just as Freud was launching into another interminable anecdote about his studies, Conan Doyle talked over the top of him and trotted out his story.

"But before you finish your story, Herr Freud, I have a burning question I must ask while I have your expertise to call upon." The Austrian psychologist seemed a little put out by the interruption, but leaned back in his chair, gestured with his cigar and grunted, "You may speak."

Thus given permission, the author of Sherlock Holmes launched into a description of the night he and Wilde had encountered the ill-fated sleepwalker. He described his fear at awakening her when they first encountered the somnambulist on the rooftop. His throat tightened as he described his unsuccessful attempt to stop her fall and her tragic plummet from the rooftop to her death. And then he related the most mysterious element of the story: in that the sleepwalker was in the commission of an act of robbery all while in a state of somnambulism. After the author had finished, Freud sat puffing his cigar for a full two minutes before speaking.

"How does one cure sleepwalking?"

Freud puffed on his cigar and then removed it from his mouth and gesticulated with the loathsome, chewed wet end.

"Sleepwalking is how neuroses exhibit in a patient. Its roots are from repressed sexual urges. Therefore, the best way to exorcise the demon is obvious."

Conan Doyle looked puzzled. "And that is?"

"To engage in the sex act to satisfy those urges. This is why it is such a problem with single women. A married woman has a husband to satisfy such needs. Whereas a young man . . . " Freud smiled archly around his cigar. "Well, we all know that young men are not shy at taking matters into their own hands . . . so to speak." He chuckled at his own joke. "But young women are encouraged to repress such impulses. Thus they are thus more likely to become somnambulists . . . or . . . even worse . . . lesbians."

The Austrian's voice was loud and his comment caused heads to turn on adjacent tables. Conan Doyle cringed as he felt the abrasive stare of strangers. He knew full well what a lesbian was, but it was not the kind of word to be bandied about in polite conversation—particularly in a crowded restaurant. He felt his face flush red.

Freud continued, "So you said that the young woman crept into the bedroom and stole the necklace from around her neck. The necklace is obviously a symbol for the vagina. The sleepwalker, due to her unconscious desires, is drawn to someone of the same sex in order to steal, in this case, a potent symbol of the open vagina. The young woman was undoubtedly a lesbian."

The people seated at the surrounding tables had all stopped conversing and Conan Doyle was certain they had all heard what Freud was talking about and had stopped to eavesdrop.

Conan Doyle now felt all the blood drain from his face. He was a well-known figure in London society, chances were good that many Londoners could recognise him by sight. And now here he was sharing a dinner table with a loud, cigar-smoking foreigner who kept banging on, in a loud and distinctive voice, the unmentionable parts of a lady's anatomy and lesbians.

"So, this sleepwalker. She was a young woman, you say? What age?"

"We later found out she was only eighteen."

Smoke plumed.

"In her sexual prime," Freud noted. "No doubt she was filled with procreative desires, as many of her sex are at that age."

Freud didn't seem to be getting the point."But she crossed many precipitous rooftops, leapt gaps between buildings, and then entered the bedroom of a wealthy widow and lifted a priceless necklace from the victim's bosom using a butter knife then put it around her own neck before leaving."

Puff. Puff.

"And you are certain she was actually sleepwalking, and not pretending?"

"I personally saw her up close. She walked right past us: two constables, myself, and my friend Oscar. Her eyes were open, but heavy-lidded and glassy. And yet she navigated the roof effortlessly, even leaping wide gaps between buildings, like the most skilled tightrope walker or acrobat."

Freud puffed on his cigar and then ventured, "I myself once shared a room with a coachman. He, too, was a sleepwalker who got up in the middle of the night and moved about. I was astonished at how he—"

"Yes, yes, you related that story at your lecture," Conan Doyle interrupted. "At one point she walked right past me and I might have grabbed her. But she was walking along a ledge above a sheer drop. I have read of the dangers of waking a sleepwalker—that the shock can cause a heart attack. And so I . . . I hesitated . . ." Conan Doyle's throat tightened, strangling his voice, ". . . with tragic results." After a pause, he cleared his throat and asked in a ruined voice. "Tell me, Professor Freud, did I do the right thing?"

Freud mulled the question for long minutes, then finally said, "I have heard of sleepwalkers reacting violently when awakened. Striking at those who wake them. The shock is very great."

"So, to ask again, in your opinion, was I wise to be cautious? I mean by not waking her?"

Conan Doyle was hoping to be justified in his actions, but instead the Austrian merely puffed on his cigar as he considered the question, then bluntly answered, "The young woman is dead, is she not? Sadly . . . that is the only certainty."

CHAPTER 14: JEAN SLEEPWALKS

It was late when Conan Doyle stepped through the front door of his Norwood home. The house was in darkness. The entire household—family and servants—were tucked up in bed. He tip-toed up the stairs and quietly slipped into his bedroom to check in on Jean. He was thankful to find her in bed and sleeping peacefully. Her beautiful face looked angelic and he could not resist creeping to her bedside to kiss her gently on the cheek, although as he pulled away, the sight of her face, surrounded by rolling folds of white sheet, reminded him of the carved stone angels and seraphs sleeping peacefully on the grave monuments at Highgate cemetery. It was a disturbing thought, and he repressed a shudder as he slipped from the room.

Despite the hour, Conan Doyle was charged with energy and so he went downstairs to his writing room/study. Once seated at his desk, he pulled out the stack of illustrations he had borrowed from Billy Brash at the Illustrated Police News. As he flipped through them, it was impossible not to notice that the sleepwalkers were all young ladies, invariably dressed in diaphanous nightgowns that clung to the curves of their ripe young bodies. Maybe Freud's sexual explanation had some merit, but then Conan Doyle thought what about young men? Surely if anyone had repressed sexual desires it would be young men. He laughed as he answered his own question as reports of male sleepwalkers would provide little titillation for the mostly male readership of the Illustrated Police News.

He next picked up the list of stories Billy Brash had provided. Taking a notepad out of his desk drawer he began to go through the articles, jotting down the date and location of each sleepwalking incident.

Finally, he dug out a map of London and pinned it up on a cork noticeboard. Rummaging in a drawer he found a box of pins and then recovered the notepad he had filched from the Boy Reporter. For the next half hour he plotted the location of each recorded case of somnambulism by pushing a pin into the corresponding location on the map. Finally, he drove the last pin into the map and and stood back to survey the results.

He was immediately disappointed.

He had hoped to discover some kind of pattern, a concentration of cases that might provide a clue of some sort. But though his eyes traced and retraced the location of the pins trying to sieve a pattern, they were evenly spread out across a wide swath of London.

Random.

Meaningless.

He stood staring at the map for some time, until he came back to himself and realised he was lost in thought and merely staring into space. Still, he did not move and continued gazing blindly at the map until the face of the young somnambulist swam into his vision. For several dreadful moments he was back on that rooftop, and once again he watched helplessly as the nightgown tore in his grip and the young woman plunged away into the arms of night. Her scream-less plummet made the ordeal all the more surreal and horrible. And then the ghastly sound of a body impacting the merciless pavement below.

A shudder rippled through him and snatched him from his dreadful reverie..

The map of London reappeared in his vision.

He was reluctant to go upstairs to bed, realising he would be seeing the young woman's face again in his nightmares.

He turned and threw a look at the clock on his writing desk.

It was late. Very late.

Reluctantly, he turned down the oil lamp and plodded upstairs to bed.

Once in his room, Conan Doyle undressed quickly and tossed his clothes onto a chair and then pulled on his nightshirt. As quietly as he could, he slid beneath the sheets and lay crouched in a foetal position, his body clenched with cold as he waited for the sheets to warm up. He listened for his wife's sonorous breathing, but she was a quiet sleeper and made not the slightest sound. Seeking the comforting feel of her warm body, he carefully slid an exploring hand toward her side of the bed, expecting to touch the curve of her back, the warmth of her hip.

But instead his hand groped cold sheets. He groped further and found nothing.

Then the dread realisation hit him.

Jean was not in the bed.

Suddenly, he jerked upright, threw the bedclothes aside, and sprang out.

He stood at the side of the bed, breathing hard, heart banging, mind racing. Where could she be? Did she go downstairs for some reason? Or perhaps she had gone to check on one of the children?

Just then he caught a strange strain of music coming as if from a long way away. His eyes were drawn to the windows. At this time of year the smaller windows were all left open a crack, but the French windows were normally kept locked. But when he looked, they had been left wide open. Conan Doyle snatched on a dressing grown, cinched the belt tight, flung the French windows wide and stepped onto the tiny balcony. Below, the sleeping streets of Norwood huddled in nocturnal shadow. The ordered procession of softly hissing gas lamps marched away into the darkness. And then he heard it again: that peculiar music—eerie, other-worldly—that raised the hackles on the back of his neck. An orange gibbous moon hung low over the rooftops, resembling a rotten pumpkin. But then movement drew his gaze to his right. He turned his head to look . . . and froze.

A female figure was gliding slowly along the roof tiles with the slow, dreamy gait of a sleepwalker. He blinked as his vision strained to make out the figure which finally resolved itself as a tall woman, barefoot, wearing only a long nightgown. And suddenly terror was a fist squeezing his heart in its grip as he recognised with dreadful certainty who the woman was.

His wife

Jean.

Moving with careful stealth, his heart pounding, he clambered over the balcony railing and quietly dropped onto the roof tiles. Jean was no more than twenty feet away, but she stood at the edge of the rooftop. Immediately before her was a sheer drop, just a half-step away. The fall to the pavement below was a good forty feet.

She would break her neck.

He thought about calling out to her, but held back. He thought about Freud's warning. Startling a sleepwalker can cause them to strike out, react violently. Perhaps she would startle awake. He crept forward one slow, agonising step at a time. At any instant he expected her to step forward into empty space. But she stood paused, as if waiting, as if listening. And then he heard it again.

The strange music.

He was close now. His throat clenched as she raised her foot, as if to step forward, but then she pivoted ninety degrees and began to walk away down the sloping roof.

Now he lunged forward and slipped his arm around her waist. He would not take the chance. She continued to stare blankly into space, gently resisting, trying to move away, trying to pull free, but he held her firmly.

"Come, Jean, my darling," he whispered in a cosseting voice. " Let's get you back into bed. You belong back in bed."

His wife resisted again, but with more force. He darted a quick look out over the darkened streets of Norwood. That celestial music echoed in the distance, floating over the rooftops and along the streets.

He brought his lips close to her ear. "My darling. Let us go back to bed. Come along now. I've got you. Let me guide you."

Slowly, and with the dreamy motion of an automaton, she allowed herself to be turned around and they moved in stuttering steps toward the balcony. At the balcony Conan Doyle encircled her slender waist and lifted Jean over the railing and set her down. Ten minutes later he had her settled back beneath the covers. He slid in beside her and laid a restraining arm across her waist. He had locked the French windows and hidden the key, also ensuring the the bedroom door was locked and all the windows tightly secured. There was no way she could escape his protective grasp. Exhausted and shaking with adrenalin, he finally lay his head on the pillow and listened as her breathing slowed, grew sonorous, and lapsed into gentle snores that deepened as she sank further into slumber.

He resolved that he would not sleep, but rather stay awake, holding her until morning. But soon his eyes closed and he started to drift. He did not remember falling asleep.

"Are you awake, my fuzzy bear?"

Conan Doyle jerked up from the pillow, blinking himself awake. His hand groped the bed beside him and found Jean's side of the bed empty.

His wife Jean stood at her dresser mirror. She was fully dressed and was just putting on a pair of jet earrings he had given her while on holiday in Scarborough. Now she moved toward the bed and smiled as he caressed his cheek with her soft hand. "Come along, sleepy head husband. Breakfast is waiting downstairs."

All through breakfast, Conan Doyle could not help darting inquiring looks at his wife. She seemed entirely normal, if not a little excessively animated as she chatterboxed her way through the meal— mostly gossip and tittle-tattle she had received second-hand from Constance Wilde.

As subtly as he could, Conan Doyle probed her with questions to see if she had any recollections of her midnight sojourn on the roof tiles. "You were rather restless last night, darling. Was there something troubling your sleep?"

His wife looked at him nonplussed. "Really? No. Nothing at all. I slept soundly all night."

Conan Doyle paused to brush the toast crumbs from his moustache and said, "Really? I came to bed rather late. I feared I had disturbed your slumbers. Do you remember me coming to bed?"

Jean shook her head blankly. "I have no recollection. Why do you ask?"

Conan Doyle paused in buttering his toast and waved the butter knife abstractly. "No reason, darling."

His wife shot him a puzzled look, but then giggled it away as she bit into her marmaladed slice of toast.

But even though Jean seemed entirely normal by day, Conan Doyle was still distressed about the previous evening's goings-on. After breakfast, he dressed for the city and gave his wife the excuse that he was going to see his publisher. But when he arrived at the Norwood train station, he bought a ticket for Piccadilly. He was going to see the Austrian doctor, Sigmund Freud, to ask him about this alarming new development.

The newspapers were right.

The sleepwalking plague was spreading.

And now it had reached his home.

CHAPTER 15: FREUD OR FRAUD?

When he stepped down from the train at Piccadilly Station, Conan Doyle happened to look up and spotted the Austrian Doctor, Sigmund Freud, walking briskly through the crowds thronging the platforms. He hurried to catch up with him, shouting "Doctor Freud," and "hallooing" as he dodged and side-stepped the milling crowd of people. He finally caught up with the doctor as he was about to step onto Platform 8.

"Doctor Freud! Doctor Freud!"

The Austrian was puffing away at one of his short cigars as he marched, head-down, toward his train, clutching a small travelling bag in one hand with a brolly tucked under the other arm. But he looked around at the sound of his name being called aloud and Conan Doyle hurried up to him.

"Doctor Freud," Conan Doyle panted, "Thank goodness I caught you in time!"

The Austrian doctor frowned at Conan Doyle's words. "What do you mean, caught me? But I have done nothing wrong?"

Conan Doyle smiled and laughed, "Sorry, it is an English expression. I mean nothing by it. But I must speak with you. It's urgent!"

The Austrian looked annoyed and shot a lingering look at the station clock. "I am hurrying to catch my train. I have but a few minutes."

Conan Doyle was deeply disappointed. He had been counting on Freud's advice, especially after the events of last night. "I'll be brief," he said. "My wife Jean . . . she too has become afflicted of the sleep-walking sickness," And then he launched into a tight-throated description of the last night's episode.

The Austrian puffed his cigar as he listened with clear impatience, tapping his toe and shooting constant looks at the station clock. Finally he lost patience and interrupted Conan Doyle. "As you should have learned from attending my lecture, sleepwalking results from the suppression of sexual desires. Have you and your wife enjoyed intimacy recently?"

The Austrian was rather loud and did not bother to modulate his voice as he asked the questions. Several passengers, including a sour-faced clergyman and an older woman, flung outraged looks at Conan Doyle as they pushed past.

Conan Doyle's face reddened visibly. He was a private man at the best of times and did not care to discuss his most intimate sex life with a brusque foreigner in the middle of one of London's busiest train stations.

"Well . . . well . . . I have been rather busy lately. I'm trying to finish a novel I am composing. I work rather late many nights and so . . ."

"There you have your answer, Doctor Doyle. Make love to your wife—morning, noon, and night—and I'm sure you will see an end to her sleepwalking."

Somewhere a whistle blew. It was clear the Austrian was in a hurry to leave. "But now I must leave you or I will miss my train."

"But where are you going?" Conan Doyle asked.

"I have family in the north of England. I am going to visit them. The doctor raised his grey Homburg and ducked a slight bow. "Good luck, Doctor Doyle. Perhaps I will see you in a week's time."

And with that Freud ducked back into the crowd, trailing smoke as he puffed away at his cigar.

As Conan Doyle walked away across the echoic vault of Piccadilly station, he could not shake off the irritation he found with Sigmund Freud. No doubt the man was very brilliant, but he was selfish and self-obsessed.

"Sadly . . . that is the only certainly," the final words Freud said at last evening's meal. They echoed in his head as he walked up to the newspaper kiosk to purchase a paper. As if there to taunt him, many copies of the *Illustrated Police News* had been arranged around the kiosk opening, their edges fluttering and growing tattered in the constant breeze all train stations seem to have. Of course it was the latest issue, with the illustration of the falling sleepwalker on the cover. Conan Doyle could not help but glance at it as he scooped up his copy of *The Times*. Both he and Wilde graced the cover of *The Illustrated Police News*, both looking manic and horror-struck as the tragic somnambulist tumbled away from his outstretched, grasping hand. In the illustration, the girl was conscious, her eyes terrified and pleading, her mouth wide open in a scream as she awakened from a dream into a living nightmare.

Although exaggerated for morbid effect, the illustration set his stomach churning.

"Here, is that you?" the kiosk vender asked, noticing that Conan Doyle was studying the cover. "Ain't you that Conan Doyle cove?"

"I only wish I had his money," the Scotsman grunted bad-temperedly and turned to walk away.

M oments later Conan Doyle stepped out of the train station onto Regent street. Once again, the encounter with Sigmund Freud had left him ill-tempered and disappointed. But then, as he stood at the kerbside, looking to hail a hansom, he happened to look up and caught sight of something that left him dumbfounded. On the far side of the street, he saw a man in a grey coat with a grey homburg dash briskly up to a waiting black carriage, open the door, and clamber inside. It all happened in flash, so he couldn't be entirely certain that it was Freud—but if it wasn't him, it was someone identically dressed in a grey hat and overcoat who was clearly puffing away at a cigar. (And the person moved with such swiftness it was obvious they were trying to avoid being seen.)

Conan Doyle determined to catch the Austrian in an obvious lie and lingered a moment on the kerb to dodge being run over by a passing omnibus. As soon as it had lumbered past, he leapt off the kerb and dashed into the street but as he did so the driver of the black carriage whipped up the horses and the carriage jerked away from the kerb. Thanks to the omnibus, Conan Doyle had been a moment too late. He still couldn't be certain it was Freud he had spotted. But as he stood on the road where the black carriage had been pulled up, he glanced down at the cobblestones to see a discarded cigar of the same type Freud smoked as it lay on the pavement, smoke curling up from it as it still burned.

CHAPTER 16: SLEEPWALK INTO OBLIVION

The moon that night was a silvery crescent, a reaper's blade scything through the high, thin clouds and the lower hanging, fossil-dark plumes of chimney smoke wreathing through the London skies.

In the early hours, long after midnight, a single black carriage clattered along the deserted streets of Kensington. The fine, six storey residences lining either side of the road testified to the area's wealth. At this hour the curtained windows were like dark eyes squeezed tightly shut. The wealthy owners were tucked up in their beds, heads resting upon feather-down pillows, and even the servants, down to the lowest scullery maid, lay sprawled on their thin sleeping pallets, lost in a world of dreams that freed them temporarily from considerations of social rank or wealth.

The horses, two brown mares, chuffed and snorted as the black carriage slowed and drew up at a point equidistant between gas lamps, purposely shying away from the revealing glare of their glowing glass shrouds. The carriage driver, an impossibly tall man in a Cossack's hat and coat, clambered down and trudged around to the rear of the coach, where he snatched loose several restraining ropes, threw aside a covering tarpaulin, and then lifted out a strange-looking musical instrument that he set down in the middle of the roadway. Next, he pulled out the metal step and then opened the carriage door and held it. A stooped, grey-haired lady stepped down, threw a shawl around her shoulders and shuffled to the waiting instrument. The Cossack returned with a chair he had unloaded from the back of the carriage and set it down for her.

Meanwhile the door on the far side of the carriage flung open and the hypnotist, Morpheus the Magnificent leapt out. He threw a black cape about his shoulder and fastened it with a chain, and then lifted his glossy top hat and resettled it upon his head.

The grey-haired matron settled at her instrument, placed one foot upon the treadle and began to pump it up and down. The glass bowls with their silvered edges reflected the gas lamps as they slowly spun. The woman paused to open a bottle of water and fill a metal tray atop the instrument, then dipped her fingers into the reservoir to wet them and placed her hands atop the rotating bowls. With the first touch of her fingers the instrument began to sing. As her hands moved smoothly from bowl to bowl, the glass armonica conjured silvery notes that rose up into the air, and swept out like a seeking voice, a celestial song as heart breaking as a choir of weeping angels.

As the music soared and swirled in the London skies, coaxing the very stars to weep with their beauty, the three of them stood looking around at the rooftops, along the empty streets, watching, waiting for any signs of movement.

And then the Cossack grunted and pointed with his long finger. Far down the street something moved toward them from the distance, growing larger. It reached the circle of light beneath a street lamp and resolved itself as a human figure: a female figure, moving with under-water-slowness. She passed through the dark and into the light, through the dark and once more into the light, so that the figure gradually accumulated form and substance, until it resolved itself as a young woman, clad in only a white nightgown, arms floating loose as she trod the cobbles barefoot.

As she approached the waiting coach, the hypnotist dropped his head as though in regret or shame. Then she reached him and he opened the carriage door and she meekly climbed aboard and sat down.

And then the hypnotist noticed movement on the rooftops above.

"There," he said, pointing, "On the rooftop."

This young woman had climbed out an open bedroom window on the top floor, and was moving along the steeply inclined rooftop. A single slip here and she would toboggan down the slope of the roof and hurtle to her death. But slowly, gradually, she made it to the very edge of the roof. But now she stood at the gable end of the roof, with no way to climb down. She stood before a sheer drop of forty feet to the cobbles below.

The music faltered and stopped for a moment. The grey-haired woman pointed and said something in Russian to the Cossack who tromped over to the base of the wall and stood looking up at the sleepwalker.

The glass armonica player played a few repetitive notes, over and over again, at first coaxing . . . and then commanding. And then she lifted one hand from the instrument and made a "come hither" gesture.

Without hesitation, the young woman stepped from the edge of the roof into thin air . . and plummeted forty feet, her night gown fluttering about her . . .

. . . straight into the waiting arms of the Cossack who caught her deftly, and then set her down upon her feet. Moments later she joined her fellow sleepwalker in the carriage. The Cossack returned the glass armonica to the rear of the carriage and securely strapped it down. The hypnotist and the grey-haired woman climbed back inside, and the black carriage rolled on down the street until it vanished into the shadows.

17

CHAPTER 17: MUSIC HALL HIJINKS

The next day Constance Wilde and Jean Doyle arrived even earlier at the box office of the Alcambra music hall, so that as soon as the doors opened they raced the inpouring crowd through the foyer into the theatre and hurried through the rows of seats so they were able to capture two seats on the very front row.

If anything Jean's second visit to the music hall left an even bigger impression than the first. She had been shy and reticent on their first visit, but now she felt confident in this environment. She looked around, smiling as she basked in the music hall's cheerful if tawdry atmosphere. The show had yet to begin and the audience was already rowdy. A slatternly woman several seats away from Jean was busily knitting away at some unidentifiable tangle of yarn while cackling over something bawdy her friend had just whispered to her. Next to her sat an immensely fat man, his red tongue greedily burrowing into the crust of a pasty as he sucked out all the gravy while glutinous brown ropes trailed down his shirt front.

A roar went up from the crowd as the curtains finally parted. The theatre manager, the same desiccated fossil who had introduced the acts yesterday, minced to the lip of the stage, cleared his throat with a rattle of phlegm, and announced several new acts that would be performing that day.

The band did not wait for him to quit the stage before they launched into a brassy blare of music. Today's show opened with the same act they had seen just the day previous: Mr & Mrs Muddle, the man dressed as an ugly woman and the woman dressed as a police constable. This time, however, Jean let her attention wander. She wondered if Morpheus would once again choose to bring her up on the stage, or if, this time, Constance would have a turn.

Jean briefly lost herself in the sing-song when the same young woman with the overly sweet voice led the audience in a sing-song of the Music Hall favourite, "The boy I love is up in the gallery."

At one point she let her eyes wander and spotted a pair of familiar eyes staring in her direction from the wings.

"Look Constance!" Jean said, elbowing her companion. "There's Morpheus, lurking in the wings. He's looking our way."

Constance quickly looked and spotted the handsome face. "Yes, I see him. He's looking at you."

"No," corrected Jean. "I'd say he's looking right at you!"

"Oh my, he is so handsome!" Constance whispered." She dropped her head. "I feel weak! I cannot look at him."

A new act followed the sing-along—a skit with a man and his performing dog; but Constance took nothing in, for every time she darted a look toward the wings, she felt Morpheus' eyes upon her, and a wave of heat flashed through her.

Finally, she risked another quick look and this time Morpheus had vanished, but then they announced him as the next act. After the same restless stir of cellos from the orchestra pit, the music stopped, opening a void that begged to be filled.

And then the curtain slowly opened to the ethereal strains of the glass armonica, the music rising from the stage and coiling itself about the seats like a sleepy serpent. The notes ascended up to the scalloped plaster ceiling, forming graceful arabesques of sound that built and collapsed.

"That music," Constance whispered to Jean. ". . . it makes me feel woozy."

But then the music changed, the lilting lyrical chords tightened in upon themselves and became a restless succession of arpeggios. It was a signal. An announcement. And then he appeared, rising slowly from the trap door in the stage: black on black in his cape and top hat. The tall and slender form and the blue eyes that flashed.

Morpheus the Magnificent.

It was obvious that, merely looking at him made Constance's stomach turn somersaults. She dragged her eyes down to the pattern on the carpet at her feet, deciding that looking at him was dangerous.

His long legs advanced and stopped at the lip of the stage. At first, Constance was afraid to look up, but then she risked a quick glance and saw that he was looking directly at her . . . and smiling.

And now she had looked, his eyes held hers, and she could not look away.

The glass armonica music ceased abruptly and he filled its echoing absence with his mellifluous voice.

"Welcome to the Alcambra Music Hall. I am Morpheus the Magnificent. For those who have seen my act, welcome. For those who have not, I must tell you that today's performance will be very different, as I plan on doing something very different. But first, as usual, I will need an assistant, a volunteer from the audience."

At first no one volunteered, but then one hand went up, and then another, and more. Mostly they were women begging to be chosen by the handsome hypnotist.

Morpheus looked about at all the raised hands and smiled, but he did not choose any. Instead he descended the steps from the stage. Now that he had broken his gaze, Constance was able to look away. She dropped her eyes to the pattern of the carpet. She dare not look up. But then she watched his polished shoes walk up to her and stop.

"Would you please be my assistant?" he asked.

Uncertain if he was really talking to her, Constance risked a quick look up and met Morpheus' gaze, and now she couldn't look away. He reached out a white gloved hand to her. By reflex, she grasped it and he pulled her to her feet.

"Applause for my volunteer," he asked the crowd and Constance allowed herself to be led to the steps and then up onto the stage. Just as Jean had experienced, Morpheus seemed to bend the light around him, so that he was the sole sharp focal point of her vision.

"Do you trust me?" he asked.

"Yes," Constance spoke the words automatically, suddenly feeling her will dissolve into his blue eyes.

Morpheus looked out into the audience and said, "And now I will use my mesmeric powers to induce a deep trance into the volunteer."

He turned to face her and in doing so leaned in close to Constance's ear and whispered, "I was not supposed to choose you, but I cannot help myself."

He stood tall and began to make motions about Constance with his hands, pushing and pulling motions that culminated in a motion where he closed his hands and then drew down sharply and commanded, "Sleep!"

Instantly, Constance's eyes drooped shut and her head lolled atop her neck as she was drawn into a deep trance.

Morpheus gently took her head in both hands and straightened it atop her neck.

"Now you are in my thrall, I am going to ask you a few questions and you must answer truthfully. Do you understand?"

"Yes," Constance spoke robotically.

What is your first name?" The hypnotist challenged.

"Constance."

Morpheus smiled, flashing his perfect white teeth. "Constance, a beautiful name for a beautiful woman."

The crowd "awwwwwwed."

"I see a ring on your finger. I take it you are married?"

"Yes."

"What does your husband do?"

"Says witty things and smokes too many cigarettes."

At her response the audience burst into gales of laughter.

The hypnotist turned to the audience and grinned. "From the description her husband must be Oscar Wilde!"

The audience laughed again, unaware of the irony.

"You are a very handsome woman and it is clear you are a very proper lady born of very proper breeding."

The question brought a murmur of expectation from the audience.

" Tell me, Constance, is your husband a jealous man?"

Anticipating where the question was going, the crowd let out a collective "oooooooooh!"

"I wish he were . . ."

"So he would not care if I were to kiss you?"

The hypnotist turned and grinned at the crowd. The risqué question titillated the audience and drew a loud chorus of oooohs and aaahhhs.

"No . . . he would not care."

For a moment, Morpheus seemed to lose his focus. He spent several moments staring into Constance's face. But then Jane noticed the hunger in his stare. He seemed about to kiss Constance, but she reasoned he could not possibly do that. She was hypnotised. It would be highly improper.

"I would like to kiss you Constance, although you are married. Would you like me to kiss you? Remember, you must answer truthfully."

"Yes. Kiss me."

The audience now responded with whoops of delighted laughter.

And with that, the mesmerist took Constance in his arms, bent her back slightly and then leaned in as his lips found hers, and kissed her deeply. It was not just a buss, but a deep and passionate kiss and Jean saw to her shock and alarm that Constance was kissing him back with equal ardour.

The crowd gasped, then tittered, which turned into laughter which became uproarious as the kiss went on and on and on and on.

Looking on, Jean watched with a hand over her mouth, feeling shocked and outraged, blushing for her friend, and wondering what Constance must be feeling—or was she really oblivious?

CHAPTER 17: MUSIC HALL HIJINKS | 107

Finally Morpheus broke the kiss and they both came up for air, but before he pulled away he leaned in close and whispered into Constance's ear, "You will remember this kiss."

As he pulled away, Morpheus placed a hand below Constance's head and began once agin the motions.

"Now I am sending you deeper and deeper into a trance. Deeper and deeper and deeper . . ."

He turned back to the audience and smiled.

"You might imagine she is a delicate flower, but this lovely lady is possessed of an inner strength that will shock and astound you."

On cue, two stage hands stepped out from behind the curtain, each carrying a simple straight back chair and set them down upon the stage.

The glass armonica music began again, filling the air with its celestial notes. Morpheus arranged the chairs back-to-back and spaced them apart. He then returned to Constance and said, "Your mind is relaxed while your body is becoming rigid, as rigid as an iron bar." He repeated the incantation while drawing his hand down as he circled her.

As Jean Doyle watched with growing trepidation, Morpheus drew the first chair closer and then cradled Jean with a hand at the back of her neck. Repeating "Straight as a board, rigid as a poker." He tipped her backward so that she pivoted on her heels, her spine board-straight and completely rigid. He leant her up with her neck supported on the back of the chair, and then moved quickly to her feet and lifted her feet free of the ground and lowered them down onto the second chair. Like a magician he swept one hand back and forth beneath her back to prove there was no invisible supports. The crowd gasped as he waved his arms over her to demonstrate that she wasn't being supported by trickery such as invisible wires.

"As you can see the subject is in a state of hypnotic catalepsy, her body completely rigid." He dragged forward a short step stool and positioned it exactly at the mid point between the two chairs.

From her seat just four rows from the spectacle on the stage, Jean Doyle was afraid, but even more afraid to look away. Her friend

Constance lay suspended between two chairs, her spine as straight as a board. Jean was terrified, expecting her friend's spine to snap at any moment. But then the feat became even more terrifying.

Morpheus continued, "But the power of the mind always exceeds what rational belief tells us is possible. Behold, as I now demonstrate the incredible powers of mesmerism."

Morpheus stepped onto the step stool, then snatched a white handkerchief from his breast pocket and opened it with a flick. He laid the handkerchief on Constance's stomach, and then, in a move that tore a gasp from the collective lungs of the onlooking audience, he stepped up onto Constance's stomach, so that his full weight—the weight of a tall, fully-grown man—was completely supported.

From her seat, Jean clamped both hands over her mouth to avoid crying out. On stage, Constance's back did not bend or buckle in the slightest beneath his weight. And now Morpheus drew off his top hat and spread his arms wide to accept the thunderous applause that was crashing down upon the stage like an ocean wave.

CHAPTER 18: A CARRIAGE RIDE CONFESSIONAL

"I was terrified!"

"Really? Why?"

"I thought your spine would snap in two!"

"Oh my! Thank goodness it didn't."

"Don't make light of it, Constance. I was very concerned. And you remember none of it?"

Constance smiled in embarrassment. "Sadly ... no ... nothing."

"Really?" Jean's voice contained more than a hint of doubt. "Nothing at all?"

"No. I remember Morpheus leading me up onto the stage ... and then taking my seat again."

"And you don't remember—" Jean Doyle stopped short, afraid to mention the kiss. The two women were riding home in Wilde's extravagant carriage.

"No. Nothing. Not a bit of it. Why do you ask so many times? Did I do something untoward? Did I compromise myself in some way? I'm afraid to ask. I did, didn't I? I can see from your face. But go on, you must tell me."

Jean Doyle could not bring herself to say any more. The entire music hall had been witness to the passion of that onstage kiss. But it was more than that. Morpheus had kissed Constance, but from her front row vantage point, Jean could plainly see that Constance was kissing him back. Part of her was shocked . . . and part was jealous. But instead of continuing the questioning, Jean merely smiled and said, "It was a very fun outing. We must do this more often."

Constance Wilde turned to look out the carriage window at the London traffic bustling around them. She released a careless sigh, grateful that Jean's interrogation had ended. She truly didn't remember most of what transpired on the stage with Morpheus. She certainly didn't remember being made as stiff as a board and then propped between two chairs while Morpheus stood on her stomach.

But she did remember drowning in his blue eyes. She did remember the warmth of his breath in her ear as he whispered, "You will remember this kiss."

And she did remember the pressure of his lips upon hers and his tongue wrestling with hers. And she knew it was a kiss she would remember for the rest of her life.

CHAPTER 19: MORPHEUS IS PUNISHED

Backstage at the Alcambra Music Hall, a dressing room door opened and the grey haired old woman who played the glass armonica shuffled inside. But as soon as she had closed the door and was out of sight of any of the theatre workers, she stood up straight (her widow's hump was in reality a small cushion sewn into the back of her dress). The woman was clearly in a foul mood and now she dug her fingers into her hair, drew out several long pins and then snatched loose the grey wig and tossed it onto the dressing table. Beneath the grey wig she was wearing a wig cap, which compressed her real hair. And now she slipped the wig cap off, revealing her dark red hair which bore a distinctive white streak slashing across her scalp. If Conan Doyle had been there he would have recognised her as Madam Xylander, the charity woman they had met at Lady Geldsach's home and who was soliciting contributions for her home for "fallen girls."

Now Xylander snatched up a rag lying atop the dressing table, doused it liberally from a bottle of mineral spirits, and then studied her reflection in the dressing room mirror as she used the rag to wipe off the grease paint wrinkles and crow's feet drawn on her face. Within seconds, without the grey wig and theatrical makeup, the woman shed several decades and now revealed her true age as in her early forties, not her seventies.

A moment later the door barged open as a hulking giant of a man entered. He was nearly seven feet in height, and with shoulders like an ox. His square features, prognathic jaw and prominent brow with an overhang like a mountain cliff, marked him as being of good Cossack stock. He was carrying the glass armonica as though it were weightless, and now he threw a questioning look at the woman who nodded at an empty space in the corner of the cramped room and grunted, "Over there." The giant shuffled over and carefully set down the delicate instrument and then looked up expectantly for more orders. Xylander snarled, "Fetch the carriage."

The giant nodded obeisance and silently trudged out of the room, being forced to duck his head through the doorway due to his height.

Madame Xylander went back to wiping off her makeup only to be interrupted as the dressing room door flung open and the hypnotist, Morpheus the Magnificent, swaggered in, his cape flung rakishly over one shoulder. His face was set in an expression of smug satisfaction as he drew off his top hat and set it upon a waiting bust on the dressing room table.

"Another triumph, if I do say so myself," he announced to the room.

It was only then that he noticed the woman's livid face.

"What's wrong?" he asked.

"You stupid child!" Xylander hissed, spittle flying as she spat the words at him.

"What?" he asked, genuinely puzzled.

The woman took two steps toward him and then struck him with an open-handed slap across the face. He reeled back, a hand to his stinging cheek where the slap had left a red handprint. His eyes pooled with tears and shock. "What? What have I done? Why are you so angry?"

She raised a fist trembling with rage and then snatched it down in a pulling gesture, which brought the hypnotist crashing down to his knees so that he cried out in pain. The woman followed up with violent horizontal sweeps of her hand that sent waves of pain rippling across his face until he collapsed to the floor and cried out, "Mercy!"

Although diminutive, the woman now towered over the prostrate young man.

"What have I done?" He babbled, cowering before her. "What have I done?"

"You arrogant little fool. You know full well what you have done. What have I told you?"

"What? I don't . . . what?"

"I know your tastes in women. You prefer the mutton to the lamb. Perhaps I share some of the blame for that. But this enterprise is not about you slaking your carnal lusts. We work the shabbier music halls for a reason. We choose young women for a reason—I repeat, *young* women. I have expressly told you—they must be *young* women: shop girls, maids, seamstresses—young, unmarried women here in London to work for a pittance. Women who have no husbands waiting at home. Women who will not be missed. In London, hundreds of these girls vanish every week—swallowed up by the dark streets and are never seen again. Home sick girls are wont to flee back to their parents, or are inveigled by a silver-tongued rogue in a tavern into a life of servitude, or who drink themselves into a whorehouse, or are dredged from the Thames by the police. Suicides. Run-aways. These are the women we want. Innocent and naive girls who will not be missed. The woman you so publicly molested today was married. And by her fine clothes I'd wager she is a woman of some wealth. If she were to vanish overnight the police and her family would come looking for her. Questions would be asked. Eventually, even the bumbling police would tumble to the fact that all the vanished girls had come to see the mesmerist at the Alcambra Music Hall. Your lust would have led them here!"

The once-dapper hypnotist lay in a twisted heap on the floor, his face quivering with agony. "I'm sorry. I forgot. Please stop the pain."

But instead she reached out with a hand trembling with rage. "See this hand? Imagine it has plunged through your rib cage and seized your heart." Her hand clenched in a fist as though it gripped the sinewy organ.

The hypnotist pressed a hand to his chest and howled with agony. His eyes were wild and rolling. Sweat ran down his face.

"Never forget, I have you in my thrall! With this hand I could squeeze the life from your body and leave behind an unblemished corpse."

"I'm sorry. I forgot. Please . . . stop the pain."

"I taught you everything you know of animal magnetism, but never forget, I am your master."

By now, the young hypnotist could not speak, his face purpling, eyes bulging, mouth wide as he fought to take a breath.

The woman twisted her hand the other way and unclenched her fist, releasing him. He fell back, prostrate on the floor and lay there, gasping.

"When I first laid eyes upon you, you and your sister were performing for pennies and sleeping on the floors of hovels. I took you both in hand. Taught you the real secrets of Mesmerism—a science far superior to the childish parlour tricks of your father's hypnotism. I turned you into Morpheus the Magnificent. Made your brother-sister act the toast of Vienna. Of the Continent. Made you what you are today."

The young man began to get up but now turned on his tormenter and screamed defiantly, "You destroyed my sister! And now you won't even let me see her."

The woman's face turned black. Once again, she reached out a hand, clenched it into a fist and gave the fist a vicious twist.

Morpheus collapsed back upon the floor, grabbing his chest and moaning horribly. As the woman twisted the fist further, his face purpled, teeth clenched in agony. And then he began to convulse, body quaking, arms and legs kicking and jerking. After his eyes rolled up, showing the whites, she finally relented, opening her fist. Morpheus collapsed back, gasping for breath. Unable even to speak.

While he lay recovering, the women who had identified herself to

Conan Doyle and Wilde as Madame Xylander stepped over to the dressing table, retrieved a baggy pair of men's trousers and stepped into them. Hitching up the middle of her skirt, she pulled up the trousers and secured them with a belt. Then she went to the coat stand and took down a long grey coat and a grey homburg hat and put them on.

Meanwhile Morpheus shakily staggered to his feet, trembling with shock as he fought to recompose himself.

Madame Xylander threw the young man a venomous look as she calmly walked to a corner of the room where a hulking object lay concealed beneath a dust tarpaulin. She snatched it loose revealing an enormous brass coffin.

At sight of it the hypnotist's face fell. "What? But can't I just come home with you?"

The woman's face hardened to stone. She replied curtly, "You have been foolish. Reckless. You must be punished."

The hypnotist's faltering composure crumbled and collapsed. "No! Please. I'm sorry. I won't—"

The woman raised one hand in a threatening gesture. "Get in the coffin."

The hypnotist's clenched jaw betrayed the hatred simmering beneath the fear, but he meekly walked to the brass coffin. It took two hands and a grunt of effort to heave open the heavy coffin lid. The inside was spacious and featured a padded satin lining. He pulled forward a step stool and then climbed inside and lay down.

The woman walked over to the brass coffin, and put one hand on the open lid.

Inside the coffin, the hypnotist began to raise his hands and plead, "No, please don't slam—." But it was too late as she gave the lid a vicious tug so that it slammed shut with a deafening bang. She was about to walk away when a thought occurred to her that made her smirk. She paused at the dressing table to retrieve the rag she had used to wipe off her makeup. Just beneath the coffin's heavy lid several air holes had been drilled into the side and now she poked the rag into the holes, plugging them.

"No! Please!" came muffled shouts from within. "Don't block the air holes! How will I breathe?"

She leaned low over the coffin lid and spoke in a taunting voice. "You must control your mind," she admonished and for the first time her face cracked in a wicked smile. "But I will leave you one breathing hole. Focus your mind. Slow your breathing and send your body into a deep trance. You'll have plenty of air then."

As she stepped to dressing room door, she paused to reach into a breast pocket and produced a humidor from which she drew out a short cigar. Next, she took out a box of Lucifers, struck one, and puffed her cigar into life. Finally she pulled up the collar of the coat so that her face was mostly hidden. From a distance, she could easily be mistaken for a man.

And with that the woman sauntered out of the dressing room as Morpheus banged on the lid of his bronze tomb and continued to plead in a quaking voice.

"Please . . I can't breathe . . . please . . ." The banging grew louder, more desperate, but she had already left the room. "Are you still there? . . . Hello? . . . I can't breathe . . . please . . . please . . ."

CHAPTER 20: THE BRIDESMAIDS OF SLEEP

From the darkness came the jangle of keys, the rasp of a key turning in a lock, and then the juddering of a door opening in a screeeeel of rusty hinges. Then a stain of light appeared and flared, dazzling in the darkness.

The light came from a lantern swinging in the grip of the giant Cossack. As he stepped inside the space, the lantern light sketched the space: an underground cellar; an arched roof of fat round cobbles, the floor, rough paving slabs, cracked and tilting. The air was chill and root-cellar dank. But the cellar was not empty, for it was filled with female mannequins arranged in rows.

The lantern revealed that the cellar was infrequently visited. Huge spider webs draped every corner and nests of black cobwebs dangled from the ceiling swaying like underwater weed in the chill air currents. Some of the cobwebs had even begun to accumulate upon the mannequins in a mockery of a woman's veil, as though the women were the bridesmaids of sleep.

More figures carrying lanterns filed into the low-ceilinged space: Madame Xylander and two strangers. The first was a bull-chested man with the bandy legs and the weather-beaten face of a seaman who has spent years treading the salt-brined decks of ships. His companion was a wizened Chinese man. He wore the traditional silk robes of China and his hair was tied in a long black braid. The small group approached the first line of mannequins and the Cossack raised his lantern high, washing the figures with a squirming amber light that falsely animated them into twitching phantoms. But they were not ghosts. Nor were they mannequins or waxworks. They stood silent and mute, each with her head slumped to one side or the other, eyes tight shut in an unnatural, death-like sleep. Each was still dressed in the nightgown she was captured in, now smudged, stained, and tattered.

"Lumme!" the sea captain grunted. "Is they all dead?"

Madame Xylander approached the nearest one and stroked a smooth cheek with the back of her hand. "Not dead, merely sleeping."

"Sleeping?" the sea captain's voice was full of skepticism. He cautiously touched the arm of the nearest and jerked his hand away. "She's as cold as death!"

"They are in a deep, deep sleep—a state of suspended animation, like an animal in hibernation. In this trance they do not hunger. Nor do they feel the cold. It is for their own safety. This way they cannot injure themselves trying to escape, ensuring the goods are as I promised."

The Chinese man moved closer, his eyes greedily roaming the living and breathing goods he had already made a downpayment on. He smiled, "They are young and fresh. My buyers will be happy." He paused as his eyes scanned the rows of sleeping girls. "I count only sixteen. Our arrangement was for twenty."

Xylander turned to face him, her face thrown into deep shadow so that only the dark glitter of her eyes showed. "We have another week before the captain's ship sails. By then, we will have your twenty girls."

CHAPTER 21: THE MORPHEUS FLYER

Conan Doyle marched up the stairs of his Norwood home and entered his bedroom. As before a thought had occurred to him as he sat at his writing desk, some detail he wished to check upon. But as he stepped into his bedroom, once again that strange trick of the mind happened again and he could not remember what he had come upstairs for, although he knew it had something to do with his dresser. At that moment, Mary, the maid-of-all-work entered the room with a pile of freshly ironed linens in her arms. Like most good servants, she stopped and froze on the spot when she saw her master, wary of having intruded upon him.

"Beggin' pardon, sir, I'm just about to change the linens."

"Mary, did you find anything on my dresser?"

"Anything, sir?"

"I set something down on the dresser, something I wanted to look at again, but I'm blowed if I can remember."

Mary frowned and shook her head. "There was a bit of rag. Just a torn bit of cloth. It was too small to use as a dust rag so I chucked it out."

Instantly, Conan Doyle recalled the torn scrap of material from the tragic sleepwalker's nightgown. He swallowed hard, ashamed that he had forgotten the ghastly memento-more and left it in plain sight for anyone to discover. He hoped his wife had not seen it. He knew the paper was important but he could not bring to mind what it was about.

"Was there anything else, Mary?"

The domestic ruminated on it a moment longer and then added, "Oh, and yes . . . there was a scrap of paper."

"Do you recall what was on the paper?"

"I think it was an advertisement for a music act. A conjurer or the like."

That was it! The memory now surfaced in Conan Doyle's mind.

"Do we still have it?"

"I fink I burned it."

"Blast!"

"Sorry, sir, have I done wrong?"

"No, no, Mary, do not fret. It's my fault. You were not to know."

"I showed it to Mrs. Doyle first. She and Mrs Wilde was looking at while they took their tea."

"Really?"

"Yes, and wait a minute. Now I come to think. I fink we still got it."

Mary led Conan Doyle down the stairs to the front parlour where she went straight to the fireplace. The fire had been laid with sticks of wooden kindling and balled up pages from yesterday's newspaper. Sitting atop them was the flier. Mary plucked it from the fireplace and handed it to her master.

"Well done, Mary!" Conan Doyle said and gently clapped her on the shoulder. "Precisely what I was looking for."

He ran his eyes over the advertisement for Morpheus the Magnificent, then looked back at Mary as a suspicion began to take form in his head. "Do you know if my wife and Mrs Wilde went to see this show at the Music Hall?"

Mary shook her head. "Don't know sir. They said they was going shopping. But I thought it was unusual they went shopping two days in a row and didn't bring back nothing. No parcels nor nothing."

"Yessss," Conan Doyle agreed. "That is very unusual. Going shopping for two days and no parcels to show for it."

CHAPTER 22 THE MUSIC HALL

Wilde was staying at his club in London, the Albemarle. Conan Doyle found him as the only diner in the dining room, having a late breakfast. He was dressed in an shiny satin dressing gown, with Turkish slippers on his feet and an embroidered puce smoking cap atop his head.

"Ah, there you are Oscar," Conan Doyle said as he joined Wilde at his table and took a seat opposite.

"I've just come from Tite Street. I had gone to see you but you're not at home."

"Really?" Wilde drawled, buttering a slice of toast and then viciously marmalading it. "I had suspected as much. So you've run me to ground."

"Yes, I had gone to ask you a question. luckily I ran into your driver Gibson, who was washing your carriage."

"Really? Haven't' been home in a while. I suppose I really need to put in an appearance. But tell me, how is old Gibson faring?"

"He's fine and it was a bit of luck I saw him without having to bother Constance, because Jean and Constance supposedly went shopping two days in a row.

Wilde's eyes looked pouched and puffy. It was obvious he'd been out carousing with his theatre friends and his voice lacked any enthusiasm about their current conversation.

"I've just awakened Arthur, is there any chance this story of yours will arrive at a conclusion anytime soon?"

"The point is that from Gibson I discovered that our wives had not gone shopping at all."

"Really? how fortunate. I'm sure my bank manager will be ecstatic at the news. I must telegram him immediately."

The Scotsman felt a wave of irritation sweep through him. "My point is that I now suspect they went to a music hall. The Alcambra music hall to be precise. I believe they went to see a specific act, this chap in fact."

Conan Doyle thrust the flier with Morpheus in front of Wilde who paused with his mouth open and his slice of toast hovering betwixt plate and mouth. Marmalade dripped onto the white table cloth. "So they went to see a magician, how droll."

"He's not a magician, he's a hypnotist."

"Ah, there's a difference is there?"

"Yes, and remember this flyer? We found it in the room of Fanny Jones, the sleepwalking girl we could not save."

"And I take it you are suggesting a connection?"

"I suspect one, especially after what Mister Freud said. He made a connection between sleepwalking and hypnosis. All manifestation of the subconscious mind."

"And all this concerns me, exactly how?"

"It concerns you because you and I are going to the matinee at the Alcambra."

Wilde laughed musically.

"Surely you jest. Moi? The doyen of British theatre? Be seen at a lowly place such as the Alcambra? Unthinkable.

"Very well. Perhaps you could wear a disguise."

"Uh," Wilde grunted at the very idea. "I am quite comfortable with the disguise I am wearing, thank you. I shall attend as Oscar Fingal O'Flahertie Wills Wilde, who else?"

CHAPTER 23: THE BOYS VISIT THE MUSIC HALL

"Ah, the music hall," Wilde said in a voice exaggeratedly dripping with milk, honey, and warm, fuzzy memories. "That most British of home-spun entertainments."

"Do I detect sarcasm in your voice, Oscar?"

"Forgive me while I pause to lubricate my mind so that I might better enjoy the delightful skits, quips, and frolics that are about to follow."

And with that Wilde drew out his silver hip flask, took a long, Adam's apple-bobbing-swig and then a second swig, just to make sure, before handing the flask to the man sitting next to him.

The two friends were sitting in a second tier box seat in the Alcambra Music Hall. From this vantage point they had a clear view to the stage below and could scan the opposite balconies and the vertigo-inducing balconies in the upper stratosphere of the third tier.

Conan Doyle grasped the hip flask and took a single quaff before handing it back. "Is that Glenmorangie?" he asked, smacking his lips.

"Umm humm," Wilde grunted, savouring his mouthful. "Yes it is Glenmorangie. Pardon me while I finish the flask. Whiskey is such a volatile liquid. I live in fear of evaporation." He gurgled down the last mouthful and savoured it as he screwed the cap back on. "Yes, good old Glenmorangie. Nothing approaching the ambrosial bliss of the *Bruichladdichm* you sampled at O'Houlihan's, but a passable substitute."

"*You* sampled, not me. If you recall, Oscar, I never actually had the chance to so much as wet my lips."

"Ah yes, that was regrettable. We really must pay a return visit to O'Houlihans once all this somnambulism palaver is behind us."

At that moment the band struck up a jaunty tune and the rather ragged safety curtain rose. The curtains swished opened to show the same Mister and Misses Muddle skit that Jean and Constance had watched with the cross-dressing performers.

Wilde recognised the pair instantly and let out a groan.

Conan Doyle threw him a look. "What? Have you seen this act before?"

Wilde waved his concern away. "Please, don't let me spoil your enjoyment. Just sit back and let the hilarity wash over you."

The two authors suffered through two more acts: Cheeky Charlie a supposed comic, who lasted only a few minutes before being jeered from the boards, and a man with a performing dog. The dog was charming as it stole sausages from the man's pockets, misbehaved, and was endearingly naughty.

"Not entirely dreadful," Wilde summed up as man and canine left the stage. "Although if I were the dog I'd sack the man and look for a fresh partner," a comment which made Conan Doyle guffaw.

And then the band played a restless stir of cellos as Morpheus the Magnificent took the stage. Conan Doyle nudged his friend and sat upright in his seat, anxious to take it all in. For the next half-hour Morpheus performed the routine hypnosis stunts that were the typical fare of such performers. But then, at the very end of his act, a half-dozen stage hands wheeled on a large mystery object draped in a tarpaulin. Morpheus snatched loose the tarpaulin to reveal an enormous brass coffin. He heaved open the heavy lid to display the padded interior within.

"In one week's time, I shall climb into this coffin . . . and be buried alive in Hyde Park before a huge audience of spectators. As you can see it is made of bronze and is incredibly heavy and immensely strong. It must be strong to support the weight of tons of wet soil. In exactly two weeks I will climb into this coffin, which will be lowered ten feet into the ground beneath Hyde park. The grave will be filled in, and will I lie interred for a full seven days. There I will discover the mysteries of the grave as I lie suspended between life and death."

The crowd let out a gasp and Conan Doyle shot Wilde an astonished look.

"There, I will remain, within the confines of the cold earth, with neither food nor water . . . buried alive, with only the air contained within the coffin to sustain me."

Conan Doyle leaned his head toward Wilde and whispered out the side of his mouth. "That would be suicide. Obviously, the coffin must be fitted with a breathing tube or he'd suffocate."

But then the hypnotist continued almost as if he'd overheard Conan Doyle's observation. "The coffin will not be fitted with a breathing tube or any similar kind of apparatus. Instead, I will survive by using the power of mesmerism to slow my heart and respiration. I will breathe only the scant air remaining in the coffin. This will be the greatest challenge I have ever faced. Should I fail to control my mind. Should my mesmeric powers fail, I will asphyxiate and in one week's time they will exhume my corpse. If I am successful, this feat will be the sensation of the age. Tickets go on sale today and can be purchased from the Alcambra box office. They are certain to sell out quickly, so mark the date on your calendar and buy your ticket early. It will be my day to face certain death or to transcend death using the power of my mind."

The orchestra struck up ominous music, the hypnotist drew off his top hat and threw the audience a deep bow, and then he stepped once again behind the curtain.

CHAPTER 24: FOLLOW THAT CARRIAGE!

When the hypnotist vanished from the stage, sucked down through the same trap door he entered, the grey haired woman who had been playing the glass armonica got up from her instrument and shuffled off after him. And then an incredibly tall man lumbered onto the stage and hoisted the instrument as through it were weightless and carried it off. Meanwhile a large gang of stage hands swarmed the stage and each took a corner as they wheeled off the massive brass coffin which sat on a robust table built from stout timbers and rolled on heavy iron casters, and the curtains closed.

The theatre manager stepped out into the lime light to announce the final act, a juggler, as the band began to strike up.

Meanwhile, sitting up in their second level box, none of this was visible to Conan Doyle and Wilde who shot a look at his friend and asked, "What now, Arthur?"

Conan Doyle turned to Wilde and said, "I want to speak with this hypnotist chap. Do you think you could get us backstage?"

Wilde hoisted a regal eyebrow. "You are speaking to Oscar Wilde, a man whose fame, notoriety and prestige amongst the theatrical world opens all doors."

Conan Doyle leapt to his feet and began to hurriedly exit the box. "Come along then, Oscar, there's no time to shilly-shally!"

"Might I not finish my cigarette?" Wilde called after him. "I've only just lit—"

But Conan Doyle had already disappeared out of the door to the box.

"Well, that was rather rude," Wilde mused and dropped his freshly lit cigarette on the floor of the box seat.

Wilde caught up with Conan Doyle in the lobby, and then the two friends exited through the front doors and traversed the facade of the music hall to the alleyway that ran alongside.

"I believe that is the stage door just head," Wilde said, pointing at a door from which a short flight of steps descended. But as they walked toward it a black carriage pulled up outside.

"Wait a minute. That's that Cossack chap," Conan Doyle observed, watching as the tall Russian clambered down from the driver's seat and stepped around to the side of the carriage where he lowered the metal step and stood holding the carriage door open.

"Good Lord," Wilde said, eyeing the Cossack. "Either the fellow is excessively tall, or that carriage and horses are Lilliputian."

"Let's see if the hypnotist comes out the stage door. Maybe we can grab him before he gets into his carriage."

But just then a male figure in a long grey coat burst through the stage door, one hand clamping a homburg to his head. He skipped down the steps and immediately dove into the open carriage trailing a wisp of smoke from a lit cigar. The Cossack slammed the door after him and climbed back up to the driver's seat.

"Wait!" Conan Doyle said, grabbing his friend by the sleeve. "I know that chap in the grey homburg! It's that Austrian psychologist fellow, Sigmund Freud. What's he doing here? He told me he was going up north to visit with family."

"Whoever it was did seem to be in a great hurry," Wilde noted.

"In a hurry not to be seen. But I recognise him by the hat and coat."

"And by the cigar," Wilde added.

"Precisely."

But at that moment the Cossack whipped up the horses and the two friends had to dodge to one side of the alley to avoid being trampled as the carriage whisked by. Conan Doyle peered into the carriage windows as it passed, but caught only a glimpse of a man seated in the carriage and the red glow of a lit cigar as he puffed upon it.

"It's him, I swear! It's that Austrian chap, Sigmund Freud. The bounder lied to me."

The Cossack cracked his whip over the horses's ears and the black carriage trundled past and then turned left onto Tottenham road.

"We must follow that carriage!" Conan Doyle looked around desperately. A hansom was just dropping off a fare outside the Alcambra. "Perfect!" Conan Doyle exulted. "Look, Oscar, let's grab that cab."

The two men piled into the cab and Conan Doyle shouted up directions to the driver to follow the black carriage that just pulled away. By the time the hansom set off, the black carriage was still in sight, a hundred feet ahead. But another two hundred yards later they entered the slow-moving sludge of London traffic. As they approached a bridge, the black carriage made it across successfully, but then a gap opened behind the carriage large enough for a stream of traffic to cut across, effectively stalling the hansom. Conan Doyle could only bite his lip in frustration as the black carriage receded and then finally vanished into the distance.

"Blast!" he said.

"Oh, dear," Wilde seconded.

"This London traffic is impossible. I'd do better with a bicycle like that Billy Brash fellow has."

"Now what?" Wilde asked.

"The hypnotist chap wasn't in the carriage, so he must still be at the theatre. Let's see if we can run him to ground. I've a number of questions I'd like to put to him."

The two returned to the Alcambra and knocked on the stage door. It was answered by the stage manager, a short, thin, hypertensive man with bulging eyes and a personality like a lit firecracker. Conan Doyle had no doubt that his bald head was undoubtedly the result of pulling his own hair out, a strand at a time. The manager wire brushed both authors with a doubting look until recognition rolled up into his eyes like pound signs ka-chinging in a till. Instantly upon recognising Wilde, the stage manager's suspicious scowl dissolved into a welcoming smile.

And so the two friends slunk into the back-stage area where they had free rein to explore at leisure. Wilde led the way down a ringing iron staircase and along a corridor, which by the name boards affixed to each door, housed the dressing rooms. They reached a closed door with "Morpheus" affixed to it where Conan Doyle loudly rapped with his knuckles.

The two stood listening for a period, but no sounds emanated from within.

"Damn! No one home," Conan Doyle said.

Wilde cleared his throat. "Unless our handsome friend Mister Morpheus is, ahem, entertaining."

"I had not thought of that. What do we do in that case?"

"Do what I always do . . . barge in! One often finds all kinds of interesting tableaus taking place, and I always always apologise after the fact." And with that, Wilde grasped the door handle, flung the door wide, and the two stepped inside.

Like most dressing rooms, this one was small, dimly lit and suffused with a tangible sense of Weltschmärtz. The two moved about the space, nosing into nooks and crannies. Although Conan Doyle noticed the grey wig sitting atop a wig stand he failed to associate it with the grey haired lady who played the glass armonica. He stood before the instrument now, admiring its blown glass array of glass cups.

Wilde stepped over to examine the hulking brass coffin.

"You consistently accuse me of overpacking on travel, Arthur, but I have never travelled with my own coffin. Should I acquire the habit, my old age may prove to be quite challenging."

"Very impressive," Conan Doyle remarked. "Im sure it must weigh as much as an elephant." He tried to lift the lid, but soon found it required two hands and considerable brawn. When he heaved the lid wide, he was shocked to find that the coffin was occupied.

Wilde and Conan Doyle looked down in horror. Morpheus lay in the coffin, eyes shut, face waxen.

Both men were taken aback.

"Good Lord," Wilde said, he looks like a sample in an undertaker's front window. Is . . . is he dead?"

Conan Doyle peered closer.

"He certainly looks dead."

"Well check to make sure. Go on, touch him."

Conan Doyle began to reach forward with a hand, but then balked. "Why don't you touch him?"

"Because . . . because I'm a playwright. You're a doctor."

"I was a doctor for living patients, not dead ones."

"Oh, now you're prevaricating. You went to medical school. You must have touched a lot of dead bodies. Did you not have lessons in vivisection?

"Yes, but I never enjoyed it."

"I'm not asking you to enjoy it now. Just touch him and see if he is still warm."

With a scowl of reluctance, Conan Doyle rubbed his hands together and then palpated the hypnotist's neck, feeling for a pulse at the jugular artery.

After several long seconds of listening, Conan Doyle shook his head, but then corrected himself. "No . . . nothing . . . oh, just a moment. Ah. No. Yes. I mean . . . he's definitely . . . dead. Oh, wait . . . no he's alive . . . I think . . ."

Oscar Wilde threw his friend a look of wide-eyed exasperation. "No? Yes? What? No he's dead, or yes he's alive? Arthur, forgive me for being rather brusque, but if you were my doctor and could not assess my current state of mortality, I would be less than reassured right now. Your coffin-side manner leaves much to be desired."

I merely meant that he's alive but only just . . ." Conan Doyle trailed off as he snatched loose the pocket watch hanging from his vest and studied it while feeling at the man's jugular. Finally he drew his hand away and fixed Wilde with an astonished look. "How very extraordinary! His pulse and respiration are incredibly slow. I've never come across anything like it. It's like he's in a state if suspended animation. His heart is beating less than once a minute. I would have said it was impossible if I hadn't witnessed it myself."

"Maybe he's waiting for the snows to melt and the spring to return. I suggest we leave in some haste. Being discovered in a room with an apparently dead man in a coffin counts in my book as a compromising situation."

Conan Doyle looked down and noticed the rag stuffed in the air holes.

"What is it,?"

These look like air holes drilled into the side of the coffin, but someone's plugged most of them. The fellow is likely to suffocate. He snatched the rag loose and tossed it on the table.

CHAPTER 25: CONAN DOYLE HIRES A BOY WITH A BICYCLE

Inspector Crumpet was the last man Conan Doyle had expected to run into. But as he stepped into the offices of the Illustrated Police News, there he was, munching away at a sausage roll while he sat in a chair pulled up to the desk of Billy Brash, Boy Reporter.

Both men were deep in conversation, heads together, but when they spotted Conan Doyle walking toward them they abruptly ended their confab.

"Ah, Doctor Doyle," Crumpet said, "Just in time." He flourished the open bag of sausage rolls and offered, "Care for a sausage roll?"

"No, thank you. I've just had my dinner."

"Well, that's never stopped me. These are the very best sausage rolls in London." He shook the bag invitingly. "Go on, you know you want one."

"No, really thank you. I recently joined the Norwood cricket team." He patted his stomach. "Got to get fighting fit."

"Ah, I see. Well, I'm sure you're here to see our boy Brash. Anyway, I must be off." He grunted up from the chair. "Police business to attend to. Cheerio."

The two watched the portly police inspector waddle away through the ranks of desks.

Conan Doyle eyed the young reporter. "I take it that was business? A tip for you, or you supplying a tip for him?"

Billy Brash smiled sheepishly. "Commerce is a two-way street around here. Sometimes I helps 'im. Sometimes he 'elps me."

"I need you now to help me."

The boy reporter shook his head and leaned back in his chair. "Sorry guv, but I am well busy at the moment. I gotta deadline for a story I'm working on."

Conan Doyle slapped down a golden sovereign on the desktop. "It's yours if you want it. I need to hire a boy with a bicycle."

Brash goggled at the sovereign and then looked up at Conan Doyle's face and flashed a wicked grin. "Well, ain't that lucky. I just so 'appen to have a bicycle right here."

When Conan Doyle looked down again the sovereign had vanished, even though he never saw Brash make a move toward it.

"I want you to follow someone."

"Ooh," Brash smiled. "That sounds spicy. A bee-you-tee-full lady, I hope."

"Not quite. There is a hypnotist currently performing at the Alcambra music hall. The chap calls himself Morpheus the Magnificent."

The Boy Reporter chuckled at the name and said, "Blimey! That's a corker of a moniker."

He travels about in a black coach with a very distinctive driver, an extremely tall Cossack chap in a grey fur hat and a long wool coat . . ."

CHAPTER 26; THE REFUGE FOR FALLEN WOMEN

The next afternoon, Billy Brash was idling at the end of the alleyway that ran alongside the Alcambra Music Hall, smoking one of his poorly-rolled cigarettes when the black carriage swung into the alleyway and pulled up outside the stage door. As Conan Doyle had described, the black growler was being driven by a giant dressed in the clothes of a Cossack. Billy guessed it would only be a matter of seconds before someone emerged from the stage door and got inside, so he took one final pull on his cigarette, which disintegrated as he took a drag, sending a scatter of ash and burning tobacco leaves everywhere. Billy ducked to one side of the alleyway where his bicycle was leaned up against a lamp post and crouched low as if inspecting the front tyre. When he looked back, he was just in time to see the stage door fly open, and then a short man in a grey coat and a homburg hat flew out the door, skipped down the steps and leapt into the waiting carriage. From his haste and the fact that he wore a hat and a long coat with the collar turned up to hide his face, it seemed obvious to Billy that the gent was intent on not being recognised. As soon as he had pulled the carriage door shut, the driver whipped up the horses. As the black carriage trundled past, Billy kept his head down and did not make eye contact with the Cossack. The carriage turned right onto Tottenham road and joined the endless stream of London traffic. Billy waited thirty seconds, then threw his leg over the crossbar and stood on the pedal, pumping hard. Within seconds, he effortlessly merged with the stream of carriages, hansoms, dust carts, brewery wagons, and omnibuses, of which the black carriage was stuck like a fly in the treacle-slow ooze. For several miles it was effortless keeping up with the slow traffic. The only hazard was the need to constantly swerve around the malodorous piles of horse manure saucing the roadway. The traffic slowed further as it squeezed through the constricted artery of Hungerford Bridge.

But as they approached the bridge, the unexpected happened. A brewer's cart laden with barrels tried to quickly turned across the stream of traffic, but its front wheel collided with the wheel of a fully-laden omnibus. The brewer's wagon climbed up at steep angle, hurling the two drivers from their seat, and then the barrels toppled out, rolling wildly across the road, two bursting open and spraying their load of beer. Moments later the cart toppled onto its side, dragging the whinnying horses to the cobblestones. Instantly, a scene of bedlam erupted. Women screamed. Men shouted. The passengers of the stricken omnibus clambered down the stairs from the top deck and joined the milling spectators. Several men rushed forward and tried to calm the horses which lay thrashing and kicking on their sides. The huge shire horses were still in harness and their flailing hooves threatening to snap the legs of anyone foolish enough to draw too close.

Worse, Billy looked up the road and saw to his dismay that the black carriage had escaped being ensnared in the fracas, and was steadily pulling away into the distance. A layer of official incompetence was added with the appearance of a constable, who blew incessantly upon his whistle and waved his arms about ineffectually without accomplishing anything to ease the snarl.

Billy made a quick decision. He jumped off his bicycle, hoisted the crossbar on his shoulder and ran down the road to a set of stone steps that descended to the embankment. He jogged beneath the arch of the road bridge and found a set of steps on the far side leading up. When he summited the steps he was now on the far side of the traffic snarl. He peered into the distance, scanning, but his heart sank when he could no longer spot the black carriage among the myriad of hansoms and wagons and omnibuses streaming in either direction. But then Billy spotted the vertical post of the Cossack at the very limits of visibility. He leapt back onto his bike and set off pedalling in pursuit. The traffic was moving even more slowly at this hour and Billy pedalled like a demon, weaving around omnibuses and growlers, earning a few flung curses as he came a little close to the horses than their drivers were happy with. With his eyes glued on the black carriage far ahead, he rode straight through a pile of horse dung, which his front tire flung up so it splattered in his face, forcing him to gag and spit out a mouthful of dung, which was still warm and fresh. But as his legs blurred on the pedals, he quickly gained upon the black carriage, until eventually he was only a few carriage-lengths behind. Finally, he slowed his pace, sucking wind as he at last eased his burning thighs.

The black carriage finally entered the Marylebone district, with its rows of middle-class houses. Here the carriage finally turned in at a residence and pulled up outside a front door guarded by tall, white Corinthian columns.

Brash leapt off his bicycle and leaned it up against a low garden wall then crouched down behind it. From here he had an unobstructed view of the black carriage and the front door of the residence. The cossack clambered down from his driver's perch and went back to close the gates. It gave Billy the chance to read the discreet sign posted next to the front door: *The Marylebone Refuge For Fallen Women.* The Cossack then marched back to the carriage where he lowered the metal step and then opened the carriage door and held it wide.

Peering over the garden wall, Billy waited for the man in the homburg hat to climb out, but instead a lady stepped down. She had fiery red hair with a prominent white streak running across her crown. She was smoking a short cigar, and now she paused to drop it on the driveway. She was also carrying a bouquet of flowers, which must have been waiting for her inside the carriage. She walked to the front door and rapped on the brass knocker. After a slight delay, the door was opened by an old woman in a babushka. The red-headed lady sauntered past, ignoring the old woman who closed the door behind her. The Cossack then returned to the carriage. Billy expected the man in the grey homburg to climb out next, but instead the Cossack slammed the open carriage door, climbed back onto the driver's seat and drove the carriage down the drive that ran behind the house to where the stables were.

Billy Brash hawked and spat. His mouth was still filmed with the taste of horse shit, but despite that he smiled. He would have an interesting tale to tell Conan Doyle for his gold sovereign. He'd watched a man get into the carriage only to turn into a woman somewhere along the way.

CHAPTER 27: BROKEN LILLY

A key rattled in a lock and then the bedroom door opened and Madame Xylander entered. The room was sparsely furnished: a single chair, and a number of small tables with a vase of flowers atop each one. The centre of the room was occupied by a child's-size canopy bed with the the bed curtains tightly drawn. Xylander was carrying a fresh bouquet of flowers and now she approached the canopy bed and lent in. "How are you my beloved?" she asked in a simpering voice. "Look, I have brought you fresh flowers to keep your room smelling sweet."

She was speaking to the occupant of the bed, whose face was obscured from view by piles of lacy pillows, doilies, rag dollies, and other expensive fripperies, so Xylander leant in closer to show off the bouquet she had brought.

"Lillies, your favourite," she said gaily. "Lillies for my beloved Lilly." She peeled back the paper and flourished the flowers so that the occupant of the bed could see. "Aren't they lovely?" She pressed the bouquet to her face and inhaled deeply. "And they smell so wonderful! Just let me put these in a vase for you."

Madame Xylander moved to a nearby round table. The table held a vase in which the flowers were all withered and desiccated. She dumped them out onto the floor and then refilled the vase with the fresh flowers she had brought. She walked back to the bed and set the vase down on a nearby table, then took a seat on the edge of the bed.

"There we are. Can you see them? Shall I move them closer?"

She got up and dragged the table closer. "Is that better? I love the perfume of flowers. It makes the room seem so . . . so fresh and clean."

She stopped a moment and cast a glance around the room. Apart from the miniature canopy bed, the only other furniture in the room was a scatter of small round tables, each holding a vase filled with a bouquet of flowers in various stages of wilting. Their combined perfumes rendered the air sticky and cloying.

She moved her eyes back to the figure in the bed and her expression changed to one of concern. "Oh, but you must be hot under than blanket, my darling. Should I remove it?"

She dragged the heavy blanket away, folded it and tossed it on the foot of the bed.

With the blanket gone, the occupant of the bed was fully visible for the first time.

Propped up on a cloud of pillows was a female of indeterminate age—she could have been a young woman or a tall child. But her emaciated form was tragically thin and her posture tortured: spine twisted in a foetal curl. Arms and legs skinny as bamboo rods. Forearms pronated, wrists cocked, hands clenched into claws, while the withered legs were clearly useless and couldn't possibly bear her weight. She was dressed in a girl's sailor suit: a white and blue pinafore with black leggings that hung loose and baggy on the stick-thin legs.

"How are you today, my beloved?" Madame reached to caress her gaunt cheek, but the startlingly blue eyes remained glassy and blank. She combed a wisp of honey-blonde hair from the girl's face with her fingers.

Madame Xylander continued to coo and fuss over the girl. "We will not be in London much longer. Your brother and I are doing well. Next week we perform the buried alive stunt. We have already sold many tickets and I expect we will earn a great deal of money. And then, after your brother is dug up and resurrected, we can sell all the dollies we have collected and leave on the night train for Europe. When we get to Berlin we will have plenty of money for your operation."

Madame reached in, lifted one of the emaciated arms, pressed the claw-like hand to her cheek, and affectionately kissed it.

"After Doctor Rüdin works his magic and restores my beautiful Lilly to me, we will live as we used to." Madame Xylander's voice became dreamy as she exulted in a future that had not yet come to pass. Suddenly, her head snapped up at a timid knock on the bedroom door.

"Who is it?" She challenged, her voice harsh.

A muffled voice murmured from the other side.

"Chodź!" Madame called out in Polish.

The door opened and an ancient woman in a babushka with a deeply wrinkled face shuffled in. The woman was Marta, a Polish servant. Xylander had hired her specifically because she could only speak Polish.

"Marta," Xylander said in Polish. "I want you to bathe Lilly and then change her clothes. She has been wearing them for two days now. And change the bedclothes while you're at it." She nodded at the desiccated flowers strewn across the rug. "And throw those dead flowers out. I should not need to tell you such things! What do I pay you for old woman?"

All through the scolding the Polish woman never responded, but kept her head down and meekly moved about the room, slowly performing the tasks she'd been admonished to perform.

Madame Xylander finally rose to her feet, but turned and addressed the figure in the bed one final time. "Good night, my darling, Lilly. I will look in on you tomorrow morning. Tonight we are making another collection run. Just two more girls and then we shall have enough. I am doing all this for you, so we can be together again."

As she walked to the door, she paused and blew a kiss to the girl in the bed. "All for you . . ."

CHAPTER 28: BILLY TELLS HIS TALE

Inspector Crumpet, along with Conan Doyle and Oscar Wilde, were sitting around a table in Mrs Wiggly's Pie Shop, listening attentively as the diminutive Billy Brash, Boy Reporter, was holding court, narrating the story of his pursuit of the black carriage.

"I watched a bloke in a long grey coat and grey homburg get in the carriage but when it arrived at a house in Marylebone, the tall Russian geezer opened the carriage door . . ."

The boy reporter paused for dramatic effect.

"Yes?" Inspector Crumpet prompted.

". . . and a lady got out." Brash ended with a knowing grin.

Conan Doyle's jaw dropped. "What? A lady got out of the carriage?"

Brash nodded. "That's wot oi said."

"Just the lady?" Wilde repeated. "What happened to the gentlemen? The fellow in the long grey coat and hat? What happened to him?"

The boy reporter laughed. "Well it's obvious, ain't it. There never was no feller."

Inspector Crumpet cleared his throat grumpily and demanded, "What do you mean? You just told us you saw a man in a grey coat and grey homburg get into the carriage."

"Yeah, but it's obvious. It were a lady all along. In disguise. Cor, you don't have to be Sherlock-bleedin'-Holmes to figure that one out."

The revelation rocked Conan Doyle back. Here this whole time he'd been certain he was pursuing the the Austrian doctor, Sigmund Freud. But it turned out to be someone wearing a disguise. But then he wondered if the disguise was just a coincidence. Was the disguise deliberate? Was it pure chance they dressed exactly as the Austrian? "Or was Freud still involved in some fashion?

"But the male figure you saw getting into the carriage was smoking a cigar," the Scots doctor asked. "You definitely saw that he was smoking a cigar, right?"

"Yeah, and the lady wot got out of the carriage finished smokin' the cigar."

"This lady," Crumpet probed. "Did you get a good look at her? Could you describe her?"

Brash pulled a notebook from his pocket, flipped it open, and squinted at his scrawl of handwriting. "About 40-ish. Around the same height as me. A little on the plump side. And, oh yeah, she had red hair with a white streak down the middle. Very distinctive."

"Poliosis," Conan Doyle added. "It's an hereditary condition, a person is often born with a white or grey streak running through the hair."

"That sounds rather familiar," Wilde chipped in. Why does that sound familiar?"

"Madame Xylander." Conan Doyle replied.

Wilde raised his eyebrows and shook his head, clearly at a loss.

"We met her at Lady Moneyb—." Inspector Crumpet caught himself using Wilde's irreverent name and stopped to correct himself. "We met her at Lady Geldsach's house. She was the woman who runs a charity for, ahem, fallen women."

"Oh gawd, the begging lady." Wilde moaned. "I have always maintained there is nothing more suspicious than charities and people who perform good works. Once again, I am proven correct."

"And yeah," Brash added, "there's a sign outside the house . . ." He read aloud from his notebook: *The Marylebone Refuge For Fallen Women.*"

Wilde steepled his fingers beneath his chin and said, "Forgive me, Arthur, if I play Sherlock Holmes for a moment, but from that I would deduce that this Xylander woman is in cahoots with the mesmerist chap. Is that correct?" Wilde laughed at his own pronouncement and added, "Cahoots, I love that word. Pity one so rarely has a chance to use it. Cahoots!" He laughed musically.

"I think cahoots is entirely appropriate," remarked Conan Doyle. "Sleepwalkers, hypnotists—a pattern is finally emerging." He shot the others with a meaningful look. I think we need to invite ourselves over to Madame Xylander's *Marylebone Refuge For Fallen Women*. I'm suddenly feeling in a charitable mood."

"Ugh!" Wilde recoiled at the thought. "Whenever an urge to be charitable comes over me I sit down and drink a bottle of my most expensive wine and that usually cures it."

Conan Doyle said, "And I suppose you don't even share that bottle of wine with anyone?"

"Well of course I don't." Wilde retorted. "That would defeat the whole purpose of the exercise. After all, what is greed if not the honest recognition of one's own worth?"

29

CHAPTER 29: JEAN VANISHES

Jean Doyle was deep asleep when something ghostly shivered across the surface of her dreaming mind. She moaned, rolled over, drew in a deep breath and released it in a languorous sigh. The bedroom's small windows had been left open to allow the heat to escape, and now the silvery chords of the glass armonica drifted in. They surrounded her, flowing around the bed in ripples of shifting colour. She opened her eyes and gasped. *How wonderful!* she thought as the brightly coloured ribbons entwined her, caressed her, so that the boundaries of her body dissolved as she became as light as a gas. Soon she levitated from the bed, and floated up to the ceiling where she tumbled weightless as a helium balloon. Here she ran her hands through silky ribbons of coloured light. And then she realised she was hearing the light, seeing the sound. The bedroom filled from floor to ceiling with an ethereal music, otherworldly as the silvery singing of angels in a celestial choir. The music had a pull upon her, an irresistible tidal draw. She needed to draw closer, to join the source of the heavenly music. She floated to the windows and tried to open them, but her sleep-clumsy hands could not release the catch, for Conan Doyle had had them screwed shut. She looked back at the bed, saw the slumbering mound that was Conan Doyle and the empty space beside him where she normally lay.

The music was coming from a distance and the volume rose and fell, but then a faint breeze stirred the curtains and as the music got louder so its pull grew stronger. She turned and moved toward the bedroom door, pushing her body through the resistant, gelid air. The door was locked but she turned the key in the lock and it sprang open. Although the upstairs hallway was dark, she could see everything plainly. She floated along to the end of the hallway. The window at the top of the stairs looked out onto the rooftop. The music was louder here and so she unlatched the window, pulled it wide, and stepped out onto the rooftop.

The slate roof tiles beneath her bare feet were still warm. A sultry zephyr blew, teasing the hem of her nightgown and caressing her bare ankles. The music changed slightly, the pitch altering as the silken notes tightened about her like a lasso. The music was irresistible, and now she surrendered to its tidal pull as it drew her along the rooftop. To Jean's dream-dazzled eyes, her feet seemed a thousand miles below her, while her head and shoulders soared so high into the night sky that the lowest stars brushed warm along her cheeks and snagged in her hair.

The roof of Conan Doyle's house abutted his neighbour's and she stepped over a low wall like a giant stepping over a matchbox. She passed the shadowy mass of a chimney, a spectre of black smoke still curling up from the dying kitchen fires. The next rooftop ended in a sheer drop and she lingered here a moment, pondering.

On the street far below a black carriage had pulled up and now three figures stood looking up at her. Morpheus, in his cape and top hat stood at the front. Behind him the grey-haired old woman sat at the glass armonica, one foot rhythmically pumping the foot treadle as her hands dipped into the water dish and then her long fingers moved fluidly over the gleaming glass bowls coaxing loose celestial notes that rose from the armonica in a shimmering aurora of colour that coiled around Jean and drowned her in its glimmering rapture.

Jean had to get closer. The music was drawing her, coaxing her closer. She looked around, desperate to join the music.

On the rooftop of the neighbour's house, a bedroom window had been thrown open to allow the heat to escape. Now Jean glided toward it and floated through its dark rectangle to find herself in a bedroom. A pair of children, a boy and a girl, were sleeping, and as she floated past their beds, the little boy opened his eyes, saw her and then ducked beneath the covers, cowering. The little girl reached out and touched the hem of Jean's nightgown before she reached the bedroom door and slipped out. In the morning both children would breathlessly tell their parents of the ghost of a beautiful lady who floated in though the window and passed through their bedroom, only to be laughed at and told they had been dreaming.

Jean floated down the darkened stairs to the front door and stepped through it onto the street. She moved dream-slow toward the waiting carriage and as she neared the glass armonica the music flowed around her and lifted her free of the ground so that she floated the last few toward the waiting carriage where the hypnotist threw open the carriage door and she was drawn inside.

The music abruptly ceased as Xylander stopped playing and stood up from the instrument. The Cossack loaded the armonica onto the back of the carriage, threw a tarpaulin over it and strapped it down. And then, their kidnapping accomplished, the mesmerists clambered back into their carriage and quietly drove away.

Back in the Doyle house, the Scots author shifted in his sleep. He awakened for a moment, sensing something he should be aware of, but then he sank back into sleep and did not stir until he screamed himself awake.

CHAPTER 30: WAKING INTO NIGHTMARE

Conan Doyle burst up from sleep with a terrified howl.

The dream again. The rooftop. The somnambulist. The flimsy nightgown fluttering. The crack of crumbling masonry. The slight form, arms flailing for balance, betrayed by weak masonry and the merciless pull of gravity.

Once again, in the dream as the woman tumbled away, he looked into her face and watched it transform into the face of his beloved wife, her eyes spilling over with starlight, her mouth open in a silent scream as she tumbled away into the darkness.

Conan Doyle surged up from the bedclothes, heart jackhammering, gasping, fighting to catch his breath. As the nightmare ebbed from his mind, he blinked and looked around dazedly. It was early, hours before the household servants got up, and the predawn gloom suffused the room. He reached an exploring hand to touch his wife, but impossibly, his hand found only cold sheets. He snatched the covers back. Jean's side of the bed was empty. He looked around the room but she was not there. He leapt from the bed and examined the windows. They all remained screwed down. She could not have gone out the windows.

Conan Doyle threw on a robe and flew from the bedroom. Perhaps she had gone to check on one of the children . . .

Lumbering from the room, half asleep, his shoulder banged painfully against the door jam as he lurched from the bedroom into the hall, the last shreds of nightmare still evaporating from his mind's eye. He was about to bang on the bedroom door of his son, Ainsly, when he felt a current of air drag a cool finger down his cheek. When he turned his head to look, what he saw made his blood chill to ice water.

The window at the top of the stairs had been left wide open. He rushed to the window and stood looking out on the pitch of the roof. Jean was nowhere to be seen. In what now seemed an obvious blunder, Conan Doyle had screwed shut all of the bedroom windows, but it had never occurred to him to do the same with this window. Now, he stood looking out the rooftop and he knew with terrible certainty that Jean had stepped through the window and vanished into the night.

CHAPTER 31: JEAN JOINS THE BRIDESMAIDS OF SLEEP

The jingle of jailor's keys.

The rasp of a key turning in a rusty lock.

The squeal of un-oiled hinges.

Lantern light spilling into a dark cellar so that the shadows cringed back and cowered in the corners.

In the gloomy cellar, the Cossack raised his lantern high, throwing forward a carpet of light that revealed an underground space with a floor of uneven flagstones and an arched ceiling of round cobbles. The ceiling was festooned with rusty hooks from where cuts of meat were once hung to season. Now the only thing hanging from them were nests of black cobwebs that dangled like hanks of witches' hair swaying in the chill breeze.

The Cossack lumbered closer with his lantern light , illuminating rows of somnambulists arranged side-by side. Each was still dressed in the night gown she was captured in, now tattered and grubby. Up close, all the women were shivering, the body's natural response to the cold and damp of the cellar, and the fact that all stood barefoot upon cold and filthy flagstones.

Now Madame Xylander moved forward with her newest capture, Jean Doyle. With a hand on Jean's shoulder, she shuffled her into place at the end of the first row of girls. Jean's heavy-lidded eyes were open but milky with sleep, and now the Madame raised her hands before her and began with her mesmeric motions, sweeping up and then pulling down as she massaged Jean's mind into a deeper and deeper trance. Finally she hovered her open hand before Jean's face, and hissed into her ear "sleeeeeeeep." Jean's eyes closed. Her neck slackened and her head slumped to one side.

Madame Xylander stepped back and smiled at her handiwork. "Now we have all twenty, we are ready." The Madame turned to look at Morpheus, who hung back near the door, unwilling to move any closer. "After the buried alive stunt we will have all the money we need."

Morpheus squirmed at her words. His eyes glittered with tears as he turned his head and looked away into the shadows, unwilling to gaze upon the spectacle of the twenty girls turned into frozen mannequins.

"This is wrong," he said in a torn voice. "This is wrong and I will be damned to hell for it."

The Madame stiffened at his words and glared at him. "You want your sister to be restored, don't you? You want Lilly as she once was? Well . . . don't you?"

At her words, Morpheus dropped his head, and nodded miserably.

"Then this is the price we must pay," Madame Xylander said. "Don't concern yourself about the fate of these girls. London gobbles up and devours a hundred girls such as these every week. Think of yourself. In two days you will be sealed in a brass coffin and buried alive in Hyde Park. You must survive a week underground. Prepare yourself mentally or we might well be digging up your corpse in nine day's time."

CHAPTER 32: MORPHEUS ESCAPES

In his small room in the Marylebone house, Morpheus lay on his bed and drew a blanket over him without bothering to undress. He lay staring up at the ceiling as the skies outside the windows darkened and his room filled up with shadows. He thought about the sleep-walker who had fallen to her death. He thought about the twenty women shivering in the cellar who would soon find themselves shipped off to strange and foreign lands to face a life of whoredom and servitude. It was a hideous fate and he measured their potential misery against his own and the combined guilt drowned him. He loved his sister Lilly but he knew she would not want this. He hated Xylander but knew that he could not go to the police because he was inextricably tied into her wickedness. He hated to abandon his sister but the longer he stayed with Xylander the more crimes he helped commit and the worse his situation became. He resolved that the only thing he could do was to run away, escape.

He lay still, listening. He heard Xylander go next door to his sister's room. Heard her cooing voice. Eventually she left after a half-hour. He heard a door opening and closing as she retired to her own bedroom. He got up, went to the corner of the bedroom and crouched down. He pulled back a loose section of skirting board and reached into the cavity behind. After a moment's fumbling he drew out a small leather purse. It contained the meagre amount of money he had been able to save and now he pocketed it. After another half hour passed, he heard the Cossack lock and bolt the front door. He crept to the bedroom door, opened it a crack, and paused there, listening. He could hear the Cossack's heavy feet, tromping around the downstairs. He could not go down that way, so he eased the door shut and went to the window. The hinges creaked as he pushed the window wide and looked out. There was a narrow balcony with a black iron railing. The Marylebone house had three floors. The rooms beneath his had the same balcony with a black railing. He smiled. This would be easy. He climbed over the balcony railing, then dangled by his hands from the balcony railing. He swung his body back and forth and few times and then let go and dropped onto the first floor balcony. He paused and listened. No one stirred. There was no sign that the Cossack had heard anything. From the first floor balcony he had a drop of maybe fifteen feet to the ground.

Again, he dangled from the railing and then dropped, hit the ground, and rolled. His feet stung from the height of the drop, but he was free. He crouched on the ground for several minutes watching the front door, but the Cossack did not step outside as he had feared.

Finally, when he deemed it was safe, Morpheus stood up, and crept to the road. When he reached it he began to run. He would run until he came across a hansom cab. Before he had released Constance from her trance, he had discovered her address and committed it to memory. Now, he was going straight to Chelsea.

CHAPTER 33: CONSTANCE ELOPES
WITH MORPHEUS

Constance Wilde had just tucked the two Wilde boys into bed and almost collided with her housemaid as she stepped out of their shared bedroom.

"Oh, Florence, you startled me!"

"Sorry, Ma'am. I was about to ask you, shall I lock up the house and bolt the doors, or do you expect the Master to come home tonight?"

Constance Wilde stiffened, her face grim. Her erstwhile husband had failed to sleep a single night under his own roof in two weeks. Even though it shamed her to admit it, Constance had no doubt that Oscar was off gallivanting with his "Oxford friends" as she euphemistically put it, unwilling to admit even to herself that he was undoubtedly in the company of one Oxford alumnus in particular, the Marquess of Queensbury's son, or as he was better known to her husband as "Bosie". Constance discovered the name after she surreptitiously read through the letters she found in her husband's desk drawer.

Constance counterfeited a smile for the housekeeper. "No, Mary, Mister Wilde's new play opened this week. I'm afraid he will be carousing—" She stopped herself. "I mean celebrating its success. He is staying at his club in London."

"At his club, ma'am," the housekeeper repeated. Constance cringed inwardly. It was clearly a veiled reproach.

The housekeeper nodded. "Very good, ma'am. Then I will lock up everything tight. Are you staying up, ma'am?"

Constance shook her head, eager to quit the discussion. "No, I have a headache. I will retire myself."

The maid ducked a curtsey and flourished the house keys. "Good night then, Ma'am."

Constance went to bed and fell into a restive sleep. Some time after midnight she was awakened by the rattle of carriage wheels and the clatter of horse's hooves on cobbles. Her eyes sprang open. A carriage had drawn up outside.

Could it be Oscar? Returned home after all?

Because of the summer heat, and the fact that her husband seldom shared their bed these days, she had taken to sleeping in the nude. Now she slid out of bed and slipped into her silk dressing gown, tightening the belt before padding to the window.

On the darkened street below a hansom cab waited, sketchily lit by the pulse and throb of gas lamps. The cabbie sat hunched over the reigns. Constance puzzled at who on earth would be arriving at her house in a cab at this hour. But then her eyes was drawn down to a tall male figure standing beside the horse. She recognised the silhouette instantly.

Morpheus!

Although the bedroom was semi-dark, the light of a gibbous moon flooded in through the window she stood at, and she knew that he must have been able to see her.

What on earth had brought him here at this hour? And how did he even know where she lived? For a mad moment she wondered if he had come to see Oscar. But then she watched him reach into his cloak and produce something and all question of who he was here to see evaporated.

It was a flower, a single red rose and now he lifted it to his lips, kissed it, and then held it out it toward her.

Constance's heart was drumming in her ears. She seemed to be under his thrall as her hands reached down, grasped the bow of her nightgown, and pulled. The knot silkily untied and her dressing gown fell open, exposing her breasts and naked body. A rush of heat swept through her as she felt his eyes upon her naked body, greedily appraising. She felt a rush of desire. Her knees quivered, threatening to buckle. It was obvious he had come to woo her. To take her away. To ravish her.

And then he raised his right hand and made a beckoning gesture. With his face masked in shadow she could not see his expression, but she somehow knew he was smiling.

He made the beckoning gesture again, this time with more animation. As if without volition, she felt herself turn from the window, slip out of the bedroom, creep stealthily down the stairs to the front door. Mary had indeed locked all the locks and shot the bolts. But Constance reached into a pocket of her robe and found her spare key on a ribbon and now she unlocked the front door, unbolted it, and then pushed the door wide and stepped out.

She did not think about her state of undress.

She did not think about her absent husband.

She did not think about her sleeping boys.

She did not think about her Housemaid or Charles the butler, or all the other servants.

She did not think about the scandal to come and the world's opprobrium for her impulsive act.

She did not even think to close the door behind her and left it standing wide open.

She no longer cared, for at that moment she knew she would never walk through the door of 18 Tite Street again. She was leaving behind the life she had lived and the woman she once was.

She was a new woman. A different woman, who now skipped down the steps and rushed to the waiting figure.

He took her hand gently and pressed it to his lips. Then he drew her into him. Their lips met in a hungry kiss that lingered for long minutes as they kissed with bruising pressure. And then he swept up in his arms and lifted her into the hansom and the two flung themselves upon one another.

CHAPTER 34: FEASTING WITH PANTHERS

For most of the jostling cab ride Morpheus spent kissing Constance's mouth, caressing her face, and nibbling her neck, chest, earlobes all while murmuring epithets of his love. For Constance his passionate attention was overwhelming. His kisses were deep and dizzying and his caresses made her quiver, but most affecting of all was how her senses were drunk with desire after years during which her husband had never laid a finger on her. After the long drought she was drowning in this younger man's passion, but most of all was how intoxicating she found it to be desired.

"Stop! Stop!" she panted finally and pushed him away.

"What?" he asked. "What's wrong?"

She laughed, a sound unfamiliar in her own ears. "Nothing's wrong. I just need to catch my breath."

At that moment she noticed that the carriage was slowing and drew to halt at the kerb. The view from the hansom windows revealed that they were in one of the less salubrious districts of the Capitol city.

"Where are we?" she asked.

Morpheus sat up in the seat and swept the hair from his eyes, although he kept an arm around Constance, unwilling to relinquish his touch. "I have discovered something . . ." He dropped his head, clearly nervous, but then added, " . . . something you need to see."

Constance looked stunned. "What? What do you mean?"

In reply, the younger man merely nodded out the carriage window and sneered.

Constance looked. Across the road was some kind of gentlemen's club. Well-dressed men in top hats and straw boaters arrived at the front door which was promptly answered by an Indian servant in a turban. Because of the greater elevation of the carriage, she was able to see through the windows a scene that would have been screened from a casual pedestrian walking the pavement. Inside was a ballroom of some type and Constance was astonished to see that the embracing couples waltzing across the floor were all men.

Men dancing with other men.

At that moment Oscar Wilde stepped out the front door with a slender younger man in his shadow. And then, although she had never seen the fellow personally, she was able to guess who the slender-wristed young man accompanying him was.

Oscar drew out his silver cigarette case from a breast pocket and held it out to Bosie, who helped himself to a cigarette. Oscar lit his own cigarette and then Bosie leaned in close and lit his cigarette from Oscar's. It was a casual, but deeply intimate gesture.

Constance choked down a sob and quickly leant away from the window, averting her gaze.

Morpheus said, "This husband of yours . . . he is a scoundrel. He is not worthy of you."

"You did not need to show me this!" Constance said in a voice choked with emotion.

"Why not? You can see what he is. Your marriage is clearly a lie."

Constance's eyes flashed liquid with angry tears. "I do not need you or anyone else to tell me about my marriage. Do you not think I have heard the gossip? The rumours? Suffered the smirks? The sideways glances and whispers that stop when I enter the room and resume before I have fully left?"

Constance reached up and banged frantically on the ceiling of the hansom. "Driver. Move on. Take me away from this place!"

Morpheus leaned forward and called up to the driver, "Driver, drop us off at the top of the road."

"Where are we going?" Constance asked.

Morpheus answered. "I have a secret place where we can be together."

"

CHAPTER 35: INSPECTOR CRUMPET
GETS TOASTED

Inspector Crumpet nearly choked on his mouthful of sausage roll when Arthur Conan Doyle stalked into Mrs Wiggly's Pie Shop, marched up to where he was sitting, and banged an angry fist down on the table top, causing the cutlery to bounce and turning the head of every customer in their direction.

"There you are, Crumpet! I suspected I'd find you here, stuffing your face with sausage rolls. God knows I wouldn't find you in the police station, or out somewhere actually doing the job you're paid to do!"

Uncharacteristically, Conan Doyle's face was purpling with rage, and he continued to vent his spleen on the portly policeman. For his part, Crumpet remained surprisingly calm. He swallowed his mouthful and then lifted the large teapot and asked, "Would you care for a cup of tea? It's lapsang souchong and rather lovely."

"No, I would not care for a blasted cup of tea!"

Crumpet took a quick sip of his tea and quietly asked, "I take it something untoward has happened?"

"Too bloody right something *untoward* has happened. My wife has vanished, that's what! Another sleepwalker who stepped out of a window onto the rooftop and vanished. I have searched the streets about my house, alerted every police station, but so far we haven't been able to find her."

"If your wife has gone missing I fully understand why you are so distraught."

Crumpet dragged one of the empty tea cups over, poured a steaming cup of tea in the china cup and pushed it toward Conan Doyle's side of the table.

"Here, sit down. Drink this cup of tea. It will restore you. Help you think straight, and then we can formulate our response."

Conan Doyle remained standing for a moment, his hands balled into fists, bristling with anger. But then he collapsed into the chair, a look of profound misery sweeping away the anger.

"I am sorry," he apologised. "I quite forgot myself. But I have reached the lowest point in my life. If anything's happened to Jean—"

"Drink your tea, Doctor Doyle."

Conan Doyle dropped two lumps of sugar into his cup. Inspector Crumpet gestured questioningly with the milk jug and Conan Doyle nodded. Crumpet added a splash of milk to the tea, and Conan Doyle gave it a stir with his spoon.

While the Scots author sipped his tea, Crumpet said, "The reason we have an empire is because we are a nation of tea drinkers. Tea requires patience. One must first boil the water, then steep the tea, and then add milk and sugar. It is a ritual that requires forethought, enforces calm, facilitates rationality. We drink tea before battles, before climbing mountains, after births and before funerals. Drinking tea allows us to collect our thoughts, deliberate our choices. plan our actions. And it's jolly refreshing, too. Trust my word, as long as the British drink tea, our empire will endure. I fear the overly-hasty, coffee-drinking nations will never amount to much."

Conan Doyle set down his tea cup and threw Inspector Crumpet a rueful smile.

"Yes, quite right. Thank you."

"Another pot, I think." Crumpet nodded to the lady in a pinafore behind the counter, who smiled as she hurried over with a fresh pot and whisked the old one away.

Crumpet pushed the plate of sausage rolls toward Conan Doyle. "Now have a sausage roll. I'm very certain you haven't had breakfast, either. Go on, don't be shy. Take as many as you like."

Conan Doyle hesitated a moment but then, spurred by Crumpet's insistence, he grabbed one of the huge sausage rolls and bit into it. After chewing his first mouthful, he wiped pastry crumbs from his walrus moustache on a napkin and breathed, "Good Lord, that is a splendid sausage roll!"

"Best in London"

"I take it you diligently sampled every pastry shop in the capitol to determine that fact?"

"And I've got the evidence to prove it!" Crumpet said, patting his rotund belly.

Both men laughed and it broke the tension. Conan Doyle apologised once again for his brusque behaviour.

"Your wife's gone missing, I can well understand," Crumpet empathised. "Believe it or not, I used to be as thin as a whippet. Then my wife, my lovely Annie, she died of the consumption. She didn't last long. Less than a year. I watched her waste away into a ghost. After that, I started eating and never stopped. I had a hole in my soul and I needed to fill it with something."

Conan Doyle gifted the Inspector a respectful moment of silence and then offered, "I well understand grief. I also lost my first wife to consumption. But as a medical man, I must advise that it would greatly benefit your health to moderate your eating."

"Yes, people tell me that I should eat less. I even hear tell of these things called salads, but I've never tried one. I'll stick to sausage rolls, because they add a moment of joy to a day that otherwise wouldn't have any. And yes, I know that many people look at me and dismiss me as a fat-arsed bumbling fool. But that is what I want them to think. I know you don't believe I've been doing anything to solve this case, but in fact I have."

Crumpet fumbled in his satchel and produced two flyers that were very familiar.

The flyer was identical to one Conan Doyle had found, with the image of Morpheus, lightning bolts quivering in the air about his hands as a woman swooned before him.

"I have personally visited the households of every vanished sleep-walker. These I found in the homes of the last two girls to vanish. I also looked in on our Mister Morpheus. It appears he's done a bunk . . . or at least he's laying low for the moment. I spoke with the manager of the Alcambra music hall. Morpheus has been missing for the last two performances. He was top of the bill, so you can imagine that the manager is furious."

"What about his companion? The grey-haired old woman who plays that queer instrument?"

"No one knows where she is, either. She is quite the enigma. No one even knows her name."

Conan Doyle finished his first sausage roll and quietly reached for another. "This Morpheus chap is also a bit of an enigma."

"Yes, but I have contacted music halls around the country where he has performed."

"Oh really?"

"Well it's obvious. He arrives at a town. A number of young women begin sleepwalking and suddenly vanish. And then he moves on to the next town or he goes to ground. Literally in this case."

"You're talking about the buried alive stunt he's due to perform?"

"Precisely. That is a new wrinkle to his modus operandi, and I'm certain he's going to make a lot of money from it—if he survives."

"I think it's a trick. I don't think he will really be buried. I'm a doctor. The coffin will not be equipped with a breathing tube. No one could survive that long without oxygen. I think its a deception. I think we'll see many more young ladies vanish during the week he's suppos-edly buried."

Inspector Crumpet took a sip of his tea and said,"I asked at the Music Hall about the brass coffin because it had to be specially deliv-ered to the music hall an account of its weight. The stage manager couldn't tell me much about it but he did have the bill of lading for its delivery. The Alcambra is the only music hall that could accommodate the brass coffin on account of the fact they got a hydraulic lift for getting heavy scenery on and off the stage."

At the news Conan Doyle raised an eyebrow. "Really? You don't by chance have a copy of this bill of lading?"

Crumpet fumbled in his satchel and produced a piece of paper which he laid atop the pile of sausage rolls. Conan Doyle snatched it up and examined it.

"The coffin was originally shipped from Austria. And there's two names written on it. Madame Xylander and . . . Berta Xylander."

Conan Doyle reacted. "Wait! We met a Madame Xylander at Lady Geldsach's house. She had a charity for fallen women. But who is Berta Xylander?"

"Indeed, Doctor Doyle, who is Berta Xylander? I fully believe that Madam Xylander is the same person as Berta Xylander."

"We need to talk to this Morpheus chap," Conan Doyle said.

"We might be a little too late," Crumpet noted. "Unless we can get to him before he goes in the coffin tomorrow we'll have to wait a week."

"We'll have to wait a week *if* he comes out alive." Conan Doyle said gravely. "I don't think even our Mister Morpheus will be able to resurrect himself."

CHAPTER 36: LOVE NEST

Constance Wilde awoke in the dead hours of the night, dredged from sleep by the strange bed, the strange street noises coming from outside, and the strange arms embracing her. She had fallen asleep with her head on Morpheus's bare chest, both of them exhausted after hours of love making. She squinted up at his face. There was enough dim light filtering through the moth-holed and raggedy curtains to make out his handsome features, looking youthful and at peace as he slept deeply without snoring.

Constance carefully laid her head back down on his chest and hugged his body to hers. The room they occupied was cheap and squalid. The lumpy bed was creaky and the bedding was rough and scratchy. Bed bugs had already bitten her three times. Still she did not care, for she was exulting in a fantasy, a dream in which she hoped the night would last forever and the dawn would never come.

She felt Morpheus stir beneath her and when she looked up again, his eyes were open and he was gazing lovingly down at her.

"Again?" he asked, his hands gliding down the dome of her belly, exploring.

"Oh goodness no!" she laughed. "You will wear me out. You are insatiable."

"That's because you excite me."

"Please . . . just hold me. I want to feel your arms around me. Our time together is so fleeting."

There was a strained silence and then he asked, "What do you mean, so fleeting?"

"I mean I must return home."

"No . . . no, you must not! We are together. I know this room is not what you are accustomed to, but I will find us a better place. A nicer place. Perhaps we could move to the country. Find a cottage. Some-place no one knows us."

"A cottage in the country sounds idyllic, but how will you pay for such a place?"

"I . . . I will find work . . ."

"As a hypnotist?"

"I am young and strong. I will support us. I would sacrifice anything for you . . ."

Constance silenced him by putting two fingers to his lips.

"I know you would. I believe you. And you cannot know how your words pierce my heart. But you forget, I am a mother. I have two young boys."

"I . . . I . . ." he started to try to argue, to reason, but then he gave up with a heartbroken sigh.

His feelings were clearly hurt and a tense silence between them prevailed. She broke the silence with a question: "Who are you, mystery boy?"

"I come from nowhere. I am going nowhere. And I am quite lost." His lips curled in a tragic smile. "Maybe you can find me . . . if anyone can."

"Your accent? You are English, but it is strange."

"My parents were show people, entertainers. They performed at country fairs, at music halls, anywhere they could find an audience. They had a hypnotist act. My father would hypnotise people cajoled from the audience and make them bark like dogs, or strut about the stage like chickens—much to the amusement of the crowd. But the special part of the act came when he would hypnotise my mother."

"Was this a sham or was it real?"

"Very real. My mother was a perfect hypnotic subject. My father would deeply induce her and then have her perform astonishing feats. She could pick up heavy objects the strongest man could not lift. She could place her hand into the flame of a gas burner and her flesh would not burn. He could thrust sharpened skewers through the flesh of her arms and she did not register pain nor bleed. His final demonstration was hypnotic catalepsy. He would hypnotise her and tell her that her spine was as rigid as an iron rod. Then he would support her solely by a chair positioned beneath her head and another chair beneath her heels. He would then stand upon her stomach while she took the full weight of his body without her back bending so much as an inch."

"That is what you did with me, at the music hall?"

The hypnotist nodded. "I have an older sister, Lilly. We started performing in my parent's act when I was only ten and my sister was fourteen. My father taught me the rudiments of hypnotism and my sister proved to be the perfect hypnotic subject, much like my mother. That was the last time in my life I was ever truly happy."

As he told the tale, Constance felt Morpheus' body tense and his voice grew taut. "What happened?"

"My parents left us in the care of some fellow show people while they travelled to the Continent to appear in Vienna. However, the return ferry from Calais sank in a storm. My parents were lost."

Constance hugged him and kissed the side of his cheek, tasting the salt tears trickling freely down his face. "How terribly sad for you."

He lifted her hand and kissed it, then gripped it tightly in both of his as he continued his story.

"With no parents. No home. No money and no relatives to take us in, we had no choice but to earn a crust by continuing our parents' act. By this time my sister was fifteen and a radiant beauty, and although our act was clumsy when compared with our parents, our youth gave the act a certain charm."

"And you are very handsome, too."

Morpheus allowed himself a pained smile at the compliment. "So some say."

"But what happened to your sister?" Constance added, although as soon as she asked the pained expression on Morpheus' face foretold that it, too, was a tragic story.

"Ah, but that is the bitterest part of my tale. My sister and I journeyed around Europe, performing in beer halls, small theatres, or wherever they would have us. We often slept on the floor of other performers' dressing rooms, in barns with the livestock, and sometimes under the stars. We kept travelling—anywhere that would let us perform. Eventually we reached Vienna, where our parents had last played. There we met Madame Xylander. She had come to see our hypnosis act because she herself was a mesmerist—trained in the Vienna school founded by Mesmer himself. Her skills as a mesmerist are formidable.

"At first we thought we had found our benefactor. For the first time we had a roof over our head and food in our bellies. Xylander recreated our act, taught us how to perform, and added showmanship. But there was a darker side as I was soon to learn. She made me her lover, but only so she could manipulate me. Madame Xylander really fawned upon my sister, and then I learned that they were lovers. As we gained fame, Xylander added new routines, ever more dangerous. Soon we outshone every other act. While other hypnotists would induce their subject in state of hypnotic catalepsy and have one volunteer sit upon them, Xylander insisted we have two volunteers take the stage and sit upon my sister. But when another Viennese hypnotist, Marvo, duplicated the feat, Madame insisted that we should have three people. I told her it was too dangerous. That my sister was frail and could not bear that much weight. But when we were booked to perform at the Viennese opera house, she insisted that I, too, stand atop my sister. I refused but her will is stronger than mine and so I was forced to do it. At first it went well. Two women sat on either side of my sister. I carefully set my weight on her stomach. The orchestra played a fanfare, but then there was a horrible crack as my sister's spine shattered beneath the weight."

Constance's eyes widened. She put a hand to her mouth. "And what became of your poor sister?"

Morpheus's expression turned wretched . . . haunted.

"My sister lives, but she is broken. A cripple. She cannot walk and cannot even feed herself. She lies in a cot all day and must be fed and washed by a caretaker. This is why we must tour constantly. Madame says that we must raise the money for a trip to Berlin to see a famous surgeon she believes can mend Lilly's spine and restore her. But it has been two years now. We have traipsed across Europe, from France to Switzerland. In that time we have visited many surgeons who have turned us away. Now I no longer believe that it is possible. In the mean time Madame Xylander forces me to do wicked things. The young women who come up on the stage as you did, they are implanted with a command so that they will respond when they once again hear the music of the glass armonica. At night they rise from their beds and they sleepwalk across the rooftops and through the midnight streets to our waiting carriage. And then we abduct them."

"How horrible," Constance breathed. "To what end?"

Morpheus dropped his head, misery screwing up his face. "Do not ask. I can say no more for I am ashamed. I have done many wicked things at her bidding and I will burn in hell for it someday." He laughed ironically. "I am already burning."

"Couldn't you just leave her? Run away?"

"I could, but I fear for my sister. When my parents left for their final performance, my father made me promise to watch over my sister, no matter what. But now it has been a year as Xylander forbids me from even seeing my sister until she is restored by the Berlin surgeon."

They both fell into a meditative silence. Finally Constance spoke. "In the morning I will need a dress."

A look of panicked concern swept Morpheus's face. "Why? Are you leaving me?"

"I am hungry. I want breakfast."

. . .

The next day, Constance sent Morpheus out to buy her a dress. He found a second hand clothes store and came back with a dress two sizes too big that fit her like a sack. He also had purchased a bonnet that was the dress's equal in ugliness, but it served a purpose as it hid her face. Constance had accompanied Wilde on many trips to the theatre and was terrified of being recognised as Mrs Wilde, a married woman, accompanying a handsome young man. They walked to the closest cafe and sought to find a secluded table in the shadowy back reaches, but the cafe was full and so they were forced to take a table for two in the cafe window. They ordered and ate quickly. Constance kept the bonnet pulled down low and seldom looked up from her plate. During the meal, Morpheus kept whispering words of love to her. He even reached out to fondle her hand during the meal, but she snatched it away and angrily hissed, "You may not hold my hand in a public place! If someone recognises me as a married woman there will be a scandal."

In response, Morpheus' face registered deep hurt, while his eyes misted with tears and he dropped his head like a scolded puppy.

As they ate in silence, Constance happened to glance out the window. There was another restaurant across the way. An unaccompanied lady sat alone at a table in the window. Constance threw her a quick glance and looked away, but then something made her chance a second look. The woman had red hair with a white streak running through it. Constance risked another glance and yes, the woman did seem to be staring at her, and her look had a feral quality that quite uneased Constance.

Minutes later, Constance looked up and once again caught the woman staring at her. She was certain now that the woman recognised the wife of Oscar Wilde travelling unescorted with a younger man. There would be scandal. She knew she had to end this mad affair . . . but not just yet.

"We must go," Constance said, jumping up from her seat. "We must go now." She suddenly turned and rushed from the table. Morpheus, taken by surprise, dithered as he rifled his pockets, threw down a handful of coins and rushed after her.

Across the street, Madame Xylander bit into a creme bun, swallowed and paused to wipe cream from her lips with a finger.

The Cossack looked down at her and grunted, clearly asking if he should pursue them both.

She shook her head. "No, Ivan, we do not need to chase them. Now we know where they are we can easily take them. But I feel the woman will flutter back to her nest soon, as she has chicks. I can tell from the way she acts. Morpheus will return to us then."

The Cossack grunted.

"And if not, you will wring her neck like a chicken and I will force our boy to return."

O n the hansom ride back to Tite Street, the two spoke little, but gripped each other's hands tightly, unwilling to let go until the last possible moment. Morpheus kept kissing Constance until she at last twisted her face away and cried, "Enough!

When the hansom drew up outside the Wilde's Tite Street residence, she at last turned back to Morpheus. Unashamed tears were running down his face. They embraced as she kissed his tears away and then they shared a final kiss.

"You are young," She said in a torn voice, "you will forget me in time."

"Never!" Morpheus replied. Constance rapped on the hansom ceiling, the doors cranked open, and suddenly she was gone in a draft of cold air. She hurried to the front door of her home and only looked back the once, as the door opened to her knock. The last she saw of Morpheus was his tear washed face, beautiful even in sorrow, and then the hansom jerked away.

As she stepped into her entry hall, her maid looked at her hideous dress and bonnet with shock and alarm.

"Where are the boys?" Constance asked her maid.

"The boys are in the parlour . . . they are with—"

The maid never got a chance to answer as Oscar Wilde now stepped from the parlour into the entrance hall. "They are with their papa." Wilde finished the maid's thought. "The question is, where has their dear Mama been?"

His stare revealed that, he too, did not know what to make of Constance's attire.

He cleared his throat and added, "I received a rather alarming telegram at my club informing me that you had vanished. That our housemaid had last seen you climbing into a hansom with a strange man and that you vanished for two days. Of course, I assumed that you were the latest sleepwalking victim. Might I ask where you've been?"

Any other woman might have been cowed by such a situation, but not Constance Wilde.

"You, Oscar, have been missing from your house for two weeks. Might I ask you the same question? How is Bosie, by the way? I understand he likes to smoke the same Turkish cigarettes as you?"

For once, Oscar Wilde, the most loquacious man in England, was at a loss for words.

Affecting a carefree attitude, Constance now ignored her husband and addressed her maid. "Florence, I would like you to run me a bath and then lay out my walking clothes. I am going to have a long soak, and then, after my bath, I am going to take the boys to the boating pond."

Constance began to climb the stairs to her bedroom, but paused after a few steps and turned back to her maid. "Oh, and I also want you to burn this dress and bonnet."

CHAPTER 37: CONAN DOYLE FRETS AFTER JEAN'S DISAPPEARANCE

The next five days were the longest in Conan Doyle's life. He haunted the offices of Scotland Yard, waiting to hear any news of his missing wife. Thanks to his fame he had used to influence to secure extra help, and several Inspectors and teams of constables were out beating the streets and going door to door in his Norwood neighbourhood. More dreadful, he had reports sent to him of any young women being received in the city's morgues. He had even visited several after receiving heart-stopping reports of young women being dredged from the Thames, but in all cases these had proven to be young prostitutes, most likely suicides who had drowned themselves in the Thames, beaten down by the ravages of poverty, despair and the merciless bullying of their pimps.

Night time was the worst as Conan Doyle lay alone in bed, stomach churning as he fretted about Jean's whereabouts. Most nights sleep was impossible and so he gave up on the bed, which only reminded him of Jean's absence. Instead, he tried to work at his desk, which often proved fruitless, and only when exhaustion overtook him, did he collapse on the leather Chesterfield in his office, or doze slumped over his writing desk. Since her disappearance, he had taken to drinking or he made up sleeping drafts for himself, and finally began to mix both strong liquor and sleeping drafts in a dangerous cocktail he knew could prove to be fatal. Still he clung to a final hope —the suspicion that Morpheus was somehow involved with his wife's disappearance. The Friday night before Morpheus was to be exhumed from his premature burial in Hyde Park, Conan Doyle allowed himself one brandy and then poured the rest of the bottle out and then he sat in his favourite chair and watched the clock as the hours unpeeled. When the clock showed seven o'clock, he got up, dressed and let himself out of the house, foregoing breakfast. (His stomach was too queasy to keep anything down.) He walked briskly to the Norwood railway station, bought a ticket and half an hour later stepped down from the train in Victoria Station.

CHAPTER 38: MORPHEUS RETURNS

It was close to noon when Morpheus walked into the parlour of the Marylebone house.

Madame Xylander was sitting on the sofa with a ledger in her lap as she calculated how much money they had taken so far in advance tickets for the buried-alive stunt planned for the next day.

Morpheus stood in the doorway, his posture penitent, his shoulders drooping. He said nothing, waiting for his upbraiding to begin. Madame Xylander did not acknowledge his presence, nor even look up from the line of calculations until she reached the end of the line and penned a final figure. Then she looked up casually at Morpheus. "So," she said, "you have returned to the fold. Did your married lady tire of you so soon?"

Morpheus's dropped his head, stared at his feet.

"Not very talkative, eh?"

Morpheus remained silent. He looked up and glared at Xylander with unconcealed hatred.

"It is always the same with silly boys like you. You indulge in these dalliances with older women, but the ones with children always return home eventually. You are nothing but a passing distraction for them."

She set the ledger aside and stood up from the sofa. "Come here," she commanded.

He did not reply, just dropped his head and shook it.

Xylander sighed and repeated the command, her voice sterner this time. "I said, come here."

She raised a hand and waved it.

Morpheus grunted as he was compelled to walk forward, his limbs moving stiffly like a puppet as he staggered across the room until he stood before her.

"Now kneel," she commanded.

At once, he crashed to his knees. She moved forward, raised one leg and then placed it over his shoulder, then seized him by the hair at the back of his head and pulled his face into her crotch.

"Perhaps I have neglected you too much of late. Tonight you will share my bed. I will allow you to pleasure me. Think of it as a little treat for you as tomorrow you begin your week-long sojourn with the darkness." She began to gyrate her hips, grinding his face into her crotch. "I know you like it when I discipline you. Tonight we will see if you can be my good little boy again."

CHAPTER 39: A NICE DAY FOR A
BURIAL

When the hansom dropped Conan Doyle and Wilde at Hyde Park, they had to push their way through thronging crowds reminiscent of a carnival. And once through the iron railings they found food and drink stands had been set up and now crowds of Londoners milled about, quaffing pints of beer and slurping down bowls of whelks, pea pods in butter, pea soup, tripe, or jellied eels procured from the many stands set up around the park. The warm summer air, usually bittered by the tang of coal fires, for once swarmed with the aromas of working class cuisine: frying onions, boiled cabbage soured by a tart undertone of vinegar, and of course the ubiquitous sausage.

Families strolled with their children, the men in caps and straw boaters and the women in their finest dresses and best summer bonnets. Children ran through the crowd, playing chase games. A brass band oompahed martial music and the scatter-tangle of laughter and voices from the milling masses soared high into the air, establishing a festive mood. Viewing stands with gaily striped canopies had been erected, providing shadow and shelter for ranks of folding chairs. These were all set with seats and now barkers were charging people a shilling to sit there. Bordering the posh seats were roped-off areas for the lower classes to stand, which cost a mere thruppence for a ticket. As with all things in Victorian England, classes were segregated by price with the pagoda seat costing 1 shilling while the groundlings were permitted to jostle shoulders behind rope barriers for a mere 3d.

In front of the stands a marquee had been set up. Sheltered beneath was the hulking brass coffin, its crushing mass supported by a double pair of sawhorses. Before it loomed the grave, black as death, a sharp-edged rectangular pit bored through the green grass and stony earth of the park. Close by sat a heaped pile of freshly dug earth impaled by the half-dozen spades of shirtless labourers who sprawled on the grass close by, waiting to shovel the grave back in.

Set up as backdrop to the spectacle was a canvas screen bearing a painted likeness of the hypnotist emblazoned with the words: *Morpheus the Magnificent, Master of Mesmerism.* As with the paper flyer, the likeness featured lighting bolts sizzling around Morpheus's hands.

It was a sun-kissed and balmy summer's Sunday and Londoners had flocked to Hyde Park to celebrate the happy spectacle of a man being buried alive.

"Blast!" Conan Doyle spat, looking at the rope barriers and police officers keeping sentinel at all the key points. "We'll never get close at this rate."

Conan Doyle watched as a windlass winch was set up directly over the grave. The brass coffin was so massive it took a team of ten broad-shouldered workmen to wrestle it from the saw horses and thump its ponderous mass down on the ground next to the open grave. A large clock affixed to the top of a pole showed but ten minutes to go before 12:00 noon, the time the coffin would be sealed and Morpheus the Magnificent confined to the underworld. The volume of the crowd increased as the fateful moment approached.

Conan Doyle paid for their tickets and the two friends *excuse me'd* as they squeezed between occupied seats to commandeer the last two empty seats at the rail.

"This is all an enormous fraud," Wilde declared, casually drawing upon his cigarette. "In my time with the theatre I have seen many such acts close up. The magician will not be in the coffin when it is lowered. He will appear to climb into the coffin and lie down, but in truth, he will drop through a false bottom in the coffin or escape via a hidden side panel. He will have escaped long before the lid is fully closed. Trust me, Arthur, we are witnessing pure music hall trickery."

Conan Doyle frowned as he eagle-eyed the proceedings.

"But look," he objected. "First of all, he is not a magician, he is a hypnotist or mesmerist, or whatever. Second, this is not taking place upon a stage. There are witnesses gathered about the coffin on all sides—police officers, a presiding physician, local officials—all at close range. How could he slip out of the coffin with so many witnesses?"

Wilde waved his cigarette dismissively. "How does any conjurer perform a successful illusion? By trickery, sleight-of-hand, misdirection—"

Conan Doyle doubted if any of those techniques would work given the outdoor location, but he let the objection die in his throat.

Just then the brass band played a brief blast of anticipatory music to set the tone. As the music echoed across Hyde Park and then subsided, the light dimmed as a cloud drowned the sun and the day turned dismal. Then the music of the glass armonica flowed out from behind the painted tarpaulin. It was an eerie sound like no other and the audience exchanged puzzled looks as the celestial chords silenced the crowd's chatter. Then the man himself, Morpheus the Magnificent, stepped from behind the painted banner of his face. As usual he was dressed in his glossy top hat and cape, black as a crow in a snow bank. Someone began clapping and then the applause built raggedly as it swept through the crowd. He stepped up to the coffin and doffed his top hat to the crowd with a regal gesture before returning it to his head. In his free hand he gripped a speaking trumpet. He raised the trumpet to his mouth and addressed the crowd in an echoic voice.

"Ladies and gentlemen, death is the final mystery we must all face. Today, I will undertake a journey to the very edge of death and peer over the precipice at the unknown bourne that lies beyond."

Many in the crowd jumped as he brought his hand down suddenly and banged on the lid of the brass coffin with a sound like a rifle shot.

"This is the vessel in which I will undertake my journey: a brass coffin. In a few moments I will climb inside and commit myself to the Plutonian depths, to the realm of the underworld where spirits go to dwell after their demise. Perhaps, in my shadowy prison, deep underground, the voices of the dead will speak to me. Whisper their secrets. Reveal unto me the secrets of the grave."

Wilde leaned close to Conan Doyle and muttered sotto voce, "This is all very nicely done. And the young fellow has a beautiful speaking voice."

"Of course the risks are enormous and I court death every second I spend below ground, for every breath could be my last. You will notice there is no breathing tube attached to this coffin. For unlike others that have undertaken similar ordeals, my aim is to prove the powers of mesmerism. Like the monks of Tibet and the Indian Swamis, I will use my powers to control my mind and thereby my body. I will slow my heartbeat so that it beats only once a minute, My breath to one or two shallow inhalations. I will place my body in a state of suspended animation, much as hibernating animals use to survive the long winter nights. I will commune with the spirits of the Underworld and learn all the dread secrets of death.

Astonished murmurs bubbled through the crowd at his words.

"This feat is so dangerous it has never been attempted by anyone in the world. I will be the first—"

"Aye, and likely the last!" An uncouth voice boomed from the crowd. A ripple of morbid laughter swept through the crowd. But instead of showing anger, the hypnotist smiled and calmly tipped his hat to the heckler. "In which case, my friend, you will be the first person I visit in the dead of night. When you open your eyes from an unpleasant dream I will be standing over you. I only hope that you don't die of fright."

The crowd erupted in an even bigger roar of laughter. The heckler's smile buckled and his face collapsed into a look of terror.

Morpheus threw a quick look at the clock. "And now, the noon hour approaches and so I must say my farewells. I hope that many of you will visit my grave during the days to come. You might be surprised to know that the soil conducts sound and I will be able to hear everything that happens above ground, so be sure to drop by and say hello. Weekday tickets will cost a mere tuppence. But I advise you to purchase your ticket for next Saturday in advance. For come the noon hour the workmen will dig up the grave, my coffin will be exhumed and then . . ." he thew the crowd a maudlin look. "Then the world will see if Morpheus lives or not. The crowds are expected to number in the thousands to see if I emerge dead or alive."

Another hubbub arose at his comments.

The hypnotist removed his top hat and bowed deeply to the crowd. "And so I say adieu for now. Please friends, pray for me and know that your kind thoughts will reach me, in this life . . . or the next."

The glass armonium music set the air aquiver as the hypnotist handed his top hat to a waiting attendant and then stepped into the coffin. He gave a single wave and then laid flat and crossed his hands on his chest like a dead man. Someone gave the lid of the brass coffin a shove so that it slammed shut with a ringing clang.

Moments later, the coffin was winched slowly into the open grave and then the winch was moved aside and the team of workman began to shovel, flinging spadefuls of dirt which drummed on the coffin lid.

Wilde looked at his friend. "Well, if he is behind the disappearance of Jean, I'm afraid he's just made a very dramatic escape . . ."

"For a week, at least." Conan Doyle muttered, wringing his hands. "What am I to do, Oscar? I am at my wits end. The woman I love stepped out a window of my house and has vanished without trace. I am sick with worry. I cannot still my mind for a cascade of dreadful thoughts. I have involved the police. Engaged several private detectives. Taken an ad in the Times to solicit the help of the public, but no one has a clue. I feel sure this fellow is somehow behind her disappearance."

Wilde sat in thoughtful silence as he watched the grave quickly filling up by the shovelful. "Had you . . ." he paused. "You are my dearest friend, Arthur, so forgive me, but I must ask. Had you and Jean had a falling out lately?"

Conan Doyle shook his head resolutely. "No, nothing of the sort.

In fact, on the advice of Mister Freud, we have been particularly affectionate of late. It is just this blasted sleep walking.

As a workman flung a final shovelful of dirt atop the settling mound, the glass armonica ceased playing and the brass band started up, oompahing a fresh tune.

With nothing left to see, the crowds began to file out of the reviewing stands. Many had purchased the single day ticket, while the aficionados of death had coughed up the extra sixpence for a full week's pass, which entitled them to return in seven days to witness Morpheus's exhumation—dead or alive.

Crumpet turned around in his chair. A quick look at the front of his jacket was all that was required to tell what he had been dining on that day. He noted, "With mister Morpheus six feet under, it will be telling if the plague of sleepwalking suddenly ceases."

"Yes," Conan Doyle nodded, "I agree. Very much so."

Wilde threw Conan Doyle a look. "Have you seen enough, Arthur? As always watching other people exerting themselves through hard work has left me hungry and thirsty. Should retire to the Savoy for Angel's on Horseback and a chilled bottle of Perrier Jouet?"

Conan Doyle shook his head, "I'm afraid I have little appetite for food or drink, Oscar, but you go ahead."But your words have made me think. The last I spoke with our Austrian friend, Mister Freud, he said he was leaving the capitol for a week to visit his family in the North and yet I am almost certain that I spotted him on several occasions climbing into a black carriage. I think And then there's the red-haired lady with the white streak. I'm not sure how she ties in with this scheme, but I believe she is deeply involved. I think we need to pay a visit to the Refuge for Fallen Women."

CHAPTER 40: INVADING THE REFUGE

"I'm afraid I've put on a few pounds since last I wore these trousers."

"A few pounds?" Wilde remarked. "Seems more like a few stones to me. Looking at how those trouser buttons are straining, if one lets go I'd say we're in danger of shrapnel wounds."

"Try to keep your gut sucked in, Crumpet," Conan Doyle advised. "Our visit should only be a short one."

Crumpet shot him a look. "My gut *is* sucked in, otherwise I couldn't have got these bloody trousers on. I daren't breathe out."

"You can breathe out when we're done here," said Conan Doyle.

The three men, Conan Doyle, Oscar Wilde, and Inspector Crumpet were standing at the front door of Number 35 Marylebone Street, having just yanked the bell pull. To remain incognito Inspector Crumpet had swapped his sergeant's uniform for plain clothes: a pair of grey striped trousers with a black frock coat. The dust marks on the shoulders of the coat testified to the fact that the clothes hadn't been worn in a very long time, and the trousers, not in many hundreds of sausage rolls.

The door was opened by a an old lady wearing a babushka and a sack-like dress.

Conan Doyle dipped his topper to the woman, smiled his most

ingratiating smile, and said, "Yes, good morning. We are here to see Madame Xylander."

The woman, who needed a shave more than Conan Doyle, muttered something incomprehensible.

"Ah, she's foreign," Conan Doyle surmised.

"Polish, I'd say," Crumpet added.

But Conan Doyle was prepared and handed the woman his calling card. "Please give my card to your mistress. I sent a telegram this morning. She's expecting us."

The Polish woman eyed the card she clearly couldn't read, but turned and left, leaving the door ajar.

They heard footsteps approaching and then Madame Xylander appeared, beaming a smile. "Do come inside gentlemen. You must forgive our informality. We only have the one maid, Sonya. She hails from Poland and is very inexpensive. But we must watch the pennies, for after all, we are a charity."

Wilde could not restrain himself and commented, "I find the whole notion of charities fascinating. Complete strangers giving you money for rather inexplicable reasons. I'm quite taken with the idea of a charity, so I'd thought I'd accompany my friends here to see how I might start my own."

Madame Xylander threw Wilde a quizzical look, but then she led them into the front parlour and muttered something in Polish to the maid, who nodded and shuffled out of the room.

Madame Xylander bade the three men to take a seat on the sofa, while she sat in the single armchair opposite.

Moments later the Polish lady shuffled back in the room carrying a tray overflowing with tea cups and milk and sugar bowls along with an enormous brown tea pot sweating condensation. The poor woman's arms were shaking beneath the weight of the tray, and all watched with bated breath until she reached the safety of the table and set the tray down with a symphonic crash of cutlery.

Xylander dismissed the maid and insisted on pouring the tea herself, and then went around the table filling everyone's cup.

Conan Doyle was sitting opposite Inspector Crumpet who now carefully lifted the cup to his nose, inhaled deeply and smiled broadly.

"Oh, that smells heavenly."

Conan Doyle shot Wilde a look and rolled his eyes as if to say, and here's someone who samples his tea the way you sample whisky."

And then Crumpet brought his tea cup to his lips and took an experimental slurp. Conan Doyle watched his face transform into a vision of rapture.

Madame Xylander sipped her tea and then offered, "I thought our visit should begin with a pot of tea and then I will introduce several of our girls."

"Sounds splendid," Conan Doyle said. On the way through the hallway from the front door he had noticed a coat stand and saw the grey homburg and wool coat hanging there.

Inspector Crumpet finished his first sip and went into raptures. "Marvellous! Simply marvellous. That is the most exquisite cup of tea." He threw Madame an importuning look. "Dear lady, you must tell me where you purchased this tea?"

The comment took Madame off-guard. "Oh, really? I don't know. My maid purchased it . . . from Harrods, I believe."

"Really, from Harrods? It came from Harrods? Fancy that, from Harrods!" He seemed incredulous, but then Conan Doyle saw him bite his tongue. "Yes, very good, indeed," he added throttling back on his enthusiasm. Judging by his face the Inspector seemed rather preoccupied for the remainder of the visit.

When they had all finished their tea, Madame Xylander looked around brightly and said, "Perhaps you would like to meet some of the girls?"

"That would be wonderful," the men agreed.

They followed Madame Xylander into a large empty room. Obviously, it had once been a dining room, but now had been stripped of all furniture. Four girls in the same plain dress stood as if they been standing in place all this time. Xylander clapped her hands to bring them to attention and then sat down at a small piano and began to play. As if upon command, the girls turned to one another, pairing up.

Madame began to play a waltz and the girls began to dance with one another. The girls whirled about the room, and their waltzing was commendable although Conan Doyle noticed that their faces were all blank and they danced like automatons. Then he noticed one girl in particular, a freckled redhead. He caught a sparkle in one of her eyes and then noticed that it was a tear. As he watched. the tear overflowed her eye and trickled down her right cheek, then fell from her chin to the oriental rug. Finally, Madam Xylander ceased playing. The girls immediately stopped and separated.

"Thank you girls," Xylander gushed, "Very nicely done." She clapped her hands again and the girls turned and trouped out of the room in a straight line. Not one of them had made the slightest utterance in the entire time.

"Well, I've think we've seen everything we came to see," Conan Doyle said with a joviality he didn't feel. He reached into his frock coat and drew out his large leather billfold.

"There we go," Conan Doyle said, handing Madame Xylander a bank note for £5.00. "That is just my first donation. I assure you I wish to become a regular benefactor. You are clearly doing a wonderful job with your girls. So well turned out and so . . . *obedient.*"

Madame smiled broadly at the compliment although the smile was quite clearly forced.

A few minutes later the three men made their excuses and left.

"Well, what do you think?" Conan Doyle asked once they were seated in Wilde's carriage and heading back to London. "I cannot believe these girls are happy. I found their behaviour most peculiar."

"I cannot believe you gave the woman five pounds," Wilde said. "Five pounds! In matters of charity, I always use the excuse that I left my wallet at home . . . or, better still, in another country."

Inspector Crumpet seemed to be mulling something over, and then he added, "The girls did seem rather—"

"Like automatons," Conan Doyle finished the thought. And then he shared is observation of the tear running down the face of the redheaded girl.

The carriage rolled on another hundred feet. Inspector Crumpet grunted and then he rapped his knuckles on the ceiling of the carriage, which suddenly jerked to a halt.

Wilde and Conan Doyle looked at him in surprise. "What is it Inspector Crumpet?"

"Tea."

Wilde and Conan Doyle shared a puzzled look.

"Tea? I don't understand. What do you mean?"

"I'm afraid I must concur with both of you gentlemen. However, I must now cast a rather darker interpretation of the performance we just witnessed. And my interpretation centres upon that rather exquisite pot of tea we were treated to."

"The t-tea?" Conan Doyle repeated, his brow furrowed in puzzlement.

Inspector Crumpet smiled a grimace and began to expound, "When I first joined the police as a beat constable—when I was young and very green—in the course of my investigations I had upon occasion a need to visit the slums in Limehouse in the London docks. The area is a very low one as I'm sure you gentlemen must know. Limehouse is a festering warren of brothels and opium houses. The streets run rampant with the ragged refuse of the empire: Chinamen, lascars and the very worst breed of Englishmen: blackguards, criminals and thugs. Many of these scallywags are ex-seamen who acquired the cursed opium habit overseas and seek out such low places to feed their addiction."

"In the course of time, I struck up a familiarity with a Chinese opium dealer, a Mister Chang. This gentleman, recognising how it was in his best interests to keep me as a friend rather than an enemy, was most hospitable on my visits. He would invariably offer me a pot of tea." The Inspector smiled wistfully at the memory, and then added meaningfully, "But not just any tea. No, sir. Not your average brown from the corner shop. No, no, to impress me, nay to dazzle me, he served me Da Hong Pao tea."

Wilde shook his head. "Can't say that I've heard of it."

"Neither I," Conan Doyle. "Is there a point to your reminiscence, Inspector?"

The Inspector nodded and continued, "Most definitely. You see, Da Hong Pao tea is the most special tea grown in China. It is worth many times its weight in gold. And I mean that literally."

Both authors spluttered at the very concept.

"The point is, gents, that the tea I sampled that day is called Da Hong Pao. And some time after I discovered why the tea was so special because, as I said, it is worth many, many times its weight in gold."

"Whaaaaat" Wilde gasped.

"Surely you are exaggerating," Conan Doyle responded sceptically.

"I jest you not gennulmen. India produces many fine teas, but the Chinese teas have no equal and Da Hong Pao is considered the finest of the finest. Small wonder that the spies of the East India Company have been trying to steal the seeds of the bush for years." He smiled ruefully. "All without success, I might point out."

"This is all fascinating, Inspector, but what is the point—"

"The point is, Mister Wilde, that how does a charity such as Madame Xylander's have the dosh to serve casual visitors the most expensive tea in the world?"

"Perhaps they came by it as a donation," Conan Doyle speculated.

"Then, as a charity, they would likely sell it. No, I think the truth is they've received the tea as a good will gesture, but they have no idea of the tea's true value. Which I think few westerners would understand. However, I would be remiss if I didn't point just how hard it is to come by this tea. To put it bluntly it is scarcer than rocking horse shit. It's hard to come by by any honest means. Mostly it is wealthy Chinese merchants who can afford to purchase it, and most of those are nefarious characters—"

"Such as opium dealers?" Conan interrupted.

"Quite."

"You don't think Madame Xylander is secretly running an opium den do you?"

"I should think that would be unlikely. However, I would point out that the ships coming in from China are loaded to the gunnels with silks, opium, jade, ivory and all kinds of rare and expensive commodities. To make the return journey profitable they need something from England, a rare commodity to fill their holds. Something uniquely English that commands a high price in the East."

Conan Doyle and Wilde exchanged puzzled frowns, but then Conan Doyle's face turned uneasy as a nascent thought percolated up into his mind.

"Wait a minute. You're not . . . I mean . . . I certainly hope you're not . . . Surely you're not suggesting . . . white slavery?"

"It does exist, sir. I know it's one of the favourite topics of *The Illustrated Police News*, as our young friend Billy Brash could attest. But like most lurid fantasies, it has its basis in truth."

Wilde raised a doubting eyebrow. "And I take it you have personal experience of this dastardly trade?"

The Inspector nodded sagely. "If you think about it, sirs, ships arrive from China loaded with tea, silks, china, and opium. Now that same ship's gotta turn around and sail all the way back to China. Are they gonna do that with an empty hold? No. They want a cargo just as priceless to take back with them."

"You aren't suggesting . . ."

"Young women . . . young, fair-skinned women . . . to be sold as wives and concubines for wealthy Sheiks, Arab traders, Chinese war lords and what not. I assure you gents, the white slave trade ain't just a lurid story."

Conan Doyle and Wilde exchanged a horrified look. "Good God, could he be right, Oscar?"

"It does fall into place with what we just witnessed. And it could explain all these young women disappearing."

And then a more horrible possibility sank in with Conan Doyle. "And what if those are the blackguards who have my Jean? The very thought sends me into a distraction. We must turn around the carriage and go back. This very moment."

Inspector Crumpet leaned forward and patted Conan Doyle's knee. 'Your wife is probably not with them. At least, not in the house. Too much incriminating evidence. They most like have girls stashed at other locations."

'You must bring more constables," the Scotsman insisted. "We must raid the place, thoroughly search it and—"

"But you saw how those girls reacted."

"They are deep under the thrall of someone," Wilde added.

"Morpheus!" Conan Doyle spat. "That blasted devil. I knew he was behind all of this."

Inspector Crumpet nodded his agreement. "Very likely, Mister Doyle. That's why we need to stay our hand for the moment. Morpheus must be taken with the girls, or he will walk free."

"What are we to do inspector?"

"I think this is a job for our boy Billy. We need him to keep Madame Xylander's under surveillance. Watch the comings and goings. If my guess is right, they will be paying a visit to Limehouse soon. Once we know where, then we can wait for them to move, and then take them all in one fell swoop."

CHAPTER 41: FREUD REMEMBERS BERTA XYLANDER

"Professor Freud, are you aware someone is impersonating you?"

"Whaaaat?" Freud jerked forward in his chair, so astonished that, for once, the cigar nearly unclamped from his jaws.

Conan Doyle was visiting St Ermin's Hotel where Sigmund Freud was staying in and found the Austrian psychologist ensconced behind a newspaper in the smoking room.

"Several times now I have had this person followed. They dress exactly like you: grey homburg, grey coat, and they even smoke the same sort of cigars you smoke, imported from Austria."

Freud laughed the idea off. "Preposterous. No one in this country even knows who I am. Who is this person you claim is impersonating me?"

"The name we have is Madame Xylander. She lives in Marylebone. Officially she runs a charity for fallen women."

"Nonsense. I have never heard of such a person," Freud maintained although, from his body language, it was clear that the name was familiar to him.

"When not disguised as you, Madame Xylander has a distinctive appearance. She suffers from poliosis, an hereditary condition. Her hair is bright red, but she has a white streak running through her hair."

Freud looked stunned and fell silent.

Conan Doyle knew he'd hit upon something. "From your reaction, I take it you know a woman who matches that description?"

"No, it cannot be . . ." Freud muttered to himself. "How old is this Xylander person?"

"Close to your age, late thirties."

The far-away look in Freud's eyes faded. He leaned forward in his chair and fixed Conan Doyle with an avid stare. "There was a person, years ago, during my student days in Vienna. His name was Wulf . . . Wulf Xylander. He was a frail, small fellow who was teased mercilessly by the other boys for having tiny hands and being rather short and effeminate. But he was a bright student, and impressed our professors. Heretofore, I had been considered the brightest student in the class, so he and I became rivals. I must admit, I was jealous of my position being threatened by this new upstart. Our rivalry grew more heated with each week, but then Xylander took to dressing like me, copying my haircut and even smoking the same brand of cigars. But when I grew my first beard he could not copy that. In fact, his face remained as smooth as a baby's. Still, my fellow students would often tease me, accusing me and Xylander of being homosexual lovers—despite my protestations that I had done nothing to encourage his attentions. Today I would dismiss it as a simple case of transference. Still, my fellow students mocked me for it, and claimed that Xylander had an unhealthy fixation upon me, much to my mortification. In truth, Xylander did seem obsessed with me in an unhealthy way. He was what you English would call a " feline who imitates."

Conan Doyle frowned until the penny dropped. "I think the expression you're searching for is "copycat."

"Yes, *copycat*, that's the term. Of course, because he copied me, I naturally reacted against him and soon became his chief antagonist. One day in class we had an argument about the efficacy of hypnosis versus Mesmerism. I argued that Mesmerism with its notions of animal magnetism and manipulating magnetic fluids were the quaint notions of a less enlightened time. At this observation Xylander flew into a rage and challenged me. We both would mesmerise a fellow student. Thus we would see the difference between the two. I hypnotised a friend of mine and proved the analgesic effect by running a large dollmaker's needle through his arm and then convincing him that ants were swarming over his face, which caused much hilarity with my fellow students. Xylander then challenged me to command my test subject to jump out an open window. Of course he would not comply as, in hypnosis, it is impossible to make someone do something he or she would not ordinarily do.

"But then Xylander mesmerised his test subject and instructed him to jump out a window. To our horror, he immediately complied, flinging himself through the nearest window. Our classroom was on the second floor and the poor fellow only escaped serious injury by falling on another student."

"That summer, after the end of our examinations. all my classmates and I went to celebrate at an inn that was a favourite haunt of students. For many of us, it was the first time we had drunk beer and schnapps.

"We all soon became drunk and so there was lots of rough-and-tumble horseplay. The inn stood on the banks of the Danube and during the horseplay, someone pushed Xylander into the river. It was only then we discovered he could not swim. One of my classmates was a champion swimmer. He dove in after Xylander but by the time we fished him out, the poor fellow was half drowned. As we attempted to resuscitate him, we loosened his clothing and it was then that we discovered the truth about Xylander."

"Which was?"

"He had breasts. Xylander was a female, a young woman who had strapped down her breasts and cut her hair short to conceal her sex. Of course, there was a scandal and Xylander was ejected from the university as we had a strict policy of proscribing females from the study of psychiatry."

"Do you know what became of her?"

"Some years later, when I was living and practicing psychiatry in the General Hospital in Vienna, I heard a story of a remarkable hypnosis act. I am not normally a frequenter of vulgar entertainment, but hypnosis has been a tool I have employed with great success. I was intrigued by the stories I was hearing and so I went to the music hall to see for myself."

"And was the hypnotist Fraulein Xylander?"

"No, the hypnotist was a handsome young man, a boy really. He performed with his sister, a stunningly beautiful young lady. They performed many astounding feats, and I began to envy the young man's prowess. During the performance he was accompanied by Xylander herself, playing a most remarkable musical instrument . . ."

"A glass armonica?" Conan Doyle interrupted.

Freud looked astounded and nearly bit his cigar in two. "Yes, a very eerie sounding instrument. But how on earth did you know that?"

"Because I have seen the self same act . . . here in London . . . and I suspect that Madame Xylander is somehow behind the plague of sleepwalking we've been experiencing."

Having extracted all the information he needed, Conan Doyle allowed the Austrian doctor to go back to reading his newspaper and smoking his cigar. But as he was about to quit the room, a thought struck Conan Doyle and so he turned back and called out to the Austrian. "Oh, Professor Freud, one last question."

The psychiatrist dropped the curtain of his newspaper and stared expectantly at Conan Doyle.

"It was you wasn't it?" the Scots author asked. "You were the one who pushed Xylander into the Danube?"

Freud was silent as he considered answering the question, but then finally nodded, muttered a quick "Ja" and disappeared back behind his newspaper.

CHAPTER 42: EXHUMATION OF
THE DEAD

The next Saturday Wilde met up with Conan Doyle who had arrived at Hyde Park a full hour early and was lurking by the gates standing next to a familiar figure bulging out of a Police sergeant's uniform.

"Good morning, Arthur. Good morning Inspector Crumpet," Wilde greeted as he strolled up.

Crumpet was busy cramming something into his mouth, no doubt a sausage roll, and then used both hands to furiously bat at his dense moustache in an effort to knock loose all the flaky pastry. He was only partially successful so that his moustache resembled the hide of a badly moulting yak.

"Morning, Oscar," Conan Doyle muttered tersely. From his pouchy and bloodshot eyes it was clear he had slept little in the week since his wife's disappearance."

"Guffff mawwnning," replied Inspector Crumpet who was still masticating his mouthful as he wiped pastry from his fingers onto the trousers of his blue serge trouser and then shook Wilde's hand.

Conan Doyle threw a quick look around at the crowd, which was swelling by the minute and then turned back to the others. "I have inveigled the Inspector to accompany us so that we might detain our hypnotist friend for questioning . . . if he's still alive."

Wilde waved away such a thought with his cigarette. "As I have assured you, Arthur, when the coffin is opened I guarantee Mister Morpheus will step out, looking crisp and relaxed after his supposed subterranean sojourn. It will all have been a trick, a bit of legerdemain. I'm sure right now he is relaxing somewhere close by sipping a brandy and water. That said, I have little doubt that, in a bit of theatre, he will sway unsteadily on his feet as he raises a triumphant hand to acknowledge the crowd's applause. I assure you, it is all an act."

The crowds were thickening as more Londoners drifted through the gates in knots. Conan Doyle looked uneasy, anxious to be ready when the moment arrived. "I shall purchase us some tickets."

And with that, the Scots author stalked off to a kiosk where he purchased three tickets at one shilling and sixpence each so that they might have the closest possible seating.

As Wilde started to walk away to join his friend, Inspector Crumpet lagged behind. "I think . . ." he looked embarrassed. "I think I may peruse the refreshment stands first. I didn't really have time to eat a proper breakfast this morning."

"Apart from the sausage rolls?" Wilde ventured.

The Inspector chuckled, setting his multiple chins in motion. "Yes, quite," he replied, quickly getting over his shame and then he vanished into the crowd.

"Where is our Inspector?" Conan Doyle asked as he and Wilde settled into their folding chairs in the viewing stands.

"I believe he is on an errand to avoid imminent death by starvation."

Moments later, Crumpet appeared from the crowd, puffing and panting and holding a paper cone filled with hot whelks. As he plopped into the empty chair next to the two authors, he spilled some whelks down the front of his uniform and then spent minutes fastidiously picking them off and putting them in his mouth.

Wilde and Conan Doyle looked on in scarcely concealed disgust, the marine aroma of hot seafood already curdling Conan Doyle's empty stomach.

Again, Crumpet spoke around a juicy mouthful of masticated

whelks. "Ashamed to say I have no other clothes to fit me. My civvies have been most carelessly shrunk by the launderers."

Conan Doyle shared a look with Wilde who stifled a laugh with a puff of his cigarette.

By 11:20 the reviewing stand was packed to capacity and the crowd surged and strained against the restraining ropes. In the week since his interment, word of Morpheus's stunt had appeared in every newspaper and spread like wildfire, so that today, the crowd to witness his resurrection had swollen to three times that of a week ago.

The brass band was, once again, on hand. And at thirty minutes to noon, it struck up with a jaunty tune that seemed at odds with the semi-sombre nature of the occasion. At precisely fifteen minutes before the hour, the band fell silent and the eerie notes of the glass armonica soared up from behind the screen.

Wilde leaned toward Conan Doyle and whispered *sotto voce*. "I'll wager that our hypnotist friend is lurking behind that banner. Expect some kind of kerfuffle when the coffin lid is opened, a diversion that will allow him to slip back inside . . . if he's not already inside."

Conan Doyle said nothing. His hands were clenched in fists so tight that his nails left deep indentations in the palms of his hands. With Jean missing, it had been the longest week of his life. No matter what happened he would soon lay his hands on Morpheus and throttle the truth out of him if need be.

The diggers came forward and began to excavate the loose soil piled on the grave. It was hotter and sunnier on this Saturday and the men soon stripped to the waist as they flung spadefuls of dirt out of the grave. At a few minutes to the hour the crowd winced at the shriek of spades scraping across the lid of the brass coffin, and then the men all clambered out of the grave as the windlass was brought forward and set up over the yawning hole.

Once the ropes slung beneath the coffin had been attached to the windlass, the men took it in turns at the crank and the massive coffin was slowly but steadily drawn back up into the light of day. As it fully surfaced, the workmen all grabbed a purchase to swing it free of the grave and onto the grass where it was thumped down.

Conan Doyle's back muscles were clenched so painfully it drove him up from his chair. Someone behind yelled at him to sit down and he sank back down on legs quivering with adrenaline.

The doctor and several officials stepped forward and then, at last, the moment had arrived. The doctor and official moved around to the front of the coffin and with the aid of two workmen the coffin seal was cracked, and then the heavy lid was slowly raised wide.

At once he saw the waiting officials, the doctor, the official, and even the work crew recoiled with horror, their faces twisting into masks of disgust. At that point the audience in the viewing stand all jumped to their feet, blocking everyone's view. Conan Doyle craned and tried to push the large man in front of him to one side, but the man turned around and unleashed a mouthful of obscenities. Unable to wait any longer, Conan Doyle grabbed Inspector Crumpet by the sleeve and dragged him along as the two barged their way through the crowd. Together they tripped down the steps and ran straight to the first constable guarding the rope barrier.

"You must let us through!" Conan Doyle insisted. "I am a doctor, and this officer is my escort. Now let us pass!"

The bluff worked, for the Constable lifted the restraining rope long enough for the two men to duck under. A wild confusion of people milled about the open coffin, blocking his view, but as Conan Doyle got within twenty feet he caught a gagging whiff of corruption. When he reached the graveside he pushed through the confusion of bodies and got his first look into the open coffin.

Wilde's confident guess was entirely wrong. The coffin was very much occupied and apparently by the mortal remains of Morpheus the Magnificent

The attending physician crouched over the body, checking the wrist for a pulse, although from even a cursory glance it was obvious that Morpheus was very much a corpse.

Conan Doyle dropped into a crouch beside the doctor and when the consulting physician threw him a questioning look, he said, "I, too, am a doctor."

"i'm afraid we're both too late," the doctor said. "Days too late. No pulse. No respiration. Rigor has come and gone. And as you can see, morbidity has set in and the decomposition is far advanced."

At first it was hard to tell if the body in the coffin was, indeed, Morpheus. Even now Conan Doyle had been holding out hope that the body in the coffin was a convincing waxwork, or the body of an unfortunate tramp, made up to look like the young hypnotist. The face was glossy with corpse wax and had turned purple and black, the result of blood pooling in the extremities. But his last hope was rudely destroyed as Conan Doyle was forced to admit that this was the same man he had seen before. This close up, the reek of putrefaction was gagging. From all the signs Morpheus had been dead for days; perhaps he had perished after only a few hours—suffocated. But Conan Doyle had no doubt that this was the man, his tall form and long, spatulate fingers confirmed it. The once-handsome face was swollen and bloated—hideously discoloured in death.

Conan Doyle touched the blackened hand of the corpse, and gave the skin an experimental pinch to assess the level of turgor, but the skin was gelid and cold as the grave.

Inspector Crumpet appeared and looked down with concern. "He's a goner is he?"

The Scots author looked up at him. "I think we have our answer. Morpheus had slipped away to a place even the police cannot follow."

Just then a handcart bearing a wooden coffin appeared. Conan Doyle and Crumpet stood back as the team of grave diggers lifted Morpheus's corpse from his brass tomb and settled it inside the wooden coffin, ready to be wheeled to the morgue.

Wilde was waiting by the grandstand when Conan Doyle and Inspector Crumpet broke free of the melee and shuffled up to him.

"You were wrong, Oscar," Conan Doyle said. "If it was all a magic trick then it must have gone disastrously wrong. Morpheus failed to escape through a hidden panel or a false bottom. He's been dead for days."

"Oh dear," Wilde said, his face registering shock. He dropped his just-lit cigarette to the ground. "Whatever shall you do now?"

"Yes," Conan Doyle nodded grimly, his face drawn and pinched with utter defeat. "Whatever shall I do now?"

CHAPTER 43: THE SHANGHAI TEA COMPANY

Billy Brash had been keeping watch outside Madame Xylander's for three hours. By now he was bursting to pee, but knew the moment he found a quiet alleyway to pee in, some carriage would leave or arrive and he'd miss it. He'd been dancing on the spot for twenty minutes, but finally he could hold it no longer. He looked around desperately.

There was a small ginnel between houses just a few feet away. He might be caught pissing if anyone came out of the house, but he was past desperate by now. He couldn't run with a full bladder and his bicycle, but he hurried to the ginnel, threw a quick look back at Madame Xylander's and then ducked down the ginnel. On the side of the house he found a down pipe that emptied into a grid and he whipped out his penis and groaned with relief as he directed a sizzling yellow stream down the grid. But then he heard a woman's voice shout, "Oi, you. Ya filthy little blighter. Be off with ya then!"

He looked up to see a woman who had just stepped from an open kitchen door. She was emptying a coal scuttle full of ashes into a dustbin and had caught him. But Billy's bladder was bursting, and once started he could not stop his fierce stream, The woman vanished back into the kitchen and reappeared with a rolling pin, brandishing it as she began to stalk up the ginnel toward him, apparently intending to do more than roll pastry with the kitchen utensil she wielded like a club. Luckily, his stream dried to a trickle, he finished, tucked himself back into his trousers, and his foot scrambled to find the pedal as he leaped astride his bicycle and escaped her swung rolling pin with only inches to spare.

As he rode back onto the street, he looked up and was just in time to see the black carriage with its tall driver pull out of the drive of the Marylebone house. Swearing, he pumped the pedals so that his thighs burned, and managed to draw closer to the slower-moving carriage. He was steadily catching up when the carriage turned onto the Strand, and they both entered the melee of London traffic.

But as the miles rolled by, he began to feel a sinking feeling as he rode into Whitechapel and the houses and shop premises lining the streets grew seedier and more decrepit. The carriage was heading into bandit country: Limehouse, where white faces were rare and stood out dangerously. As he reached the docks area, the denizens of Limehouse stared at him as he rode by, or rather, they stared at his bicycle and he readied himself to be set upon by the gangs of rogues and thieves who idled on every street corner. Finally, they reached the warehouses lining the river where, thankfully, the carriage drew up.

Billy wheeled his bike into the cover of stacks of tea chests that were being winched onto the deck of a merchant ship, ignoring the cold stares of the leather-faced British sailors and the Chinese coolies loading them.

He watched as the towering Cossack clambered down from the driver's seat and opened the carriage door for its occupant. Xylander stepped out, threw a quick look in both directions, and then entered the nearest premise. She obviously had business there because she was gone for the best part of a half hour. By then the sailors loading the ship had noticed Billy and were shouting oaths and questions at him, "What's yer business 'ere, sonny", and more "oi, fuck off out of it!"

When the threats grew to the point it was clear he could not longer tarry, he stood up on the pedals of his bike and began to ride toward the waiting carriage. The Cossack stood guard, the huge head moving back and forth on a swivel as he gave any of the locals who ventured too close the evil eye. Billy did not want to be spotted, but if the Russian giant happened to glance up at the street he would be in plain sight. Luckily, just then several street thugs—two Englishmen and a pair of Chinese men—converged on the Russian in a coordinated attack. The Englishmen flourished long-bladed knives while the Chinese attackers wielded rough clubs. But in a flash, an even longer club appeared in the hand of the Cossack. As one of the Englishman thrust a knife at him, the Cossack brought the club down on his forearm, and from the piercing scream the man let out left little doubt that his arm bone had just been shattered. The man staggered away, his face twisted in agony as he held his broken ar,. The Russian next seized one of the Chinese by the pigtail and and used him as a shield as the second knifeman struck, and the unfortunate Englishman took the blade his back. The Cossack moved with surprising speed, swinging his club left and right, raining devastating blows each time. Seconds later all four were sprawled on the ground, stunned or seriously injured. Billy stopped his bicycle to watch. At that moment Madame walked out of the doorway and gave the prostrate victims the most cursory of glances as she stepped over their bodies. She was carrying something in an ornately decorated black lacquer box. She waited while the Cossack lowered the metal step and opened the carriage door for her and then climbed on board. Within seconds he was back in the driver's seat and gee'ed up the horses with a crack of his whip. He wheeled the carriage back in the direction they had come from and soon was rattling back along the cobbles toward central London. As Billy rode his bicycle back to the scene of the fracas, one of the Chinamen was helping his comrade stagger to his feet. The Englishman remained slumped on the floor, still unconscious. Billy stopped his bicycle outside the building the Madame had just left.

The Shanghai Tea Company was painted on the front door alongside a presumed translation in Chinese characters. Billy now had what he'd been hired for, following Madame Xylander and finding out where she was going to, so he stood up on the pedal and rode away up the bumpy cobbled street, tinkling his bicycle bell manically.

CHAPTER 44: WAKING THE DEAD

By the loudness and frenzy of knocking, someone was trying to wake the dead. The night watchman at the morgue had just unwrapped the stained and holed tea towel containing the cold meat pie he had brought for his dinner and looked up sourly at the impatient-knuckles-on-wood summons and then at the clock on the wall. It was well past one o'clock in the morning. No normal visitors would appear at this hour. He reasoned it must be the police, delivering another body. As the frantic hammering continued, he hurriedly rewrapped the tea towel around his pie and slipped it in a desk drawer. This intrusion into his peace was an unwelcome irritation. He had taken an unsociable job with unsociable hours because he was an unsociable man. Compared to the living the dead were far easier to work with. Occasionally the dead groaned, gurgled, sat up, or eructed foul-smelling gases, but usually they were as silent as the grave they were heading for.

He turned the key in the lock and cracked the door slightly. Peering out with a single eye, he glimpsed two shadowy figures lurking in the doorway; the short one was clearly a woman and in the sketchy light she seemed to be wearing widow's weeds—a clear sign of mourning. But the figure that lurked behind her was a giant—the tallest man he had ever seen. He was dressed in a thick overcoat and his head was capped by a fur hat as if he had just shaken off the snow of the Russian steppes from his boots.

"We're shut," he called through the cracked door. "Come back in the mornin'. Morgue opens at nine."

But as he went to push the door closed, the tall figure lunged forward and pressed a hand against it, holding it open.

"Please, sir," the woman spoke in a lachrymose voice. "I've come to see my poor son. I only want five minutes with him. Just to say goodbye."

The watchman eyed the tall figure nervously. He was a huge brute of a man. If he wanted to he could likely smash the door to splinters with his bare fists, locked or not. Body snatchers usually stole from graveyards. He had never heard of them stealing a body from the morgue.

"We're shut I said," he repeated.

"But I cannot wait," the woman said. "I just heard the terrible news about my poor son. I must see him with my own eyes. Please . . . my poor heart is breaking. Won't you have pity on a grieving mother?"

After his initial fear subsided, the watchman's irritation at the interruption returned. He wanted to get back to his meat pie.

"Sorry, ma'am. but you'll have to wait. I can't let no one in at this—"

His words were cut short as the woman in mourning thrust out a small purse toward him.

The night watchman looked at the purse and swallowed, his mouth suddenly dry.

The widow shook it and he could almost tell from the jangle of coins the denomination of each one.

He relented a moment, and then took the coinpurse from the woman and now he shot the bolts and opened the door to them.

"If anyone asks, I never let you in," the watchman said as he led them down the darkened corridor by the quivering light of a candle on a brass dish. He paused at a closed door and used his jailor's ring of keys to unlock it. Then he handed the woman the candle and said. "I won't charge you for the candle, seein' as you . . ." he didn't finish the sentence and pushed the door wide for her. "He's the only one we got tonight. I'll leave you with him. When you're done, follow the light to my office and I'll unlock the door to let you out."

And with that, the night watchman left and traipsed back along the darkened corridor toward his office.

In the morgue, only one slab was occupied by a naked body and now the two figures stood around it. The woman laid a hand on the corpse's throat and pressed her fingers against the jugular vein.

"Is dead?" the Cossack grunted.

After a long pause the widow shook her head. "No, the pulse is there but extremely slow. Extremely faint. He is very deep. It will take a while to revive him." She opened the corpse's mouth, reached in, and drew out the large clumps of cotton wadding stuffed in the cheeks to give the face its bloated appearance.

The woman then began to make gestures in the air over his prostrate form. Hands pulling down, and then drawing up his body, as if the drawing the blood back up from the extremities, pressing her palms against his forehead and then drawing back, as if drawing his consciousness back into his mind. After several minutes the body made a horrible choking sound and then let out a deep sigh and the chest began to rise and fall as the corpse's breathing quickened and deepened. Her gestures quickened and became more intense as she flailed the air around him. Finally, with a death-rattle moan, Morpheus's eyes flickered and opened.

"I'm cold," he rasped in a dry, distant voice.

The woman cracked a smile. "Yes . . . cold as the grave, but you will soon be warm again."

She looked at the Cossack who handed her a blanket, and now she draped it over his naked body.

"You did well, Morpheus. At first, I did not think you had survived. But you have surpassed all others. A full week."

"It was horrible," he said in a wisp of ruined voice. "I dreamed constantly of the grave. It was . . . worse than death . . ."

"Yes, but now you are dead. Morpheus is dead. They will not look for you. We will be gone in the morning and no one will think to look for us."

As warm blood returned to his extremities, he slowly recovered the ability to move his limbs, and now he pulled the blanket tighter around his torso and huddled into it as shivers wracked his body.

The watchman had been making his rounds and had only just returned to his office and finally started chomping on his meat pie when the door opened and three figures shuffled into the office.

When the watchman looked up and saw the dead man standing before him, flanked by the widow and the tall man, he gaped in terror and half-chewed pie fell out of his mouth.

The hypnotist flashed him a ghastly smile, which made the man gibber and quake with terror.

Finally the woman stepped forward and set down a bottle on the desk before him. "The bottle contains laudanum," she said matter-of-factly. "I recommend you drink it. It will soften the memory of this night. In the morning this will all seem just an unpleasant dream."

The three then departed the office and left by the front door. As soon as they had, the night watchman ran to lock the door behind them, and then rushed back to the office where he snatched up the bottle of laudanum, yanked the cork, and gargled down a mouthful of the bitter liquid.

As the black carriage rolled away from the morgue, the hypnotist and woman conferred inside. Morpheus had a rag and was wiping off lurid black and purple grease paint thickly daubed on his face that had counterfeited the colours of death.

CHAPTER 45: INSPECTOR CRUMPET HAS INDIGESTION

That afternoon Conan Doyle answered a summons from Inspector Crumpet to meet at Mrs Wiggly's Pie Shop. When he stepped inside, he found the rotund Inspector ensconced at his usual table, a giant pot of tea and a plate of the inevitable sausage rolls close at hand.

"My wife, Inspector," Conan Doyle asked. "I am very anxious about her. Have you had any luck in locating her whereabouts?"

"Ah, Doctor Doyle," Crumpet greeted. "Just in time!"

Conan Doyle eyed the wreckage of the plates scattered about the table. It seemed obvious that Crumpet had been indulging in his favourite food. "I hope this meeting is germane to the investigation, and not just gustatory."

There were three uniformed Constables sitting at the table or at neighbouring tables, along with a couple: a man and a woman in plain clothes.

"It is very much a strategy meeting, although feel free to help yourself to a sausage roll. They're very good, aren't they lads?

"Bloody lovely!"

"Very toothsome.

"Best I've ever 'ad."

"I couldn't bake better meself!" the woman, tee-heed, who proved to be a plain clothes constable who had shaved his moustache and dressed as a woman.

Billy Brash was also there, sitting in a chair turned the wrong way around. He had his elbows resting on the chair back and when he saw Conan Doyle, he tipped his newspaper boy's hat to him and flashed a cheeky grin.

"These are the lads," Crumpet said, introducing them. "The Chief would only let me have five, but they should be plenty. There's only Xylander, Morpheus, the big Cossack chap and the maid to deal with. We don't need to go in mob-handed."

"Not a precise location as such, But I believe that, tomorrow morning, Madame Xylander and her crew will lead us to her location, where I fully expect to find all the other disappeared young ladies."

Crumpet reached into a leather satchel at his feet and drew out several papers. He slapped the first one down on the table. I did a little bit of poking around about the business of Mister Morpheus and also of Madame Xylander.

Conan Doyle dropped into the chair opposite Crumpet. He helped himself to a cup of tea but then pushed the heaping plate of sausage rolls away—lest he start to resemble the portly Inspector.

Crumpet threw a look around at his assembled team. "I believe I have now established a time line that Madame Xylander and her entourage will follow. First, I enquired at the Alcambra Music Hall about the fate of the brass coffin as recently used the late Mister Morpheus." He slapped down the first sheet of paper before Conan Doyle.

"What's this?"

"A bill of lading for when the coffin was delivered to the Alcambra. Note where it was shipped from."

Conan Doyle's eyes roved over the paper. "It was shipped from Germany—Dusseldorf, in particular."

"Originally, I figured that, with Morpheus having snuffed it, the coffin would have been sold for scrap someplace local." He slapped down another piece of paper next to the first. "But I was wrong. It ain't being scrapped, it's being shipped to Berlin in Germany. Funny that. The coffin weighs a bleedin' ton and it's costing them a fortune to ship it. But why ship the coffin when Mister Morpheus is dead? He ain't gonna need it for his act. That is, if he really is dead."

Conan Doyle pushed his chair back slightly and stared at the portly Inspector. "What on earth do you mean, *if* he's really dead. You saw the body inspector: the stench of corruption, the blackened and bloated face. The other physician found no pulse. He was very dead."

Crumpet reached for a sausage roll, took a bite, and slowly chewed, making Conan Doyle wait until he'd swallowed the bite.

"I say *if* he was dead because of what I found out yesterday."

Shock washed across Conan Doyle's face at the news.

Crumpet continued, "The morgue's night watchman reported that the deceased's mother visited the morgue in the early hours. She wanted to see her boy one last time . . . and she was accompanied by an extremely tall Russian chap. Rather unusually, after they had viewed the body, the corpse got up and accompanied them home. The night watchman was found the next morning, out of his mind on laudanum with a fat purse of coins in his pocket. Of course, the authorities figured he'd been paid off by body-snatchers and had made the rather fantastic story up, but now I've changed my mind."

"So Morpheus is still alive!"

"So it would seem."

Crumpet paused to sip his tea. "So then I followed up on the brass coffin as I was curious as to what would become of it. Turns out it was returned to the Alcambra Music Hall until its final destination could be determined. But, of course, the coffin still stunk to high heaven, so one of stage hands was given the rather horrible task of cleaning it out. Turns out that he found a dead cat hidden in the lining. The cat was a month past ripe and that's what the source of the stink was. They checked the lining further and found a number of grease pencils, mostly black and blue in colour. I woulda said he faked his death but for the doctor who couldn't find a pulse."

"Damn!" Conan Doyle banged his fist down on the table in frustration. "That's my fault, Inspector. Oscar and I previously discovered Morpheus in his coffin. Apparently he was practicing for the buried alive stunt. He had slowed his pulse and respiration down to a point where I, at first, could not tell if he was dead or alive."

Conan Doyle frowned as his eyes scanned the documents before him. "Well we know that for certain. Morpheus is ling on a slab in the morgue. Maybe they will replace Morpheus with someone new."

"Maybe." Crumpet conceded, but then he placed another piece of paper before Conan Doyle. "This is a copy of a booking I obtained from the railway. Someone, they are anonymous, has reserved a private car on the train that runs to Dover. It's a through ticket so they will take the cross-channel ferry and then board the train from Calais for Germany, specifically Berlin."

Conan Doyle's face lit up. "So we know that someone with associations to the brass coffin is also traveling to Berlin."

"Five tickets have been purchased. At the moment I am slightly at a loss to understand why they needed five tickets. With Morpheus, Madame Xylander, the Cossack and the Maid, that's only four."

"Another accomplice we haven't met yet?"

"That's what I'm guessing." Crumpet stabbed a fat finger on the ticket receipt. "You'll notice the time of departure, 1:15. I figure they are doing a bunk. I think they will make the exchange for the girls tomorrow so the boat can sail on the afternoon tide. They will then go directly to Victoria Station where they will board a train and they will arrive in Berlin the day after."

"The Emerald Star, a clipper that runs from Shanghai to London, docked four days ago. It's unloaded its cargo of tea (and presumably, opium) and is currently loading cargo for its return journey. It sails on the morning tide around noonish tomorrow. I think they will wait for the last minute to load the girls aboard. We can't move before then. I'll have Billy and his bicycle staking out the house. We'll arrive with a growler and a Mariah before dawn. Billy will be equipped with a Bull's eye lantern. As soon as Billy sees their black carriage leave the Marylebone house, He can flash us . . ."

All eyes focused on Billy, who picked up the Bull's eye lantern on the table in front of him, and demonstrated by flashing the group with it.

" . . . to signal that the carriage has set off. We will then follow at a discrete distance. If Billy flashes once, it means they've set off. If he flashes twice it means the carriage has stopped. If he flashes 3 times it means he's certain they have arrived at the place the girls are being held. We then swoop down and arrest the lot of them."

"And what if he doesn't flash at all?" Conan Doyle asked.

"It means he's dropped the lantern."

"I checked with the railways and someone's booked a private first class carriage for six people that goes to meet the Calais ferry. That must be them."

"Wait, you said six passengers. Who are the fifth and sixth?"

"That I don't know."

"I've got the tide table here.

I reckon they'll move early, around dawn. We can't follow them in a Police Mariah or they'll rumble us straight off. Plus, we can't have two many white faces lurking about—it'll tip the locals. But they won't notice a young messenger boy on a bike. I purchased a copy of the tide charts. The Emerald Star, a china clipper, docked four days ago and unloaded its tea, purchased by the Shanghai Tea company. It's currently loading its new cargo, and will sail out on the morning tide, about noonish. That's when the young woman will be loaded aboard.

After listening to Crumpet's plan, Conan Doyle felt somewhat relieved, but he still let out an anguished sigh.

Inspector Crumpet slapped a reassuring hand on his shoulder. "Don't you worry none, Doctor Doyle, we'll have them all soon enough. And you'll have your darling wife back."

"I certainly hope so."

But then, after delivering his stirring speech, a strange look came over Crumpet's face, a terrible vacancy where he seemed over-whelmed by uncertainty about the mission they were about to embark upon.

"What?" Conan demanded. "What is it inspector? You suddenly seem riddled with doubt."

The rotund inspector turned to look at Conan Doyle.

"Wind," he said in a strangely squeezed voice.

"Wind?" Wilde repeated. "You mean the winds for the shipping? Is that something you hadn't accounted for?"

He shook his head. "Wind," he repeated in a strangled voice.

Inspector Crumpet's eyes watered, his mouth fell agape, the face reddened his blue eyes bulged. Conan Doyle from his medical training, recognised the symptoms of an incipient heart-attack, rose to his feet, ready to spring into action.

Crumpet's mouth widened even further and then he loudly eructed. It was the longest, loudest belch Conan Doyle had ever heard, and it went on forever, filling the air with a meaty pork aroma. It seemed about to stop, but then resumed, gaining volume and liquidy substance. When it finally ended out, with an abrupt burpy flourish, the faces of those clustered around the table betrayed their collective disgust. Unperturbed, Crumpet thumped his chest with a fist several times, as if to knock loose the final clinging clods of his belch. "Ah, that's better," he remarked with obvious relief. "Perhaps one sausage roll too many."

CHAPTER 46: THE FLIGHT

In the pre-dawn gloom, the occupants of the Marylebone house were assembling on the front drive. A few moments later the Cossack drove the black carriage onto the circular drive and stopped before the front doors.

He climbed down the driver's seat and Madame Xylander spoke curtly to him, "Go fetch Lilly. She is in her travelling crib."

The dour Cossack nodded and tromped back inside. One look at the carriage revealed that the inhabitants of the house were flitting. Heaps of baggage were lashed tight to the top of the carriage.

Morpheus moved close and spoke to Xylander. "And the contents of the house, and the carriage and horses, we're just going to abandon it all?"

She shook her head dismissively. "Most of it is rented. And besides, we don't need it any more. We have plenty of money. When we get to Germany we will just buy again what we lack."

He watched as the Cossack loaded Lilly's crib into the carriage. It stretched from the front seat to the rear seat leaving only room inside for two additional passengers.

"Morpheus moved to the crib and began to pull back the hood so he could look in at his sister.

"Stop!" Xylander commanded. "What are you doing?"

"I have not seen my sister in over a year. Can I at least look at her?
"

"No! You cannot see your sister until she is restored . . . as I have promised you. I have deeply induced her for the journey. You will only upset her. Now get up top."

'But can't I ride inside with you and Lilly?"

"No, there is no room. You will ride up top with Ivan."

At that moment they heard the clop-clop of hooves and all looked up, squinting into the coach lights as a boxy moving van drawn by two mares clattered into the driveway and drew up behind their carriage.

Madame Xylander waved to the sea captain who was driving the boxy van. "Good. The van is here. Come, we must hurry. We cannot be late."

Madame Xylander and Marta climbed into the carriage.

Morpheus clambered up onto the driver's seat next to the Cossack who flicked the whip over the horse's ears and the carriage rumbled forward.

From where he was crouched behind a garden wall, Billy Brash watched the black carriage roll out of the driveway followed the hulking moving van. They had left the front door to the Marylebone house standing wide, the lights still burning brightly inside. He turned around and flashed the police growler which was parked discreetly a hundred yards back, trailed another hundred yards by a Black Mariah with four officers in it. Then Billy threw his leg over the cross bar of his bike and peddled off in pursuit of the black carriage. Inspector Crumpet, Conan Doyle and Oscar Wilde were all inside the growler.

"Right, off we go, Lads" Inspector Crumpet called up to the driver. "Don't get too close. If they see us, we're rumbled. But don't let them get too far ahead." He looked around at the two writers. "Get a firm grip on your knickers, gents. This next bit might be a bit dicey."

CHAPTER 47: THE CHASE

And so the police growler containing Oscar Wide, Conan Doyle and Inspector Crumpet rolled slowly up Marylebone and snugged up to the kerb six or so houses down the road from Madame Xylander's home for fallen girls. Following a discreet distance behind the growler, a police Mariah with four constables in the back drew up to the kerb a hundred feet back.

In the tense waiting, Conan Doyle, sick with concern about his wife, was anxious for them to swoop down and arrest all concerned. "When do we move?" he asked Inspector Crumpet.

"We do nothing until we're certain the girls and your wife are with them."

"And you are very certain they are not in the house?"

The Inspector shook his head. "I am not certain of anything. I am convinced those girls we met had been brought in specially to put on a show for us. But I strongly suspect they're being kept at some other location. Which would mean it would be harder to prove kidnapping if they were discovered."

He reached for something next to him and then offered around a bag of sausage rolls.

Wilde deferred, again asserting that he never ate that early; Conan

Doyle's stomach was churning with concern for his wife, Billy Brash and the Inspector were the lone pair noisily consuming sausage rolls, the sounds of their juicy mastication, smacking lips and the smell of pork unfurled in the cramped carriage space, curdling Conan Doyle's stomach.

Suddenly Crumpet spotted something out the carriage window and came alert. "Allo allo," he said. "They're beginning to stir."

Conan Doyle peered out at the carriage window. The Cossack had drawn the black carriage out of the stable and had just pulled up in front of the house. He climbed down and went in through the front door and a moment later the door reopened and he emerged with both armfuls of something that looked like a giant cradle. Madame Xylander (or Berta Xylander as Conan Doyle now knew her real name to be) followed him outside and watched him as he manoeuvred the large cradle to fit inside the carriage. "There's something in that cradle from the look of things," Wilde noted. "A baby?" the Inspector speculated.

"More like a invalid," Conan Doyle noted. "Notice they've got a bathchair strapped to the back of the carriage along with that glass armonica."

"And there's that little Polish lady. I take she is looking after the invalid."

And then a horse-drawn moving van appeared. The boxy shape pulling into the circular driveway and drawing up behind the black carriage.

"Now who's this?" Conan Doyle said.

"A moving van!" Crumpet said. "That proves my belief They are going to collect the missing girls and your wife. How many can they have if they need a van that size?"

They watched Morpheus climb up on the seat next to the Cossack driver.

"They're doing a flit," Inspector Crumpet said, his voice ratcheting with tension. "Lookit the baggage tied to the top of the carriage. "They're doing a flit and they ain't never coming back."

As if to confirm the Inspector's speculation. Berta Xylander climbed into the carriage. The Cossack closed the door behind her and then clambered up to his driver's seat.

They saw a flash of light from the darkness.

"That's the signal from Billy," Crumpet said. "Looks like they're making for the off."

And now the Cossack cracked the whip over the horses's ears and the carriage rounded the circular drive and drove onto the street, heading directly toward their carriage.

"You're right, Inspector," Conan Doyle noted. "Look, they've not even bothered to close the front door. They really have no intention of ever returning."

As the black carriage approached, Inspector Crumpet suddenly urged. "Put yer heads down lads, they're coming this way. I don't want them to spot us!"

All in the carriage ducked as low in the seat as they could as the black carriage passed. They popped back up as soon after.

"They'll see the Mariah!" Conan Doyle worried.

"Can't be helped," Crumpet said. "It's parked at the side of the road. It's still dark out. They may take no mind of it."

They had to duck and hide a second time as the lumbering moving van rumbled past, following the black carriage.

A second later Billy Brash whizzed by on his bicycle, pedaling hard, and threw them a wave as he passed.

Now they had to turn both the growler and the Black Mariah around to continue the pursuit. By the time they set off again the black carriage and the moving van were no longer in sight.

"Blast!" Conan Doyle fumed. "We've already lost them."

"Never you mind, sir. We've got Billy doggin' their tracks. And if they're headin' where I think they're headin', we'll soon catch em up." Crumpet wrapped on the ceiling with his knuckles and shouted up to the constable who was driving. "Jonesy, "make for Limehouse as quick as you like."

The growler picked up speed, and within ten minutes the rear of the moving van hove into view with Billy casually pedalling behind. Meanwhile, Inspector Crumpet kept throwing glances behind them and fretting. They had left the Black Mariah with the extra constables far behind.

Conan Doyle kept throwing furious looks at him. They had only just begun and already Crumpet's plan was falling to pieces. If they could not find them again, he despaired at finding his beloved wife again. He threw an agitated look at the Inspector. "The Mariah, where is it? I don't see the Mariah."

"The Mariah's a great, lumbering thing. But don't worry. They'll catch up."

Billy Brash followed the carriage and its attendant moving van as it entered the Limehouse district. There were no gas lamps here and the moon was cloaked in thick cloud, throwing a blinding blanket of darkness across the streets. Billy was careful to stay tucked in behind the moving van, while not getting too close.

Finally they reached an area of warehouses and slowed down. Suddenly, the doors of the nearest warehouse flung wide, spilling a rectangle of light into the dark road. And then the furniture van swung into the warehouse and the doors were shut fast behind it. The black carriage pulled up a dozen yards away, waiting.

Billy had hooked the bull's eye lantern over his handle bars, but having swung about for several miles the flame had gone out. He felt at his pockets for a box of Lucifers to relight it. But when the opened the matchbox, of course, it was empty.

Now Billy dithered, uncertain what to do. The plan had been for him to flash his Bullseye lantern back at the following carriage when they reached where the sleepwalkers were being kept. But now the moving van had pulled inside a warehouse. Billy couldn't tell what was going on. This might not be the right place. He climbed off his bicycle and wheeled it into a pool of impenetrable gloom in the shadow of the nearest warehouse. He could ride back to tell Inspector Crumpet, but was afraid to move away, as relocating the correct warehouse in the darkness would be risky. And so he watched and waited in the shadows, worrying.

Back in the police growler, the others watched in puzzlement.

"What's happening?" Conan Doyle asked. "Billy's stopped, but he hasn't flashed us. Perhaps we should go."

Crumpet squinted out the window, straining to see what was gong on, but the street was in blackness. "We must be certain. If we swoop down and the van is empty we can't arrest them, but we will alert them and they might slip away."

CHAPTER 48: THE SLEEPWALKERS ARE COLLECTED

Keys jangled. A lock starved for a drop of oil rasped grittily and then clunked open. Madame Xylander, accompanied by the Cossack and the sea captain entered the dungeon-like cellar of the warehouse. Before them, twenty women stood motionless in the gloom. The sea captain's head nodded as his eyes flickered up and down their rows, counting. He finally finished his count and smiled a gap-toothed grin.

"Sure enough, twenty, just loik we agreed."

Xylander held out her hand. "So you have your girls. Now I shall require payment."

The sea captain smiled slackly and shook his head. "Payment upon delivery," he insisted. "Once we get dockside and get the merchandise loaded on board ship, Mister Chan will pay the bill in full."

Madame Xylander swallowed in vexation. "Very well, but you had better not try to cheat me . . ." She threw a quick glance at her Cossack and then back at the sea captain, in an unspoken threat.

Xylander moved amongst the ranks of sleepwalkers and began to wave her hands, making pulling motions. "You will all open your eyes. You are still in my thrall and will hear and obey more orders."

The women began to stir. Their slumped heads straightened, their eyes flickered open but remained glassy.

"And now you will follow me."

As the Cossack held his lantern aloft, Xylander and the sea captain left the cellar, followed by a procession of sleepwalkers. Together they trooped up a set of stone steps to the warehouse above where the moving van waited, its rear doors thrown wide. Xylander then commanded the somnambulists to climb aboard the moving van. Jean Doyle was among them and after a week in the cellar she looked the worse for wear. Her white nightgown was smudged and torn, and her honey-blonde hair was draped in cobwebs. When the last girl had been loaded aboard, the Cossack opened the double warehouse doors and then hurried back and clambered up onto the seat beside the sea captain.

CHAPTER 49: END GAME

Billy Brash was standing in the middle of the roadway, waving his arms and hoping that the men following in the police growler would see him. But then the warehouse doors flew open and the horses dragged the moving van back out onto the road. Billy dodged into the shadows before he could be seen. The moving van halted a moment in the roadway while the Cossack jumped down, rushed to the black carriage, and climbed up into the driver's seat. Then both set off again.

Moments later, the police growler rolled up and Billy waved it down. When the carriage window lowered, he stepped up and gave a breathless report. "They just left here. The pair of them."

Crumpet grunted as he leaned his bulk out the window. "Did they have the women with them?"

Brash shrugged. "I dunno, the moving van pulled into that warehouse there and a few minutes later pulled out again. I couldn't see nuffink."

Crumpet pulled back into the carriage and shot Conan Doyle and Wilde a look. "I'll wager they stopped to load the women inside."

"Can we not just stop them now?" Conan Doyle asked, frantic to get his wife back.

"We're almost at the docks; it's just a few hundred yards up the way. I wager they'll go straight to where the Emerald Star is docked and unload there."

At that moment, the Black Mariah, which had been lagging far behind until now, suddenly rattled past.

"Blast!" Crumpet said. "The blithering idiots in the Mariah just passed us. If they see the Mariah they'll know we're onto them."

Crumpet hammered on the ceiling of the carriage and shouted up at the driver and they set off in pursuit.

The Inspector proved to be correct. When they arrived, the black carriage and moving van had pulled up at the slip where the Emerald Star lay waiting to take on its human cargo. A groups figures huddled around the moving van. Madame Xylander had her hand held out and was just about to receive a bag of money from Mister Chan when they all looked up at the sound of an approaching carriage and were horrified to see a Police Black Mariah clattering toward them from the darkness.

Instantly, a scene of panic ensued. Mister Chan withdrew his money and quickly melted away with his two enforcers. The sea captain and Xylander exchanged a look of horror and then both ran back to their respective carriages. The Cossack clambered back up to his seat and lashed the horse's ears most cruelly, sending the black carriage vaulting forward.

The sea captain jumped back behind the reigns of the moving van and set off after the black carriage. The police growler soon caught up to the Mariah but couldn't pass as the road was too narrow.

The ponderous moving van was a poor choice for an escape vehicle. Plus the sea captain had never stopped drinking since his ship put into port and had half a bottle of rum swilling about in his belly. The moving van also had twenty hypnotised sleepwalkers standing in the back of it. The somnambulists inside were thrown violently back and forth with every turn and twist of the road, so that the van's wildly shifting weight prevented anyone from passing.

The drunkenly-weaving pursuit soon took them out of Limehouse and they entered Whitechapel, heading back toward London.

Conan Doyle cursed aloud, "Damn and blast! We'll never get past on these roads, and with that moving van careering about."

"Yes," Wilde agreed, as he attempted unsuccessfully to touch a burning match to the tip of his Turkish cigarette, "and I can't light my cigarette."

The rough hovels of Whitehouse soon fell behind and were replaced by handsome six storey residences as they entered London proper.

"We're heading into Westminster," Conan Doyle noted. "Where can they be making for?"

"I doubt they have a destination in mind,"Wilde speculated. "I think they're just running away blindly."

Conan Doyle disagreed, "I wager the black carriage is heading for Victoria Station."

"You're right! They're trying to catch the train," Inspector Crumpet speculated. "They must be mad if they think they can get away in that moving van."

Crumpet was right, for as the van turned the sharper bends it would raise up dangerously on two wheels before crashing back down again.

"Where on earth are we?" Wilde asked as the growler careened back and forth as it tried to keep up.

"I believe that's Westbourne Gardens," Conan Doyle said and a moment later was proven correct.

Westbourne Gardens was a small triangular square so named for the small, but lushly treed park at its centre. The square was surrounded by Regency-Style white mansions of five storeys. The road ahead turned sharp right, and as the moving van careened around the bend it heeled up onto two wheels and then its outboard wheel crashed into the raised kerb, snapping the front axle. The front right corner of the van dropped and crashed to the roadway, bringing the van to a grinding standstill. The sudden stop launched both Morpheus and the drunken sea captain from the driver's seat. Morpheus managed to land on his feet and run it out, but the drunken sea captain hit the pavement face-first and knocked himself unconscious. The black carriage had been following close behind and it collided with the side of of the moving van and inextricably locked wheels.

The pursuit was over . . . only it wasn't.

As the the police growler drew up, those inside watched as the Cossack jumped down from the driver's seat and then the carriage door flew open and a figure climbed out—Madame Xylander. They both hurried to the back of the moving van. The Cossack unlatched the rear doors and threw them wide. They saw Xylander making hand motions before the hypnotised women and then she turned and hurried toward the park in the middle of the square with the somnambulists following.

"Jean! That was Jean! I just saw my wife!" Conan Doyle excitedly blurted. "She's among those young girls."

Conan Doyle, Crumpet and Wilde leapt down from the growler. They tried to follow Xylander into the park, but the Cossack stepped in front of them, blocking their way, and now he reached into the folds of his long overcoat and drew out a skull-crushing club.

The Black Mariah arrived moments later and the extra constables poured out. Inspector Crumpet pointed to the Cossack and shouted, "Come on lads, take that fellow!"

The five constables now drew their truncheons and cautiously advanced upon the Russian, who flashed an undertaker's smile and beckoned them closer with one hand. The policemen looked at one another uncertainly. The Russian was a towering bear of a man and their regulation truncheons seemed like toothpicks compared to the bone-breaking club the giant was wielding.

The constables were wary, but decided a mass attack was the best strategy. One of them gave a shout and then all five charged the Cossack at once. The first received a broken arm from a club blow. One of the constables thwacked the Russian across the head with his truncheon, but the Cossack shrugged off the blow with a mocking smile, and then clubbed the Constable senseless. The remaining constables piled on, grabbing the giant's arms and trying to manhandle him to the ground. After a moment's struggle the Russian bellowed like a bear and flung them all off. Just then, Conan Doyle heard a shouted cry from behind. When he looked around, he saw Inspector Crumpet bent horizontal, running pell mell straight toward the Cossack. The Russian swung his club but missed and Inspector Crumpet's bulk struck him full in the lower abdomen, sandwiching him up against the back of the moving van. The Russian expelled air with a prolonged oooooof, and crumpled to his knees, both hands holding his stomach, before toppling over to the pavement, unable to fight anymore.

"Well done, Crumpet!" Conan Doyle said as he reached down a hand to help the Inspector back to his feet. The rotund policeman took one look at the Cossack's crumpled form and patted his belly, smiling. "Looks like all those pork pies came in handy after all."

Wilde appeared. "Xylander led the women through there," he panted excitedly, pointing to the open gateway leading into the park.

When Conan Doyle dashed through the gates, he found Xylander surrounded by sleepwalkers. And then she played her last card. Xylander stood before the group of mesmerised women and began making fierce hand gestures, then called out. "Go! Scatter! Climb to the highest point of every rooftop." At her command, the mob of women split apart like blobs of mercury and each set off in a different direction.

But the somnambulists were slow moving, and so several were quickly captured and gently led back to the safety of the moving van. But others managed to make it to the surrounding houses. Westbourne Gardens was an affluent neighbourhood. The area was well-policed and very safe. Consequently, not many people locked their doors at night. So now the sleepwalkers walked up to the surrounding houses and simply opened the front door and went inside. If the door was locked, they moved on to the next building. Moments later they appeared at an upstairs window, which they opened and climbed out onto the roof and relentlessly made their way up to the highest point.

Conan Doyle looked around the square and his heart plummeted. Figures in white—sleepwalkers in white night gowns—could be seen on every rooftop. He looked from one to the other, desperate to identify his wife. Although the constables had rounded up many of the young women, he counted twelve or more still loose on the rooftops.

"Quick, Oscar, you take one house I'll take the other!"

Both men hurried off. Conan Doyle reached the first house, snatched open the door, and rushed inside, surprising the servants, a footman and two maids. Without bothering to explain his presence he shouted, "Emergency! How do I get onto the roof?" The servants mutely pointed without speaking and Conan Doyle dashed up the stairs. Moments later, he climbed out the top floor window onto the roof, breathing hard. He looked around frantically, desperate to save his wife. And there she was—the tall, willowy shape, the honey blonde hair he recognised so well. He raced to the rooftop's edge and flung an arm around her waist, restraining her, but when he saw her face his spirits sank.

It was not Jean.

He guided the young woman back in through the window and downstairs. The astonished servants were still standing at the foot of the stairs.

"This young woman," she shouted. "Look after her. Don't let her go." And then he dashed out of the house.

"I managed to catch mine," Wilde said, just exiting the next door residence holding a young woman by her arm.

"Well done, Oscar, but don't stop now. There's plenty more out there."

Wilde, who considered striking a match an exertion, and who was red-faced and panting, threw a horrified look at Conan Doyle. "More stairs? Perhaps a cigarette first."

"No! Hurry, for my sake, one of these girls could be my wife."

On the next residence, Conan Doyle saw another fair-haired woman standing at the very highest point of the roof top and ran toward her, praying that this time, it would be Jean.

Morpheus had been missing during the entire melee, for he had climbed into the black carriage where he crouched over the cradle and peeled back the curtain. He was shocked when he saw his sister's emaciated form. "Lilly!" he said in a breaking voice. "Lilly, it's me, your brother Richard." But when he touched her arm, he realised the terrible truth and let out a howl of despair. Tenderly, he pulled his sister from her crib and cradled her in his arms, where he sobbed unconsolably.

When Conan Doyle reached the rooftop, panting for breath, he looked around, but there was no sleepwalker. And then he saw her, on the rooftop of the neighbouring residence, standing like a statue at the edge of the rooftop. He advanced toward her but found a twelve-foot gap between houses—unjumpably wide.

"Jean!" Conan Doyle called. "Jean, it's me, your husband. Jean, wake up. Step back from the edge."

Madame Xylander now stepped from behind a nearby chimney. "So, this lady is your wife? How very useful."

She waved a hand before Jean Doyle's face and beckoned her to step forward, so that her toes touched the very edge of the roof."

"Tell your police friends to leave, otherwise I will bid your wife take a step forward and you can watch her plunge to her death. And then the others, one by one."

Conan Doyle's voice failed him. He swallowed and tried again. "Have you no compassion? Release my wife, and all the others."

Suddenly, a male voice shouted, "No, she has no compassion. Do you Xylander?" Conan Doyle looked around. It was Morpheus. He had followed him onto the same rooftop. "No compassion. No feelings. For me . . . or my sister."

Xylander's eyes flared. "I love your sister . . ."

"My sister is dead. Lilly is dead. You destroyed her!"

"What? No. She is in a deep trance. I placed her in a deep trance . . . to protect her. So that she might heal."

"She's been dead for a long time. You broke her. You killed her. But I won't let you hurt anyone else."

Morpheus called out to all the sleepwalkers and raised his hand and began the motions, pulling from side to side and then the downward drawing motions. "I release you all. You will all awaken when I count five. One, two—"

"STOP!" Xylander commanded. She raised her hand toward

Morpheus and began to once again make the motions. "Do not chal-lenge me. I taught you everything you know. You are a weak child."

Morpheus kept his hand up, but the strain on his face showed the inner battle he was fighting . . . and losing.

Conan Doyle looked at the distance separating them and wondered if he could get to Jean in time to save her. He would have to climb back though the window, navigate the stairs. Got out through the front door run across the street and through the park. Then go in through the door of the far house, back up the staircase and find an open window. Conan Doyle had been cycling and walking, trying to get fit for the cricket season. Still it was quite a distance and seemed impossible to do in time, but now he turned and hurried to the open window.

Xylander was intensifying her attack on Morpheus. "I am opening a hole in your ribcage. And now I reach in with my hand and seize your heart and begin to squeeze."

Sweat beaded on Morpheus's face and began to trickle. His raised hand lowered a few inches. His mouth stretched into a grimace and his knees trembled and threatened to buckle.

"And now I squeeze the last drops of blood from your heart. You will die and that will be an end of you."

Morpheus dropped to his knees; he could no longer hold his arm up and it drooped, and then his eyes rolled up into the back of his head and he collapsed to the ground.

Madame Xylander lowered her hand and smiled triumphantly.

"Sorry, but that's not going to do you any good." A voice to her right announced. She looked. Conan Doyle stood a few feet away. His hair was wildly mussed and he was panting with exertion.

Xylander released a snarl and raised her hand toward him, but too late as Conan Doyle took two steps forward and swung an uppercut that caught her neatly on the point of her chin and snapped her head back. The punch knocked her cold, and she crumpled like a doll that's had all its strings cut.

A moment later, Morpheus staggered to his feet. He raised his hand and began the motions again. "Hear me!" He called out. "I now release you from your sleep. At the count of five I will clap my hands and you will awaken. Five . . . four . . . three . . . two . . . one. AWAKEN!"

As Morpheus's hand clap echoed across the square, the sleep-walkers suddenly opened their eyes and looked about themselves.

Conan Doyle threw his arms around his wife and folded her into his arms. "Oh Jean, my beloved." He hugged her to himself with a force that threatened to crush her ribs. "I will never let you go again!"

Jean looked around in amazement. "Where am I?" And then she gasped as she realised she was dressed in her nightgown.

CHAPTER 50: THE TRIAL AND A SURPRISE WITNESS

The trial at the Old Bailey court did not go well for Madame Xylander. Although she could not be tried for murder in the case of Fanny Jones, the young sleepwalker who fell to her death, she was found guilty of death by misadventure. That plus twenty charges of kidnapping meant she would likely go to prison for the rest of her life.

But then, at the last moment, a surprise witness entered the dock—an immaculately-groomed Austrian gentleman. He had a small cigar jammed into the corner of his mouth, although he was not allowed to light it inside the courtroom. Surprisingly, he was appearing as a witness for the defence, despite the fact that Xylander hissed at him from the dock.

Freud testified that the judge should find Xylander incompetent to stand trial as she was mentally unbalanced. He testified that he had a long, shared history with Xylander and spoke of her cross-dressing and imitating him. And then he gave his professional opinion as a psychiatrist to point out that Xylander had carried around the mummified corpse of Lilly Thomson for two years, and had deluded herself into believing the girl was still alive.

Prior to the trial, Conan Doyle had consulted with Freud. The Scots author was concerned that, because of Xylander's mesmeric powers, no prison would be able to hold her for long. Together they had reasoned they should convince the judge that Xylander should be found criminally insane and committed to Bethlehem hospital. As Freud had stated during his lecture, hypnosis had no effect on the insane, and as in the very worst parts of Bethlehem, even the warders were mad, it offered the most secure place to keep her.

As for Morpheus, née Richard Thomson, Conan Doyle argued that he and his sister had been under Xylander's thrall since they were children, and thus Richard should be shown mercy, especially as he had been instrumental in saving the lives of the twenty sleepwalkers, including his own wife. And so, the young man known as Morpheus walked free at the trial's end.

In fact, as soon as he was acquitted, Morpheus walked out of the courtroom without uttering a word to anyone and disappeared into the capitol city's swarming mass of humanity.

CHAPTER 51: STEP INTO THE ABYSS

Although Conan Doyle and Oscar Wilde searched the streets around the Old Bailey Courthouse, Morpheus had vanished into the dark streets and alleyways of London.

In truth he wandered the streets of the Capitol for hours, seeking solace. He had no money. No family. No home. And no where to go.

Finally he found himself at St Paul's Cathedral. Here he used his powers of mesmerism to bamboozle a verger and so was able to slip into the inner staircases where he climbed the 378 steps up to the stone gallery that encircled the outside of the dome.The sun was sinking in the West when he walked out into the cooling air of dusk and sat down upon the sun-warmed stone. As hours passed, he watched the sky darken and the first wan stars light up the bowl of sky.

In sorrowful contemplation, he considered his life. He had no one. He had lost his parents when he was scarcely into his teens. His sister was dead. And even Madame Xylander, who had been an unhealthy pairing of part mother/part lover to him was gone. Now it seemed that even prison didn't want him.

After ruminating for several hours, he decided he would welcome oblivion.

Release from the world of loss and sorrow.

Morpheus stepped to the very edge of the rooftop, his legs pressed up against the stone railing, and stood looking out. Below him, the flying buttresses and sublime architecture of St. Pauls darkened into shadow shapes as the sun sank into the Thames. As the skies darkened, lamp lighters moved about the city, kindling the gas lamps to life, and lighting up the streets and avenues in an arcane scatter of constellations.

He felt the moment of decision rushing toward him, gathering momentum. He climbed up onto the stone railing, rocking slightly as his knees trembled and he fought for balance.

A flock of honking geese flew past, their wings rhythmically pumping the air. Noctilucent clouds glowed on the horizon. As the first stars sparkled in the twilit sky, he looked up to drown his mind in their beauty. It would be the last sight that ever filled his mind. He knew there would be the fall. The dreadful rush of air. And then a moment's pain as his body smashed and his soul rushed free.

Finally, he felt it—the moment had arrived.

He lifted one foot, leaned forward, and and stepped out into the abyss . . .

CHAPTER 52: PULLED FROM THE BRINK

... but then a strong hand grabbed him by the sleeve from behind ...

CHAPTER 53: RETURN TO O' HOULIHAN'S

The powerful hand dragged him backwards, backpedaling him down from the railing and away from the abyss.

Morpheus jerked around to discover the owner of the hand that still gripped his sleeve.

Conan Doyle and Wilde were standing there, looking at him. The Scots author had hold of his sleeve and wouldn't let go.

"There's no need for that," Conan Doyle said gently.

Morpheus (what was his real name? He could scarce remember himself) looked about him, his eyes stunned and impossibly distant.

"Wu . . . wu . . . why . . .?" It took a while to find his voice. To regain his equilibrium. "Why did you stop me? I was ready to die. I had prepared my mind . . ." He looked from Conan Doyle to Wilde as emotions rippled across his features. "After what I did to your wife? Those poor innocent girls? Why would you save me?"

"You saved the other girls . . . and my wife."

Wilde stepped forward. "You and your sister were under the thrall of that horrid woman. I never trusted her as soon as I learned she had a charity. Such people are always untrustworthy."

"You are a young man," Conan Doyle said. "You just temporarily lost your way—through no fault of your own. But I know you are fundamentally decent. You can start your life over again. I understand what you are going through, but we can find a better way. Oscar and I will help you."

Morpheus stood speechless, utterly at a loss. "I . . . I don't know what to say. You offer me kindness when I don't deserve it." He shook his head in bafflement. "I don't know what to say."

Wilde clapped a hand on the young man's shoulder and smiled. "Although I admit I am perhaps the least qualified man in the world to give this advice, sometimes silence is the apropos response."

After descending from the roof of St Paul's, the three men climbed into Wilde's carriage and journeyed across London to O'Houlihans, the whiskey bar where their first sojourn had been so rudely interrupted. They staked a claim at the small bar and now three freshly poured tumblers of *Bruichladdichm* whiskey sat before them.

"I've never drunk whiskey before," the young man admitted. "I've never drunk any alcohol before."

"Oh good," Wilde said, "then you should prove to be a cheap date."

"What do I do?" Morpheus asked.

Wilde clapped his hand on the younger man's shoulder. "First, you must engage all your senses before imbibing."

"Oh, not this again!" Conan Doyle lamented.

"Tush!" Wilde scolded his Scots colleague. "I am providing our young friend with a valuable life lesson."

With that, Wilde resumed his lesson. "You must begin by engaging all your senses. First you must look, I mean really *look* at the whiskey. Study it. Note the Peaty colours, the ocherous depths. The way the light dances off the surface . . ."

When Wilde had concluded his lesson, Conan Doyle and Morpheus were finally given permission to taste and the author of Sherlock Holmes finally took his first sip of *Bruichladdichm*.

"Oh my!" Conan Doyle exclaimed, "That really is special Oscar. Full marks to you."

Predictably, at the first sip, Morpheus exploded in a coughing fit. "Oh ... oh ... that ... that is ..."

"Yes it is, isn't it?" Wilde agreed. "Don't worry, you'll soon get the hang of drinking, but it requires commitment. I am dangerously close to forty, and I still practice diligently every day."

Conan Doyle was just taking his second sip when from outside the bar came the shattering scream of police whistles and the drum of truncheons being pounded on the pavement.

"Oh gawd, not again!" he lamented.

The pub door flew open and a constable stuck his head inside, his face wild with alarm. "The building's on fire. Everyone out!"

The other patrons jumped up in a scraping of chairs and rushed out the door, followed soon after by the Leprechaun bar tender who vaulted over the bar and followed them out. Already a grey haze and the smell of burning was beginning to fill the air.

Morpheus looked back and forth between his companions, who remained standing resolutely at the bar. "The building's on fire. Shouldn't we evacuate?" Morpheus asked.

Conan Doyle took another sip of his drink, savoured it, and then shook his head. "I'm not moving until I've finished my whiskey."

"And most likely a second," Wilde added.

Conan Doyle looked around casually. "I don't see any naked flames yet." He nodded at the roof beam above the bar. "And that beam is solid English oak. Probably take four hours to burn through."

"Yes," Wilde agreed. "We have plenty of time ... although it might be a bit warm and flamey in here by then."

As it turned out, the fire was simply a blocked chimney flue, which caused smoke to back up, and which was soon cleared. The doors were propped open and the smoke swirled out. The barman returned and then the rest of the patrons filed back in and found their whiskeys patiently waiting for them.

After his third whiskey, young Morpheus fell asleep with his forehead on the bar.

Conan Doyle and Wilde clinked classes as they toasted one

another and another job well done. They polished off the bottle of *Bruichladdichm* between them, and though no one was hypnotised, neither could remember a thing about the experience the next day.

T HE END

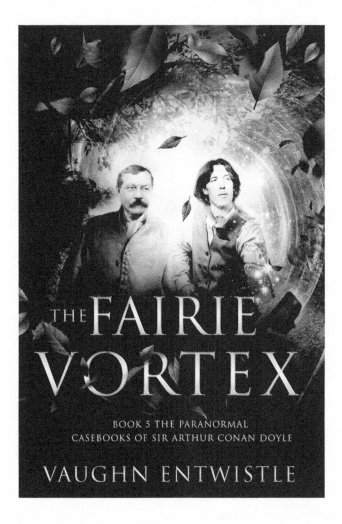

Did you love this book? If so, preorder the next book in series, The Faerie Vortex; Book 5 The Paranormal Casebooks of Sir Arthur Conan Doyle. Due out in September 2021

THE FAERIE VORTEX

CHAPTER ONE: A RATTLING DISCOVERY

Oscar Wilde skipped up the steps of the British Museum, swept through the heavy bronze doors, and plunged from brilliant summer sunshine into a cool and gloomy corridor lazed by sleeping shadows. Here he paused to scratch a Lucifer and puff one of his Turkish cigarettes to life, then followed his own echoing footsteps into the circular expanse of the library reading room. Seated at the radiating spokes of the readers' tables were dusty men and dusty women perusing dusty tomes taken down from dusty shelves. A studious hush filled the great domed space: a quiet disturbed only by the susurration of turning pages.

The Irish wit had come neither to write, nor to idle away the hours with a casual morning's read. Instead, he scanned the downcast faces seated at the blue leather topped tables, searching for the person with whom he had an assignation.

He flinched as a hand touched his arm and a voice spoke so close to his ear he felt warm, stale breath wash the side of his face. "A friendly reminder, sir, no smoking in the reading room."

He turned to find a tall, rather desiccated figure in a worn suit and round spectacles lurking at his elbow. Undoubtedly a librarian—he had the constipated face and unnaturally long index fingers of a man born to *shusssssshhhhh!*

"I'm afraid you'll have to put that out," the librarian insisted.

"I'm sorry? Ah, the cigarette. For a terrible moment I thought you were referring to my genius, which is inextinguishable." Wilde flashed a smile, counterfeiting affability.

"You know the rules, sir. No smoking."

The Irishman's long face fell. "Oh, really? Must I? As you can see the cigarette is Turkish, rather expensive to obtain in England, and only recently lit."

"Sorry, sir. But rules are rules."

"Ah . . . Very well, then," Wilde huffed an exasperated breath and extinguished the cigarette on the inside of his silver cigarette case then slid it into one of the elastic holders. He would save it for later. He bowed his head and threw a gesture of obeisance at the librarian. "Thank you, noble guardian of the printed word . . ." adding in a mutter as he walked away, " . . . for saving me from a moment of joy."

The stacks of the reading room, three tiers high, held the works of some of the greatest writers in the world. As he orbited the circular room in a counter clock direction, the literary canon unwound in reverse alphabetical order: Zola, Wilde (he could not suppress the urge for a quick glance at the shelf which held his own, *Picture of Dorian Grey*) Tennyson, Shakespeare, Poe, Melville, unalphabetizing until he reached the Ds where he found his friend Arthur Conan Doyle, sitting (appropriately) at the reading table at the end of C-through-E.

As it was the height of summer, Wilde was sportily kitted out in a white linen suit with a straw boater and a cane. By contrast, Conan Doyle was overdressed for the heat in his work-a-day tweeds. He looked up as Wilde stepped to the reading table. The Scotsman's expression was even gloomier than his dress.

"Whatever's wrong, Arthur? You have the face of a man unfashionably late for his own funeral."

"Sit, Oscar. I have something of grave importance to share with you."

Wilde eyed the straight-backed chair with doubt. "For once I prefer to remain standing. I was playing horsey-rides with the boys last evening and believe that I have ruptured my spleen or one of those other equally obscure organs that somehow performs a vital function."

"I recommend you take a seat. What I have to say will soon make you forget your back ache."

Conan Doyle opened his leather portmanteau and drew out a familiar leather-bound book held closed by a strap and a lock. He showed it to his friend. "You know what this is?"

"Of course, "Wilde replied, settling into a chair opposite. "One of your casebooks." He drew off his straw boater and tossed it on the table, set down his walking cane, and smoothed back his chestnut-coloured hair with a large hand. The long wavy curls of his aesthete days had been trimmed by a recent visit to his barbers, and now he wore his hair short and brilliantined into place.

"Look at the cover, Oscar."

"Yes, I am looking."

"Take special note of the number."

The Irishman frowned and hunkered forward, eyes asquint. "Casebook Number 5," he read aloud. "Is that all? Can we go now? I am quite famished and you lured me here with the promise of standing me breakfast."

"Lunch."

"Breakfast," Wilde insisted. "I arose from my bed at the crack of 11:30, a full hour earlier than usual. Just in time for breakfast."

"We had agreed to meet at ten. It's now almost one o'clock." Conan Doyle pointed out in a peevish voice.

Wilde laughed dismissively. "The Wildean stomach is the most reliable chronometer I own and it tells me that is still breakfast time."

"Very well, but first I must read the contents of this casebook to you."

The Irish wit's eyes widened in alarm. "Now? The entire book? Surely not? Could we not adjourn to the Savoy where you could synopsize over oysters on horseback and a chilled bottle of champagne? I was never one for idling in libraries, particularly this one, where I am jostled by the ghosts of literary giants criticizing my punctuation and mocking my abhorrence of the semicolon."

Conan Doyle held up the casebook again. "Read the full title, Oscar. All of it."

Wilde sighed and leaned forward, peering. "Casebook Number Five: The Faerie Vortex. Yes. Very nice. A spanking good title. Has a definite ring to it."

Conan Doyle set the casebook down and drummed his fingers atop the cover. "Do you remember two year years ago when you and I went on a little adventure in the southwest of England? Our visit to a picturesque old village named *Wyrme-Hallow*?"

"Wilde's pursed his generous lips and knitted his brows, nonplussed. "No, I don't recall that."

"Come now, you must remember staying in a rustic inn with a thatched roof?"

Wilde's frown deepened. "If I did, it quite escapes me now."

"So you don't remember us going down there to investigate the disappearance of two village children?"

Wilde released an exasperated sigh. "Examine my face, Arthur, this is the most puzzled expression I can make without straining a muscle."

"Then you don't remember fishing for trout in a stream?"

Wilde laughed musically. "Now you are being ridiculous. Fishing is one of the many manly outdoor pursuits Oscar Wilde does not participate it . . . and with great enthusiasm, I might add. When it comes to the pursuit of fish, I prefer my catch to arrive on a plate, poached, with a slice of lemon and a tureen of hollandaise sauce."

"So you don't remember posing for this photograph?"

Conan Doyle flipped open the casebook, turned it around, and slid it across the table. Wilde studied the photograph glued into the pages and his mouth dropped open. There, rendered in sepia tones, was the most famous playwright of his generation in hip waders, standing in the middle of a stream, a large trout dangling from the end of his fishing rod.

Wilde's eyes widened with bemusement. "What? I don't understand. I never . . ." He trailed off, mid-sentence and cast a suspicious glance at his friend. "Is this some kind of clever prank, Arthur? I have read that there are ways of altering photographs. Is this a new hobby you've taken up? Are you dabbling in trick photography?"

But Conan Doyle's face looked anything but mocking. "No tricks. I'm afraid I am in deadly earnest. You know I keep my casebooks behind a hidden panel in my writing desk?"

"Yes, and if you die before me I am to remove them and find a similar safe hiding place. The books can only be made public five years after the last one of us dies. That is our agreement."

Conan Doyle nodded. "A few days ago, I opened the secret compartment—there was something I wished to refer to in the second casebook, a name I had forgot. That was when I discovered the book you see before you—Casebook Number Five. Like you I was baffled. I have written two casebooks to date. I certainly did not remember writing a third or fourth. And definitely not a fifth. But the handwriting is undeniably mine. Plus, there are a number of telling artifacts pasted into its pages: stubs of train tickets, photographs, a tattered map, even the pressed blooms of some unidentifiable flowers. And yet I have no recollection of any of it. No recollection of the train journey. No recollection of visiting the rustic village of Wyrme-Hallow. No recollection of posing for the photographs in the book . . ."

He paused and glanced down, gathering himself before looking his friend in the eye. ". . . and no recollection of you being arrested for murder."

The color drained from Wilde's already pallid complexion.

"What? Murder? Arrested? Oh, this is all a joke is it not? It is, isn't it? What are you saying? It's quite impossible."

Conan Doyle flipped to a newspaper cutting pasted into the pages and held the book out for Wilde to examine. The Irishman read the headline and recoiled: FIEND RUN TO GROUND. Accompanying the article was a reporter's sketch—drawn looking through the bars of a prison cell—of a forlorn and disconsolate man perched on a wooden cot. The drawing bore an unmistakable likeness to the face that greeted him each morning in the mirror.

"I have read the clipping," Conan Doyle went on. "It describes the arrest of one Oscar Fingal O'Flahertie Wills Wilde for the rape and murder of two village girls."

Wilde jumped up from his seat, fidgeting with distress. "Stop this, Arthur. You're frightening me."

Conan Doyle looked at his friend with bloodshot eyes that testified to a sleepless night of pummeled pillows and bedclothes wrestled into knots. "You are right to be frightened Oscar." And then he added in a voice torn to rags. "Because I, too, am frightened."

Oscar Wilde looked into his friend's face, a face that always held a calm resolute certainty. But now, the look of hopeless uncertainty he found there chilled the summer sweat on the back of his neck to a skimming of ice. His knees buckled and he sagged back into his chair.

"Are you still in a hurry to dine?" Conan Doyle asked mildly.

"No . . . my appetite is suddenly gone. What is all about, Arthur? What does it mean?"

"That I cannot fully fathom. I have grappled with this hideous discovery all night long. Just before you arrived I came to a rather unsettling conclusion. As I have written in my Sherlock Holmes stories, "Once you eliminate the impossible—"

"Yes," Wilde interrupted, finishing the quote. "Whatever remains, no matter how improbable, must be the truth. But what does that mean?"

Conan Doyle's shoulders heaved as he sucked in a deep breath and let it out. "It means that, two years ago, you and I had an experience that has somehow been erased from our minds. We must find out what that experience was, and why we have no recollection of it."

For a long, long time Wilde sat in stunned silence. When he finally spoke, his voice was brittle with panic. "Bu-but how do we even begin to go about such a task?"

Conan Doyle slid the book back from his friend and turning it around, opened to the first page. "First you must become familiar with the story. Or at least, the story thus far."

And then Conan Doyle began to read aloud the words he had no recollection of writing.

 * * *

PLEASE LEAVE ME A REVIEW

Did you enjoy this book? If so, please leave a review on Amazon and/or GoodReads. Reviews really help build readership and ensure more books in the future.

Thank you in advance and warmest wishes.

Vaughn Entwistle, Cheltenham, England 2021

To leave me a review: CLICK HERE

ABOUT THE AUTHOR

Vaughn Entwistle grew up in Northern England, but spent many years living in the United States, first in Michigan, (where he earned a Master's Degree in English at Oakland University), and then in Seattle (where he worked as an editor/writer and also ran a successful gargoyle sculpting business for ten years. (Yes, really!) He currently lives in the English spa town of Cheltenham.

Find out more about the author and his books. and sign up for his newsletter at his author website: www.vaughnentwistle.com

GET A FREE BOOK!

Get a free copy of my Kindle short, *The Necropolis Railway*, by signing
up for my occasional newsletter at my author website:
www.vaughnentwistle.com

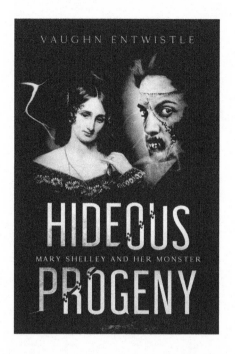

Hideous Progeny: Mary Shelley and Her Monster

It never had life . . . but now it must die . . .

During a night of apocalyptic thunderstorms, 18-year old Mary Shelley's imagination birthed a nameless monster that would make her name famous and haunt the world for generations. But since the dark nativity of her "hideous progeny", Mary's life has been cursed by tragedy, loss and grief: a dead sister, a dead husband, and three dead children. Now aged 48, and suffering debilitating headaches from the brain tumor that will finally claim her life, Mary sees her monster as a malevolence that has cursed her life and which now threatens her only living child. Seeking release, Mary travels from London to the Somerset estate of Andrew Crosse, the gentlemen scientist who first inspired her Dr. Frankenstein. Crosse is an electrical experimenter known to the terrified locals as "The Thunder and Lightning Man". Mary has sought him out in hopes that the same *Dread Engine* that conjured her monster can finally lay that ghost to rest.

Made in the USA
Monee, IL
06 November 2021